THE CLEANSING
A THRILLER

R. G. HUXLEY

This is a work of fiction. The characters, names, incidents, places, and plot are products of the author's imagination or are used fictitiously. Any resemblance to actual persons, companies, or events is purely coincidental.

Cover Image: *A Silhouette of an Angel over the glow of a fire* Copyright © A&B Photos, 2012
Used under license from Shutterstock.com
Cover Design © 2012 by R. G. Huxley

Copyright © 2012 R. G. Huxley
All rights reserved.

ISBN-10: 1475147910
ISBN-13: 978-1475147919

DEDICATION

To my wife, Heather and daughters Taylor, Hannah Grace, and
Reagan. This one's for you. Promises to keep.

ACKNOWLEDGMENTS

Three authors gave me the encouragement I needed at the right time and this book is what it is because of them. John Sandford, Douglas Clegg, and Jonas Saul. I will forever be thankful to you and I know I am here because I met you at the right time in my life and along the way in writing *The Cleansing*. I wish the three of you all the success and joy life has to offer.

Jonas, a personal sense of gratitude to you and you know why. You really are the essence of what a true friend is. You're one of the main reasons this book exists today. Thank you so much.

My friends and family: Philip and Pam Buckles, Jack and Elaine Davis(my mom), M. Wayne (my dad) and Judith Huxley, Carl and Amy Huxley, Joel Huxley and Ryan King, Aaron and Liu Huxley, Abbey Huxley, John and Shauna Davis, Patrick Toler (Best Friend A Guy Could Ever Have), Patricia Toler, Chris Toler, Jesse Moyer (first person to ever read *The Cleansing*), Jodi Horton Dascalos, and Tammy Rowland. Thanks so very much for everything!

This novel is what it is because of all of you. All the mistakes are mine.

THE CLEANSING: A THRILLER

"...Then the priest shall bring it all and burn it on the altar; it is a burnt sacrifice, an offering made by fire, a sweet aroma to the Lord."

- Leviticus 1:13 New King James Version

SUNDAY

2

1

Sunday. 11:30 AM EST.

Pastor Tom Sullivan was just minutes away from taking his life. He was going to pay for his transgressions in front of his congregation for what he had done and his soul was at ease with this decision.

It *had* to be.

Community Christian Fellowship had a size of 1,500 plus people before Tom Sullivan accepted the pastoral position. Now the number had shrunk. Members left in droves and the congregation became an anemic 237. The elders, during staff meetings, tried to reassure Tom it wasn't because of his leadership, but Tom knew otherwise. He would humbly thank them for their words of encouragement, but again, the numbers didn't lie. There was no more growth. Only defections. Calls from the church for Tom's resignation grew over the last four months. He tried to remain steadfast through the turmoil, but it soon became too much to emotionally bear on his heart and the heart of his family.

He put out his resume to other churches seeking a new pastor. His applications went unanswered or he'd receive a courtesy letter basically saying, "Thanks, but no thanks."

He had enough of the ministry.

He committed heinous acts in secret he wasn't proud of.

Now, today would be the day Community Christian Fellowship got their wish. Tom would no longer be their shepherd.

3

The congregation finished singing the offertory song and sat down. Tom scanned the body language of the remaining faithful attendees. They didn't want to hear his messages anymore. Their stony bodies were rigid with disgust in him as their pastor.

Occasional coughs sprinkled throughout the sanctuary along with the rustling of papers. Some were looking at their bulletin to appear they cared what today's message would bring to their pitiful lives. Others checked their watches as if starting a stopwatch to let Tom know he better finish in thirty minutes and not a second more.

Pastor Sullivan stood and walked over to the podium and looked out at the crowd. Instead of seeing smiling faces, he detected their eyes boring into him, dissecting his heart. Some of the faces seemed to contort and twist. The featureless faces had black holes in the sockets, which used to hold their eyes. Tom closed his lids hoping the faces would return to normal when he opened them. He decided it was best to keep staring at his Bible instead of looking out at the congregation. The horror he might witness would be immense and he had to go through with his plans. The consequences awaiting him were immeasurable if he didn't.

They know, he thought to himself. *They're already aware of what I've done.*

Tom Sullivan flipped through the thin pages, found the morning's passage, and began speaking. "Surely there is a day that is coming. This will be a day that will burn like the intensity of a furnace. The smell of brimstone. The heat of fire. The pain of the unrighteous at their final judgment. The haughty and conceited. The sexually immoral. The ignorant. All evildoers alike, they will become hot burning coals in the lake of fire. The Psalmist in the eleventh chapter and sixth verse wrote, 'Upon the wicked he shall rain snares, fire and brimstone, and a horrible tempest: this shall be the portion of their cup.'"

He paused.

"Amen!" a few people shouted out.

The Cleansing: A Thriller

Pastor Sullivan took a sip of water from the glass on the podium and continued, "Rest assured fellow church family; these people will become the ashes beneath your feet. You will be able to walk over their burning retched flesh and not feel the lick of the flames that has already consumed them. You will walk to glory. On that day, the day that sets the evildoers on fire, you will either be the one consumed by flames and try to flee like frightened animals from a burning stable or become the one walking over the fire and into victory."

Once again, Pastor Sullivan paused to allow the expected shouts of *Amen*.

He reached into the podium and pulled out a 1-gallon milk jug filled with a brownish liquid resembling watered down tea. He twisted off the blue cap and began pouring the contents all over himself. Gasps from the congregation sucked up the air in the room.

"And the devil that deceived them was cast into the lake of fire and brimstone, where the beast and the false prophet are, and shall be tormented day and night for ever and ever. And when they came to the place to which God had told him, Abraham built an altar there, and laid the wood in order, and bound Isaac his son, and laid him on the altar, upon the wood, and took the knife," Tom paused, swallowing hard, knowing what was coming and then continued. "…and took the knife to slay his son."

Pastor Sullivan reached inside his sport coat and pulled out a lighter. Screams pierced the silence throughout the sanctuary. "But the fearful, and unbelieving, and the abominable, and murderers, and whoremongers, and sorcerers, and idolaters, and all liars, shall have their part in the lake which burneth with fire and brimstone: which is the second death. Yes, the lake of fire will become *my* second death."

While he spoke, he flicked the lighter and immediately flames consumed his body. The congregation stood to their feet in disbelief. Some of the elders ran up on stage trying to put the fire out. Pastor Sullivan continued to shout through his flamed ravaged body, "See I shall send thee the prophet Elijah

5

before that great and dreadful day! And when they shall have finished their testimony, the beast that ascendeth out of the bottomless pit shall make war against them, and shall overcome them, and *kill them*! THEION!"

Pastor Sullivan fell to the floor and writhed in pain as his flesh burned and melted away as the fire consumed him and devoured his soul.

***

Across the city, at the same time, two other pastors committed the exact same act. Saying the exact same words. Wanting to die in the exact same way.

MONDAY

2

Monday. 6:30 AM EST.

Jack Angel flipped his legs over the side of his double bed, and while sitting only in his Fruit of the Loom briefs, he smacked his pasty lips and slowly rubbed the hangover from his groggy eyes and disheveled hair. Decker, his yellow lab, perked up and began walking towards his owner for a morning rub on the head.

"Mornin' Deck," Jack said half awake. "You sleep better than me last night?" Decker let out a quick sneeze as if he understood his owner. Jack turned and looked at his nightstand, which stood as a testimony of his drunken evening: a half-empty bottle of Evan William's Bourbon and a few pills scattered next to the glass that still held a shot of the eighty-proof liquid that escaped Jack's mouth when he passed out on the bed.

Decker started circling the room, occasionally sniffing the floor. Jack knew this was his cue to get up and let him outside. "Can I at least take a leak first? Then let you out?"

Decker whined his disapproval, but obediently followed Jack out of the room and into the hall. He sat by the bathroom as if to remind Jack of his priority when he finished taking his morning leak.

As promised, when Jack flushed, he walked out and Decker sprinted and headed towards the door to relieve himself all over the yard.

Still in his briefs, Jack stumbled into the kitchen to get himself a cup of coffee. He was annoyed to find out he forgot

9

to pre-program the coffee maker. He grabbed a filter, placed it inside the maker's filter holder, poured in the water, and clicked it on. While he waited, he stared at the pile of three-day-old dishes in the sink and reminded himself again that he needed to get them washed. He turned and opened the refrigerator to get some orange juice and noticed the jug only had a sip left at the bottom. He twisted off the cap, swished it around, and drank the last bit.

After ten minutes passed, his coffee stopped brewing and he poured his cup. When Jack sat down at the table, he began gently sipping his morning kick-start so not to burn his upper lip. After he settled in to his morning ritual, the phone rang. Not wanting to get up to answer it, instead he looked at the caller ID to see if it was worth his effort. Recognizing the number calling, he decided it was. "This is Jack. Go," he said answering the phone quickly.

"Mornin Jack."

"Good morning Frank. Hey, if this is about the hundred I owe you from Saturday's fight night, I'll get it to you this week okay?"

"No this is something a little more on the serious side."

"More serious than gettin' your hundred bucks from me? Then I don't think I want to know what it is."

Frank Madiolie was the lead homicide detective for Dayton P.D. "Yeah, I'm afraid it's serious."

"Then why are you bothering me with it? You know I don't do this stuff anymore. Besides, I've got things to do today."

"No you don't Jack. Trust me on this, you'll want to hear what I have to say."

Jack huffed. "Fine. What is it?"

"Did you hear about the pastor suicides yesterday?"

"Yeah who hadn't? Pretty damn bizarre if you ask me."

"What details do you already know?"

Jack took another sip of his coffee as if it would help jog his memory. "Basically what the news said. Two pastors preached on the same message and then lit themselves on fire in front of their congregation. Both of them died. Like I said, pretty damn bizarre. I must admit, it does put a completely new spin on, 'This little light of mine. I'm gonna let it shine.'"

"Funny Jack," Frank replied not laughing and giving Jack the satisfaction of his rude humor. "What if I told you there were supposed to be three suicides? Three pastors, preaching the same message, and all three were supposed to die the same way, but one didn't?"

"I would say you need to find that lone survivor, assuming he hasn't already become the next Human Torch, and interrogate his ass until you get the information you need."

Frank was silent.

Jack continued to sip his coffee.

"Well, we don't have to worry about trying to find him."

"Why did he already off himself while quoting scripture elsewhere and somebody phoned it in?"

"Not exactly."

Jack heard scratching paws at the back door. "Hold on a moment Frank. I need to let Deck in."

Jack laid the phone down and walked towards the sliding glass door where Decker sat as if he had a huge smile of relief on his face. Jack knew he could've left Decker outside, but he needed to gather his thoughts because he knew where this conversation was going to lead and he didn't want to break the bad news to his friend and former colleague that he had zero interest in helping in the investigation. Not even as a paid consultant.

He returned to the table after warming up his coffee and picked up where Frank left off. "Okay, what's not so exact about what I asked?"

"We received a phone call yesterday from a few deacons across town pleading for us to come and help restrain their pastor who was trying to kill himself. They were able to subdue him during his sermon before he had a chance to set himself on fire. We went and picked him up and he's been in our custody ever since. His name's Ray Stevens. Does that name sound familiar to you?"

Jack thought for a moment. "Not really. Besides, even if it did, you know how to handle guys like this. I don't know why you're calling. You don't need me Frank. Just break him down and get the information you need."

"I understand, but the reason I'm calling is because you've been personally requested."

Jack grew irritated, "You know I don't get involved in matters like this anymore. Not since Dani left. I want to be there for you Frankie, but I have to say no. Not right now. So don't ask me to do this."

"I'm not the one who's asking."

"Then who?"

"Reverend Ray Stevens."

"What?! I don't even know this guy! Honestly, I have no desire to come and see him."

"Then will you at least come and read his file? See if there's something that jogs your memory. Can you at least do *that* for me Jack?"

"Why the urgency?"

"Medi-Port's coming to pick him up in a couple hours and take him over to county for a psyche eval." Frank paused hoping to hear an answer from Jack. After a moment of silence, Frank continued. "Seriously Jack. Just come and look at the file for me. I need to have something...*anything*...before he leaves."

Jack looked down at the floor at Decker who was whimpering in his dream-filled-sleep. "*Dammit!* Fine," Jack said giving in. "I'm only doing this because it's you Frank."

"I know. And I appreciate that."

"I'll be there sometime before he leaves. When I get there, I'm just looking at the file and that's it! Then I'm gone."

"Thanks Jack."

But Jack didn't hear it because he'd already hung up.

3

Jack Angel arrived at the police station within an hour of hanging up with Frank Madiolie. The police station lobby hadn't changed since Jack had left it when he resigned from the force. Wives with their fatherless children, waiting to visit with their current incarcerated boyfriend. The occasional cuffed-perp walking to the holding cell. And the sad mother sitting and wondering where she went wrong with her child that he or she would end up in a hellhole like this.

When Jack walked through the front doors a familiar face greeted him. "Hey Jack! Long time no see," Sergeant Marcus Rand greeted from behind the front desk.

"Good morning Sergeant Rand. How's life?"

"Can't complain."

"Wife and kids okay?"

Marcus nodded. "The little ones are doing well in school. Bradley's getting ready to start first grade and so Gwendolyn will go back to full time at the hospital. They said her schedule will be during the days, so that will allow us to see each other in the evening instead of me coming home and watching her leave to work. So that'll be nice."

"Sounds good sarge." Jack replied.

"And you?" Marcus waited a beat. "How have you been?"

Jack knew Marcus meant well, but he wasn't prepared to talk to his former colleague about his personal life. "Let's just say, it's a day-to-day ritual for me. Some are better than others."

"Gotcha."

"Hey have you seen Frank around?" Jack asked wanting to change the subject.

"I'm headed your way!" Frank shouted from across the lobby. "Don't bore Jack with your stories sarge!"

"He wasn't boring me. Just giving me the family update." Jack turned towards Marcus. "Keep your family happy sarge and cherish every moment."

"Will do."

Jack shook hands with the sarge before walking away from the front desk and towards the door Frank had propped open for Jack to enter through. They both walked silently down the hall and into Frank's office. Frank shut the door behind them to keep their meeting private.

"Can I get you some coffee?"

"No, I'm good."

Frank walked around his desk and sat down. He pulled out a manila folder with the name Stevens, Ray written across the label. "Here's what we have on the rev."

Jack reached across the desk and took the file from Frank. He opened it and skimmed through the typed records already contained within the folder.

"I don't understand. Why did he mention me? Seriously, I don't know this guy from Adam. So what else has he said? Anything?"

"He keeps quoting verses from the Bible. That's it. Nothing more."

"You know, sometimes, mentals like this could actually be talking to you by not directly answering your questions if you know what I mean."

"I know what you're saying. Like through the verses he quotes."

"Exactly."

"Well all of his verses deal with blood, rain of fire, pestilence, rapture, and judgment. You know, the typical radical end time's mantra. Other than that, only your name has come up."

Jack nodded his head taking in all Frank was saying to him. "I admit. I'm curious as to how my name came up."

The Cleansing: A Thriller

"I told him we weren't getting anywhere with him constantly referring to us as liars, thieves, and whoremongers and asked what he would like us to do. He sat silent for a good five minutes and said he will talk to only one person. I asked who that was and I would see what I could do. He looked up, stared at me, and said your name. That was it. He hasn't spoken since. Not even an apocalyptic verse."

Jack didn't say a word. He kept reading the file hoping something would jump out at him to see if he could recall who Ray Stevens was or how he may have met him before.

Nothing.

"So let me ask you, do you want to see him?"

Jack flipped between the same pages in the folder acting as if he was studying them, but in reality, he was deciding whether to meet with Ray. After a few minutes, he relented. "Dammit! Fine! But after that I'm leaving. I mean it! I don't want anything to do with this investigation. I'm just here out of curiosity to see how he knows me. Are we clear?"

"Absolutely."

"When I'm done, I'm walking out the front doors and going home."

"I understand Jack." Frank stood and walked towards his office door and opened it. "He's in room two."

Jack stood and walked out the door, turned left and headed to interrogation room two.

"I'll be watching from the other side of the glass. You know the drill. He won't see us, but he'll know we're watching."

Jack turned back towards Frank. "I mean it Frank. No more. I'll talk to him, but no more. I'm out. I've been out for awhile now and I want to keep it that way."

"Okay Jack," Frank replied sounding frustrated. "You've made yourself clear. I won't ask you for anything more."

But something on Frank's face let Jack know in all likelihood this wasn't going to be it. There was something more. Something about the rev didn't sit well with Frank and it was obvious.

15

Something awfully dark.
And dreadfully cold and extremely calculated.
No, this was just the beginning for both Frank and Jack.

4

Jack entered interrogation room 2, motioned for the officer standing guard to go ahead and leave them alone, and when the officer left, Jack took a seat at the other end of the long aluminum table. He sized up Reverend Ray Stevens. He was medium build and still wearing his Sunday morning white Oxford with a burgundy red paisley tie. Ray's brown hair was receding on top and so Ray preferred to slick it all back. Jack noticed Ray was wearing a wedding band with his right hand donning a beautiful gold pinkie ring that had diamonds arranged to form a cross. Ray was very tan and had a leathery look to his face. Even though Ray was in his mid to late forties, he appeared to look ten years older. Jack also recognized the cologne Ray had bathed in for Sunday morning, Aqua Di Gio by Armani.

Jack stared at Ray waiting for him to speak first. It was a tactic he learned while at the academy prompting the other party to decide where they should start the conversation. Ultimately, it would lead down the right path. It was the same tactic some psychologists used when counseling patients. Instead of asking questions, let the client open up freely. Eventually they would spill everything. It may take awhile, but it would happen.

Sometimes, one's own self-conscious can be their worst enemy.

Ray looked across the table at Jack Angel. He smiled arrogantly at him and then slowly closed his eyes.

"Come to me, all of you who are weary and loaded down with burdens, and I will give you rest."

Ray opened his eyes and looked back at Jack, but this time there was no smile on his face. Just simply a cold, blank stare.

Jack folded his hands and leaned in towards Reverend Ray, "Look," he said stone-faced. "I'm only here because you asked for me. I don't know shit about you, your family, your church, or anything else. What I do know is that you and two other preachers decided to become Roman candles yesterday during your church service with the other two dying and only you surviving. If you want to sit here and play "How many verses can you and I quote?" I am out of here and you can rot for all I care. I want to know how you know me, why you wanted to see me, and what that has to do with what happened yesterday. You got one minute to start or I leave. Starting now."

Jack turned his left wrist and watched the seconds tick down. 60...59...58...57...56

"I was naked, and you clothed me. I was sick, and you took care of me. I was in prison, and you visited me."

"Times a-wastin. Forty-five. Forty-four. Forty-three."

"Then I noticed the appearance of His loins and upward something like glowing metal that looked like fire all around within it, and from the appearance of his loins and downward I saw something like fire."

"Thirty. Twenty-nine. Twenty-eight."

"Then I looked and behold, a hand was extended to me and lo a scroll was in it. When He spread it out before me, it was written on the front and the back, and written on it were lamentations, mourning and woe."

"Thirteen. Twelve. Eleven. Ten."

"I am a sign to you. As I have done, so it will be done to them."

"Five. Four. Three. Two. One. Times up," Jack said standing up. "Thanks for the verses. I'm sure they will really help in their investigation."

Jack walked past Reverend Ray and started to turn the knob to leave the room.

"Your daughter." Jack felt his blood run cold. "You miss her?"

5

Jack didn't expect to hear those words about his daughter.

Ainslie, how I miss you so much. Why were you taken from your mother and me? Why?

Is this what Reverend Ray wanted to talk to him about? His seven year old daughter? The abduction? The subsequent investigation which led to the discovery of her remains?

Jack's body stiffened angrily. Reverend Ray's question had got to him. The Rev knew what to ask. This is what he wanted. He seemed to know what buttons to push on Jack to get a reaction from him. His tactic worked.

It wasn't a secret about his daughter's abduction from the playground. The event was all over the news with many in the community joining up and passing out flyers and posting them in every store window hoping someone had any information to help find her. Days turned to weeks with no sign, no leads, and no Ainslie.

Until finally one day the call Jack and Dani feared most came. They went together to i.d. the body. Dani couldn't bear to look, so Jack went into the coroner's room by himself...

"I asked you a question Mr. Angel."

Jack gathered his composure and returned to his original seat. He didn't want Reverend Ray to feel as if he was in control of this conversation. He couldn't lose the upper hand and cede control over to Reverend Ray.

"Yes," Jack said coolly. "I miss my daughter, but we're not here to talk about her. We are here to talk about what happened yesterday. If you don't want to do that then I'm afraid I'm not needed here any longer. You're simply wasting my time."

Reverend Ray laughed. "Do you believe all events are connected somehow? For every action there is an equal or even greater reaction?"

Jack wondered where this was going. He decided to humor Reverend Ray. "You mean like someone playing with fire? Eventually they'll get burned?"

"Exactly," Ray said emotionless. "Let's use that scenario. A little boy gets into a box of matches. He's curious, so he swipes them from the cupboard and takes them outside into the backyard. He gathers some sticks and dead leaves and decides to make a little brush pile. He scrapes one of the matches against the striker and a flame ignites. A little harmless right? Wouldn't you agree?"

"To an extent." Jack wondered where this was going.

"Then the little boy takes the small flame and sets it to his brush pile. Within seconds the pile begins to smoke and burn. What the boy sees excites him. Even to him it seems harmless. He hasn't caused any damage. What harm is there in what he's done?"

"So far none."

Reverend Ray continues. "So every day during the summer he goes outside and makes another brush pile and he burns it, and every day the piles seem to get bigger and bigger than the pile the day before. He's no longer happy with the size of the pile he could control. He wants bigger and better. But you see, the boy can't control the outside sources that could effect his burning. The summer has been dry. The grass around him is dead and becomes a tinderbox. One day the boy creates his best pile yet and when he sets it on fire, a gentle wind comes along, and begins to blow one of the burning embers onto the dead grass. And before he knows it, his burning pile has engulfed the ground around him, burning everything in its path. Including the little boy."

"So what does this have to do with yesterday?" Jack asked beginning to lose his patience with Reverend Ray. "Quit talking to me in parables."

"It has everything to do with yesterday. It has everything to do with what was and what is yet to come. You want me to give you answers, but yet if I did that you wouldn't even begin to understand the depth of our actions and the ultimate reactions."

"Then why did you call for me?"

"Because I'm confident that if you personally do the necessary investigating that needs to be done here, you will not only find the answers you've been seeking since your wife left you, but you will also understand the reactions that took place."

"So why not just tell me? Save us all wasted time and energy?"

"You're pathetic! Your choice is a simple one Mr. Angel. Don't do a thing and stay holed up at home and die a slow, lonely alcoholic death. No one misses you. No one cares. Life goes on. It's what you want isn't it?"

"Or what?"

Reverend Ray smiled at Jack. "Seek, and ye shall find. Knock, and it shall be opened unto you."

Reverend Ray lowered his head, closed his eyes, and began praying silently to himself. Jack stood up and walked past the now praying Reverend Ray. When he was next to Ray, he paused and bent down next his ear.

"If this has anything to do with my daughter, make sure you offer up a prayer to the soul or souls responsible. They will need all the prayers they can get when I find them."

After Jack left the room, closing the door behind him, Reverend Ray Stevens lifted his bowed head, stared at the now-empty chair once occupied by Jack Angel, and felt the sides of his mouth become a smile.

It had begun.

6

"Jack I think you need to reconsider this!" Frank boomed while following a visibly frustrated Jack into his office. He shut the door behind him and sat at his desk. Jack refused to sit and paced around the room while fishing out a cigarette from his pocket.

"I don't care what you think Frank! If this somehow brings closure to Ainslie, then I'm in. Dammit! Don't shut me out on this one Frank!"

Frank watched as Jack paced hurriedly from one end of his desk to the other. He knew this was hard on him. The investigation into Ainslie's killer ended with no leads and no suspects. It had been two years and now the case was considered cold. The long drawn out process, coupled with the emotional toll it took on Jack and his marriage to Dani, saw Jack drinking heavily, quitting the force, and finally separating from Dani after ten years of marriage. Now Jack scraped by from what little savings and investments he had, and the occasional odd job being hired as a private investigator to help make ends meet.

Frank hoped Jack would soon start to get his life back together and had contemplated hiring him some day as a consultant to help out with an investigation - just to see his friend doing something other than sitting in his apartment and getting drunk. Now Frank started to question bringing him in to talk to Ray Stevens. At first, it seemed like the right choice, but now in hindsight Frank didn't know.

"Jack I know this was the last thing you expected today when coming here. Hell none of us knew what he wanted you for, but I really think you need to reconsider. You're emotional right now. Not thinking straight."

"Hell yeah I'm emotional! Who wouldn't be Frank?"

"Please Jack. Take a step back and reconsider what you're asking."

"Why? Why should I reconsider Frank? You heard what he said in there!"

"Because of your motives."

"*My* motives!" Jack shouted. "What do my motives have to do with any of this? My daughter's killer was never found. He may be the link to finding her killer."

The volume from Jack's voice shook the thin office windows. People in the hallway paused in front of Frank's office trying to steal a peak at the confrontation between Jack and Frank.

"Jack, lower your voice please."

"I was told the case is cold. No leads! No suspects! Nothing! So if you think I'm motivated by getting the answers *you* never could, then you're damn right! And I'll be damned if you think I'm going to sit back while you play Vacation Bible School with Reverend Ray!"

"You have to let us do our job," Frank said calmly hoping it would settle Jack down.

"But no one here did their job when it came to Ainslie!"

"Please Jack," Frank said pointing with an opened hand to an empty chair.

Jack finally took a seat. "You know you can't hold the Rev unless you charge him," Jack stated with his tone calming down. "So tell me Frank, what's going to happen to him?"

"Like I said earlier when I called you, we are transporting him over to county for a psyche eval. The guy tried to kill himself and with all these other ramblings of his, I'm confident he'll be admitted."

Jack reached across Frank's desk and grabbed the picture frame that was sitting next to the computer monitor. The picture was Frank and Jack on a fishing trip, taken at the end of the day with both holding up their stringer of walleye. It had been a trip they planned to Lake Erie all year. They limited out on fish within a few hours with Jack catching a fourteen-pound trophy sized walleye.

His biggest ever.

That was the last time Jack remembered smiling. Shortly after the trip, his daughter came up missing and Jack felt his life took a turn for the worst.

"Frank, what did you enjoy most about our trip to Erie?"

"I'd have to say seeing your face when you landed that behemoth of a fish."

"You know I haven't smiled since that day?"

"Yeah, that's why I keep that photo of us on my desk. I'm actually reminded that you were happy once and I hope that happiness comes back again."

Jack placed the picture between his hands and stared into Frank's eyes. "Then you have to let me do what I do best. Let me help investigate this. If what happened yesterday with those pastors is somehow connected to what happened to Ainslie, then I want to know."

Frank leaned back in his chair, exhaled loudly as if he had no other choice in the matter, and held up his hands, "I don't see how they're related."

"I know, but Ray suggested that I would get the answers I seek."

"And what if you don't?"

"I can't think like that. Not at this moment. I need to try. It's all I have going for me right now. I need to do this Frank," Jack pleaded.

Frank let out a second enormous sigh. He knew what Jack was saying and deep down he would do the same thing if he were in Jack's position, a child taken from him and then his wife leaving soon after. Jack wasn't acting any different than any other rational father in his state of mind.

Frank folded his hands and placed his elbows on his desk, resting his head on his folded hands. "Okay Jack. I'll bring you in on this, but I need to talk to Lieutenant Richards first and let him know. I don't think it will be a problem."

The Cleansing: A Thriller

Jack stood up and stuck his hand out towards Frank. "Thanks. I owe you one."

Frank shook Jack's hand. "You don't owe me anything except a hundred dollars from Saturday's fights."

Jack chuckled and turned to leave.

"Hey Jack." Jack turned towards Frank. "I hope this brings the closure you're looking for."

Jack nodded, not saying a word. He exited the office closing the door softly behind him. When Frank heard the door click shut, he picked up the phone and called Lieutenant Richard's extension to let him know about his conversation with Jack.

7

Monday. 2:15 PM EST

William Brookings had been the Associate Pastor of Community Christian Fellowship for three years. He was thirty-eight years old with a theology degree from a southern Christian university. He met his wife Jana while in his senior year and two years after graduating and saying their nuptials, they brought home a baby boy, Jonathan Patrick Brookings. Three years later Jana gave birth to twin girls, Madison Kate Brookings and Amanda Marie Brookings. William and Jana celebrated their twelve-year anniversary prior to William taking the Associate Pastor position. Jonathan had turned ten and the twins would turn seven within a few months.

William weighed about one-eighty with a blonde flattop hairstyle. He wasn't as athletic as others, but he did make sure to play for his church's summer co-ed softball league with his wife Jana.

William had been gathering Pastor Tom Sullivan's belongings, reminiscing about some photos before placing them in boxes to give them to Tom's wife Kathy, when he heard a knock on the now deceased pastor's door.

"Come in," William announced still boxing up items.

"Sorry to bother you, but I was wondering if I could have a moment of your time."

William looked up and saw a man who stood six-two, dark hair that was stylishly messy on top, and a nice athletic build to him. The man also had a confident air about him that William rarely saw in people these days. A confidence that let others know he wouldn't back down to anyone. *If he is here to ask about church membership, I need to enquire about his softball abilities*, he thought to himself.

"Is this something that can wait?" William asked. "We had a tragedy, so the church office is closed today. Hope you can understand our situation here."

"I figured it would be closed, but I decided to drive by anyway. I saw a car out front and tried the doors. They were open and so I let myself in. I hope you don't mind."

"Like I said, we are closed today."

"I don't plan being too long."

"Can I ask what this is about?" William continued to stand by Tom's desk, not moving.

"I'll get to that. Can I have a seat?"

William hesitated then nodded reluctantly. "Can I get your name?"

"Absolutely. My name is Jack Angel," Jack said reaching out to shake hands. "Yours?"

"My name is William Brookings," he said extending his hand and returning the gesture with a limp handshake.

"Can I call you William?"

"Sure."

Jack sat down and pulled out a mini-tape recorder. "I hope you don't mind if I record our conversation."

"That depends on what our conversation is about. I've already talked to the news enough already."

"Don't worry this isn't a news interview. I'm actually here investigating the suicides that occurred yesterday and seeing if you could shed any light on the matter."

William rolled his eyes. He was tired of talking about what happened. He couldn't understand why people just wouldn't let the grieving process see itself through. It was a tragic day for the congregations and the families involved. "Look, this is a hard time for the churches that suffered yesterday. I don't think *now* is the right time to talk about it. Let us mourn and get through the bereavement and then I can answer any questions you have."

Jack sat back in the black leather chair and crossed his legs signaling to William he wasn't going anywhere. Not anytime soon that is. "I understand your concern William, but you see I need to get as much information I can while it's still fresh in your mind. I'm sure you understand the urgency of the matter."

"So you're not going to respect my wishes?" William huffed.

"I'll respect your wishes soon after you answer a couple questions I have. I promise to be brief and then I'll let you be."

"And what if I don't want to? Then what?"

"I was hoping you'd ask me that. You see William; I already called one of the news stations to do an exclusive interview with me in about fifteen minutes down the street at the Pub and Eatery. The topic was on how this church's administration is obstructing justice and didn't want to get to the bottom on why three pastors lit themselves on fire with two of them dying in front of their congregation."

William was stunned. "Three? I thought there were only two."

"Maybe you should talk to me then. You know, while it is still fresh in your mind. Questions need to be answered and it appears we might be able to help each other understand what happened yesterday."

"I really don't know. Not at this moment. Sorry Mr. Angel."

"Like I said, I can either be here or at that interview. It's your call William." Jack waited for William to make a move.

Reluctantly, William walked away from the moving box and sat at the cherry wood desk of his former pastor. *Three pastors? What was going on with Tom and the others to want to do this to themselves?* "Fine," he said reluctantly. "What do you want to ask me?"

8

He is a drifter.

A transient.

To look at the Gray Man, he appeared to be in his sixties. He had shoulder length greasy gray stringy hair which he always wore in a ponytail. His six-one lean body appeared more skeletal than muscular. The appearance of his skin was a mixture of ashy white and gray covered in dark sunspots which had lost is elasticity years ago. The only facial hair was his neatly combed and trimmed goatee.

Probably the only hygiene he experienced.

His stained teeth and unclipped dirty yellow fingernails resulted from decades of chain smoking Camel unfiltered. The heavy stench of smoky clothes, rotten meat, and charred animal fat created a less than comfortable presence.

No matter the weather outside, his clothes were the same everyday. Whether it was sweltering hot or frigid cold he wore dirty, almost worn out, blue jeans, a jeans shirt, tattered rattlesnake skin boots, and a pale gray dirty trench coat.

He never carried a wallet with him and therefore he had no identification to show, if asked, which rarely happened. The police found the Gray Man's aura to be something more lethal than what they may have encountered before and didn't want to find out what kind of fight he would bring to them.

His intimidating demeanor seemed to keep people away. At first glance, he might look like an easy target for muggers or someone in a bar looking for a fight, but within moments their minds would know better.

The Gray Man was someone not to test one's strength. Few had tried in the past and quickly shown the error of their ways, with none given the chance to apologize. Bones broken. Quick slashes of a knife to vital organs or arteries sliced. Ashy gray hands crushing the attacker's esophagus.

The Gray Man had killed before. That's what executioners do.

And he would kill again if provoked or felt the necessity to end one's life. With each death, the Gray Man felt more powerful, and never did he feel sorry for taking the life from the wretched.

He had a purpose to serve in this life. He knew it from the beginning. He came with one purpose in mind.

To judge the vile and kill if necessary.

Tattooed in Old English capital letters on his right forearm beginning at his elbow and ending at his wrist was the word REVELATION.

On his left forearm was 6:8, which was the chapter and verse from the book of Revelation.

"And I looked, and behold a pale horse: and his name that sat on him was Death, and Hell followed with him."

He's the Gray Man.

A drifter.

A transient.

A killer.

...And Hell followed him.

9

Jack was once again in his element. He almost forgot the rush of adrenaline the job brought him. This was his zone, his element, sitting across from the Associate Pastor and trying to get the details to push the investigation towards a conclusion. Whether it was a suspect, or a witness that had crucial information that could help connect the dots, Jack would get the answers he needed. This is what he loved to do best, and the fact was, he was exceptional at it.

And he knew it.

He was confident.

Frank knew it and that's why he called him in. No one could see into the mind of a criminal better than Jack or could question a witness or suspect better than Jack. Jack seemed to get inside their mind and their heart.

Their heart.

That was the key.

You had to become one with their heart. The heart births the emotions from love, to fear, to happiness, to anger, and malice. The eyes were the mirror to the soul. The heart and soul were connected. By watching their eyes, Jack could tell what the heart was saying.

Jack learned early on in his career that a suspect was lying by the way their eyes blinked. It was a self-conscious reaction to questions asked. When a suspect answered, they would somehow look away or blink their eyes. This was always coupled with a shift in composure. Jack's interest was not just the answers given, but how those answers were delivered.

But there was more to Jack than just his interrogation skills.

Somehow, he was able to visualize the crime as it occurred. He wasn't psychic. He would be the first to say that. He just knew how to put his entire being into the scene of crime – the murder – and witness what the victim felt, from their perspective.

"You have a unique gift," Frank would always say to him. "You see what others can't. You feel what the victim's felt. Somehow, you put yourself at the scene."

A unique gift.

At times, it felt more like a curse.

Nevertheless, the gift seemed to vanish with Ainslie's death. He couldn't do it anymore. He lost his ability and desire to get inside the heart and mind.

Ever since her death, he retreated inside himself and didn't have much energy to do anything except to get up in the morning, maybe shower, eventually eat, smoke, and drink bourbon. He always had time for alcohol, which is why Dani left him.

"*Forget her!*" Jack would say to himself when trying to cope with Dani leaving. "*I had to grieve too, but all Dani seemed to care about was Dani!*"

Now here he was. It had been two years. Called in by his friend and former colleague to question Reverend Ray and given a second chance at starting over. Jack didn't want to second guess himself whether or not he could do what he needed to find the answers to the pastor suicides. He knew this was more than just a strange coincidence, like the news tried to spin it.

It had to be.

Something inside his heart nagged at him that around the corner a terrible event was going to take place. Something greater than just pastors setting themselves on fire. There was a reason for that. Jack had to find out why. Once he did, he was confident it would open the door to these unexplained suicides and prevent something more tragic from happening.

The Cleansing: A Thriller

But one feeling Jack was certain about.

And this was a feeling he couldn't get away from, no matter how hard he might try.

He knew this investigation was on a timetable.

The next tragic event was not months or weeks away.

No, he couldn't be so fortunate to have more time.

Somebody or *some group* was trying to make a statement and they wanted to make that statement now.

But what? What was being said for every ear to hear or eyes to see?

Jack had to find that reason and fast. He knew if he didn't on his own, he feared the next tragedy would only be in a matter of days.

10

Associate Pastor William Brookings leaned forward with his hands folded on the giant cherry wood desk. His eyes, now fixed on Jack, with the occasional glance at the clock hoping that Jack's appointment with the news reporter would be a no show. William was tired of having to answer for what Pastor Tom had done, but he also knew that his church didn't need any more bad publicity. Attendance would be low this Sunday and probably for many weeks for sure. He prayed the church would stick together as a family through the dark valley they were walking through at this time. They trudged through these waters before and didn't sink. Regrettably, because of Tom's suicide, this time it was different and William didn't know if the church could make it. He prayed they would, but his heart told him he was certainly wrong. He just needed to remain steadfast and guide the flock through the pain.

And that was something he could do.

Jack leaned forward, placed the mini recorder on the desk, and hit the record button. He stated the date, time, place, and who was present at the interview.

"William, can you please tell me where you were in the sanctuary during Tom Sullivan's message?"

"Where I always am, sitting on the front pew with my wife Jana."

"And tell me what was going through your mind when Pastor Sullivan started pouring gas all over him?"

"I thought it was part of his sermon. I didn't know it was gasoline. None of us could tell what was in the jug and so everyone in the sanctuary thought it was just a prop for his message. By the time he pulled out the lighter, we were all in a state of shock and disbelief. I couldn't move. I tried. I kept thinking, surely this isn't real. He isn't going to set himself on fire."

"But he did."

"Yes he did. Many were screaming while others of us ran on stage to try and put him out, but it was too late. The fire was too much. It was the most horrific experience of my life. I watched not only my pastor die in front of me, but he was my friend."

"Did you talk to him that morning?"

"Yes."

"And how did he seem to you? Did you see a change in his mood or personality?"

"He did seem a little distant, but I know he's been under a lot of stress lately."

"Really? How so?"

"Well our numbers are way down. Have been for some time. And since our budget is based off of what we take in offering, the giving has been low."

"Sounds like a normal problem to me, but not one that would cause a pastor to kill himself in such a display. Let's not forget, two others tried to kill themselves as well. Fortunately, one congregation saved their pastor. "

William nodded. "And praise God for that! I wish our church could say the same. We can't." William leaned back in his chair. "I do want to add, I agree with you completely. You're right. It's not usual for a pastor to become so dismayed over the offering and budget that he'd want to kill himself. "

"That's why I think it's something more than just the lack of giving from people."

"Well you asked if I knew why he would have a change in mood or personality and that's all I can think of right now. Our church has been going through a financial crunch. If there's anything more, I simply don't know."

"When did you hear about the other pastors?"

"A few hours after."

"And what did you think when you heard about it?"

William's brow furrowed while he chewed on Jack's question for the next few minutes. "Disbelief and confused," he finally answered. "I didn't think it was possible to feel any more numb after watching Tom die, but I did."

"You're aware that each of the pastors, including Tom Sullivan, were all preaching the same message?"

"Yeah I heard that."

"You know, rumor has it, they weren't just preaching the same message in context, but they used the same verses."

"Yes, I was aware, but with the thousands of sermons delivered every Sunday by thousands of pastors, I'm sure that's bound to happen from time to time. It's coincidence."

"Well then, let me go one step further. On top of the fact they gave the same message and used the same verses, did you know they lit themselves on fire at the exact same time. Did you know that? Would you say that's a coincidence too?"

"No I wouldn't, but I don't know what you're getting at Mr. Angel. All I know is what I told you."

"You see, I'm having a difficult time wrapping my head around all this. When I look at some of these other churches, I don't see a problem in their attendance. I see very large numbers of people. So I don't think yesterday had anything to do with not being able to afford your next potluck luncheon or ice cream social. I'm confident there's something more going on here. A lot more. And either you all are too naïve to see it or you choose to be blind and not see it at all. So which is it?"

Jack sat back in the black leather chair and studied William's face. He studied William's body and how it might change positions in the chair. *His hands.* Where does he place them? Does he scratch his head or ears? *His eyes.* Does he look away? Is he nervous? All signs that he might not be telling the entire truth.

He wasn't able to detect anything.

"Mr. Angel, what happened to this church and the others yesterday is a tragedy and one that will take a long time to heal from. I wish I knew why Pastor Sullivan and the others did

The Cleansing: A Thriller

what they did, but I don't. If I had any sense of what was going to happen, I would've prevented it. I don't know what else you want to know from me, but if it's all right with you I would like to get back to packing up my pastor's belongings for his mourning wife."

Jack nodded as if he was processing William's words. Parsing them. Filing them away in his mind to recall later when he needed to.

"Absolutely. I will get out of your hair then."

Jack stood and grabbed his recorder, but not turning off the record button. William stood as well. "Thanks for coming by. I hope I answered your questions."

"For now you did."

"Well, I'm glad."

"One more thing."

"Yes?"

"Do you all record your Sunday sermons? I know churches do that nowadays either on video or audio."

William wasn't expecting the question. He stammered, "Uh...yes...we record them."

"Can I get a copy? I would like to review the sermon and see if there is anything that might be able to help."

"Well sure. I already gave one to the police though."

"I understand that. I guess I want one for my own personal library."

William was annoyed. "Fine, you can come with me and I'll dub it for you right now. It will only take a few minutes."

"Great. And while you're doing that, I'll be in your sanctuary looking at the crime scene."

"Ummm, I don't think..."

Jack held up his hand. "Not to be blunt, but I don't care what you think. I won't take too long, but I *am* going to stand down there and get a sense of what was going through Pastor Sullivan's mind. Do we understand each other?"

"Fine," William said obviously irritated. "I'll take you there and then meet you back after I have your copy ready."

Jack smirked. "Sounds like we're on the same page."

37

Within a few minutes from leaving the church offices, William Brookings led Jack to the sanctuary doors. Following behind William, he walked down the aisle and then up on stage, staring at the empty pews.

So this is where it happened? Talk to me Tom. What was going through your mind?

11

Jack walked onto the stage and stood in the middle of the charred area where Pastor Tom Sullivan fell to the ground and burned to death. The burned area still had the residual smell of gasoline, burnt carpet, and the remnants of burnt flesh.

Jack walked up to the podium where Pastor Sullivan delivered his message. The once shiny oak podium now had the black scars from flames around the edges.

He stood at the podium, gripping the sides, as if he was about to deliver a sermon. Taking in his surroundings, he reached inside his jacket, pulled out a sterling silver flask, took a swig, and closed his eyes.

He inhaled the air around him deeply, still getting the nauseating pungent stench of gasoline. "What did you see when you looked out at the crowd Tom? How did they see you?"

It had been a couple years since Jack had tried to get inside the mind and heart of another person and knew this may take awhile. He continued to keep his eyes closed and repeated the same questions as if at any point the words would act as a key to unlock this mysterious door.

What did you see when you looked out at the crowd?

How did they see you?

When the door was unlocked, he would know it. At first, the deep blackness he was peering into would begin to flash a bit and then as if dreaming, his mind, with a series of rapid flashes, would begin to create a picture.

Often times people had made the mistake of thinking Jack had a psychic ability.

He didn't think so and was quick to remind them of that fact.

He just had the uncanny ability to put himself at the scene and peer through the eyes of those present and tried to profile what the victim or assailant saw.

Jack asked under his breath again, *What did you see when you looked out at the crowd? How did they see you?*

Nothing.

Jack wasn't getting anything, but a black void.

He knew it would take some time, but hoped he hadn't lost his profiling ability.

Not receiving any connection, Jack decided to go and sit on the front row of the center pews. He hoped it might trigger something inside. He sat down and leaned back as if he was sitting there on Sunday listening to Pastor Sullivan.

Once again, he closed his eyes and attempted to peer through the eyes of Pastor Tom Sullivan. He envisioned the pastor scanning the crowd, pausing in his message to give emphasis on the words, and preparing himself for the inevitable.

What did you see when you looked out at the crowd?

How did they see you?

Jack waited.

C'mon! Talk to me.

Now getting visibly frustrated, *What did you see when you looked out at the crowd?*

How did they see you?

And then, as if out of nowhere, he got a quick pop.

Faces. Distorted faces.

That's all he was able to see.

Nothing more.

Like the flash from a camera, as quick as the image came, it left.

Feeling defeated, Jack looked up at the ceiling. "Dammit," he said aloud. "Why can't I get anything more? Have I lost it?"

Jack knew the answer to his question, but wondered how long it would take for his ability to completely recover.

Time.

It was going to take time.

But time he did not have and something had to give.

"I got yesterday's sermon for you Mr. Angel."

William Brooking's voice startled Jack as he flipped his head around to see the Associate Pastor walking down the aisle towards him. He stood up and met him half way.

"I appreciate that."

"Sorry it took longer than I thought it would. I went ahead and burned it to a DVD for you. Not many people have VCRs anymore."

"Thanks." Jack took the DVD, glanced over it and shook hands with the Associate Pastor and then handed him his business card. "If you happen to come across anything or think of something missed, don't hesitate to call me."

"Will do," William agreed, trying to get on Jack's decent side, letting him know he will give his fullest cooperation. Jack didn't buy the sudden change in attitude. "And Mr. Angel, if you need anything more, you can call me. Understand please, I may not be able to answer your call because of funeral preparations. So just leave a message and I'll call you back."

"Better yet, I'll come and see you in person if I need anything more."

The look on William's face was obvious, *I was afraid you'd say that.*

Jack turned and headed towards the doors leaving the pastor and his bereavement time behind.

12

Susan Clevenger was walking home from school when the black Honda Accord pulled up beside her. Her mind wasn't on what she was going to do when she got home. She wasn't thinking about the exams she had the next day. She wasn't thinking about the party at Rhonda's house on Friday. Her mind was elsewhere entirely.

Jeff Sarshay, captain of the high school football team.

Throughout three years of high school, and not by choice, Susan hadn't had a steady boyfriend, unless someone counted her relationship with Eric Campbell. Which Susan didn't. She and Eric dated for a month, but they never went out on a real date to dinner and a movie. They would occasionally talk on the phone or pass notes to each other in the hallway in between classes. That was it. Finally, Susan, after a few weeks of boredom, passed Eric a note between second and third period to end the juvenile relationship. When she saw him at the end of day, he already had a new girlfriend standing at his locker. She looked at him disgustedly and he turned away. Not since Eric had a boy even given her the time of day.

That was last year.

Now it was her senior year.

Over the summer her pimples seemed to disappear, she grew out her hair, spent lots of time at the pool, and traded in her glasses for contact lenses.

Then something happened she wasn't expecting. Jeff Sarshay started smiling at her in the hallway and would give a sheepish wave. She couldn't believe it! She thought she noticed

42

him paying a little more attention to her lately and asked Rhonda if she noticed it too.

"I think he likes you."

"Why would he be interested in me? He's been dating Teri off and on since our sophomore year."

"I don't know. Maybe he's tired of dating little girls and wants a real woman."

"Well I am far from that Rhonda."

"Well, not in the boob factory you're not."

"Rhonda!" Susan shouted with embarrassment at her friend's observation and comment.

"Well, it's true sister! I say flaunt 'em!" They both laughed, but Susan didn't think about it anymore until today when Jeff decided to gather up the courage and sat down at lunch with her and asked her for her phone number.

Susan had been sitting with Rhonda and Ashley when he pulled up a chair to the table. He greeted everyone politely. At first he made small talk with Rhonda and Ashley, and asked finally asked Susan if it would be okay to call her some time.

Blushing, Susan said, "Yes. I would like that."

She gave Jeff her number and ever since lunch her mind was only thinking about when he might call. She hoped when she finally did talk to him she didn't want to sound retarded and make him second guess asking her for permission to call her. She could live down the Eric relationship. This was something else entirely.

The Honda beeped at her bringing her out of her daydream. She quickly glanced at the car and turned away thinking it wasn't her getting honked at and kept walking. When she heard the horn again she stopped and turned and saw the passenger window coming down.

"Susan," she heard the driver say.

"Oh hey!" she laughed feeling stupid and leaned into the open car window. "I didn't recognize you at first. I thought you were honking at someone else."

The driver laughed. "No I saw you walking home and thought about giving you a ride if you needed."

43

Susan seemed to ponder the gracious offer. "I don't know. I don't want you to have to go out of your way. My house isn't much further really."

The driver couldn't help not looking at her young soft breasts and how they seemed to press together delicately in her shirt. He thought for sure she was doing that on purpose to tease him. He felt himself get aroused in his pants and hoped she didn't notice.

"It's really no problem at all. I don't mind."

Susan tossed around the proposal in her mind and finally nodded. "Okay, I live a few blocks up on Clifford and then turn right."

She slid into the passenger seat placing her book bag on the floor between her legs. The driver couldn't help but notice her smooth tan legs and wondered if later on she might let him kiss her inner thighs.

He would have to consider that option after eating dinner with his wife and children, but knew he would have to come up with a reasonable excuse to leave the house for the night. Probably say he had unfinished work he was pressed to complete on time. Then he could go and enjoy some alone time with Susan who would be waiting for him tied up in the cold basement he had prepared for her. The place he was taking her to instead of her home.

13

Jack was on his second shot of bourbon at The Town Tap. He stopped in for a drink after leaving Community Christian Fellowship. It was just going to be one drink so he could relax and get his thoughts together. But as always, one drink led to another. Deep inside, Jack knew there would be one more before he needed to leave, and possibly a fourth because he couldn't stop thinking about Ainslie.

He threw back the second shot and swallowed the 80 proof corn liquid and motioned to the bartender he wanted one more by pointing to his now empty shot glass. Reluctantly, the bartender nodded and set Jack up with his third shot, reminding him of his overdue tab, then made a mental note to call Jack a cab when he was ready to leave.

With a new shot poured, Jack's cell phone rang. He looked at his phone's caller ID and after trying to recall the number through glassy inebriated eyes, he answered.

"This is Jack," he said slurring a little.

"Hey Jack. Frank. Where are ya?"

"Town Tap."

"Figures," Frank replied sounding frustrated. "Stay put I have something I want to bring you."

"What?" he asked dreading Frank seeing him like this again. "Can't you just tell me?"

"No. I need to see you in person. Plus, I need to talk to you about my meeting with the Lieutenant."

"What did he say? That he doesn't need me? The department has it handled?"

"Not at all. He actually thinks it's a good idea."

"Then what is it?"

"He has some valid concerns."

"Like?"

"Well, take a look at where you're at and it's only the afternoon."

"Damn Frank, sounds to me that he's not the only one concerned."

"If you're talking about me, you're right."

"Well, don't worry about me. I'm fine. I'm handling it."

"Doesn't sound like it."

"Look, you wanna have an intervention wait until we are done with this case then you can call a group of my friends and family and some former alcoholic now turned counselor and we can all get together."

"Stay put Jack. I'll be there in a few."

Jack closed his phone without saying goodbye. He threw back his shot and then motioned to the bartender for one more.

I'm handling this just fine.

At the other end of the bar, the Gray Man watched as Jack Angel waited for his fourth shot of bourbon.

14

Frank walked inside the smoky bar and spotted Jack through the carcinogen fog that hung in the air. He looked as if he hadn't budged since they last talked. He was still sitting at the bar trying to convince the bartender his credit was good and would pay for his fourth shot.

"Sorry Jack. No more," the bartender said with his arms crossed leaning against the shelf of beer glasses. "Gonna have to cut you off until you pay your entire tab."

"Just one more Tommy. I've only had three today."

"Well, sorry, but three's enough and your bill includes last month. Get you some coffee on the house instead if you'd like."

"Coffee will be fine Tommy," Frank said walking up to the bar trying to spare his friend from being thrown out.

"Anything for you Frank?" the bartender asked.

"I'll have some coffee as well. Black. Three sugars and no cream." Frank tapped Jack on his arm and motioned for him to get off the stool. Jack complied and followed Frank from the bar to a secluded booth away from other patrons so the two could sit and talk privately.

"I thought you said you could handle it," Frank commented while sliding into the booth. He wanted Jack to know he was disappointed.

"I can," Jack replied, slipping in the seat across from Frank. "So what did the Lou have to say?"

"He wants you on," Frank said dispassionately.

"You don't sound as if you're okay with it."

47

"As long as you're drinking doesn't interfere. Like what I'm seeing right now."

Jack's eyes became stone-fixed on Frank, "It won't. This is too important. I need this."

"Then I'll forget what I'm seeing right now."

"I slipped. Old habits can be hard to break I guess."

"That's what I'm afraid of."

"Seriously Frank, it won't happen again. Not like this."

Frank retreated. "Okay, just make sure of that. I don't care what you do afterhours, but don't embarrass me or the department while you're working. Agreed?"

Jack nodded. "Fair enough. What'd you want to show me?" Jack asked quickly changing the subject.

Frank pulled out a long yellow envelope with the words Ray Stevens Transcript written across the front. He unwound the string on the back and pulled out the document from inside. "Here's the transcript from your conversation with Reverend Ray."

Jack took the transcript from Frank and started skimming the contents.

"I thought it might be of some help. Maybe we can bounce some ideas and figure out if he is telling us something through his cryptic verses you alluded to earlier."

"I think it's a great place to start."

"Okay, let me inside. What are you thinking?"

"He quoted a verse to me. I can't remember word for word what he said." Jack started flipping through the transcript running his finger up and down the pages looking for the exact quote from Ray Stevens. "Here it is. 'I am a sign to you. As I have done, so it will be done to them.' I didn't even give it a second thought at first, but now that I think about it, I'm certain he was trying to tell us something."

"Or warn us."

"That's what I'm afraid of."

Jack slid the transcript back into the oversized envelope.

"What are you thinking Jack?"

"I think what happened yesterday could possibly be the beginning of something bigger to come. Look Frank, you and I have been around the force a long time. We both know two people don't just set themselves on fire. They're sending a message of some sort and anyone with half an IQ can figure that out. Just like he quoted in this verse, 'As I have done, so it will be done to them.'"

"Any thoughts?"

Jack shook his head. "I met with Pastor Sullivan's Associate Pastor, William Brookings today. He couldn't think of any reason why Sullivan or the other pastors did what they did."

"Figures."

"Yeah, but he did give me a DVD copy of the sermon. So I'll watch it later on and see if I get anything from it."

"Sounds good. Are you going to visit the other churches?"

"That's my plan. Maybe I can get the audio or video recording of yesterday's sermon. Try to see if there's anything in their message that might lead us somewhere."

Frank sat back in the booth and stared at Jack. They were both silent. Frank searched for the words he wanted to say to his friend.

"Jack, listen…"

Jack held up his hand to stop Frank. "If you're going to lecture me, I'm not in the mood. I'm fine."

Frank leaned forward and looked into Jack's eyes. "I'm not going to lecture you. You're a big boy."

"You're right. I am."

"But…"

"But what?"

"If I think at any moment this is too much or if your drinking gets in the way, I'll personally pull you off the case and I won't regret doing it. Am I clear?"

Jack nodded.

Frank stood up and grabbed the check. "I'm going to cash out my bill. I'll take care of yours too. The *entire* tab. When you get home, watch that DVD and continue to look at that transcript and see if you can sift through his religious mantra and find something useful."

"Okay. I'll call you if I find anything. Thanks again."

Frank walked away, paid their bills, and left a generous tip. Jack continued to sit in the same booth after Frank left and replayed his conversation with Ray Stevens trying to get an image in his head. Nothing was coming to him, just like when he was at Community Christian Fellowship. He couldn't help but wonder if his ability was ever going to come like it did before. His one concern, if his ability ever did return, would it be too late?

He dismissed the thought as soon as it came.

He couldn't think along those lines.

He had to focus. Get in his zone. He knew time would be his enemy.

As he left the Town Tap, Jack hailed a cab to take him home. If he had been completely aware and not so narrow-focused, he may have noticed the Gray Man following him out of the bar after spending time at the Town Tap watching and studying Jack Angel and wondering what kind of adversary he would be.

Only time would tell. And the Gray Man had all the time he would need.

15

Jack sat in the back of the cab, eyes closed, and thinking about man's heart.

The *heart* of man.

The one place where evil was born. Jack knew people often confused the heart with the soul. But he knew different. Evil planted itself, then grew, and then eventually harvested its fruit in the heart. Not the soul.

Evil was always born in the heart.

Never is a timetable set when evil finally decides to reveal its face. It manifests and then exposes itself, often in different ways. It grows at its own rate, and finally exposes itself on that day. Jack knew that no matter the face it decided to show, it was all evil.

The longer evil lay dormant, the more treacherous it became. How it planted itself and the manner it was sown determined the severity when ultimately reaped.

To understand the purest nature of evil, Jack contrasted it with *Good*. Jack believed evil existed as an active force. Many believed evil was the complete embodiment of Satan, the Devil. Often times, people accepted evil as the exact opposite of God; therefore, it was viewed by some scholars as the shadow of God. Many believed and accepted the fact that one, *Evil* or *Good*, couldn't exist without the other.

Therefore, evil encompassed a duality.

Without evil, there could be no good.

Without good, there could be no evil.

Jack read once that the Swiss psychiatrist, Carl Jung, depicted evil as the "dark side of God." Therefore, without the Devil, there was no God.

Many debated where evil truly began, but most everyone agreed where it eventually ended. The consequences of evil and its acts were always upon the lives of others.

Jack knew reclamation from evil began with the heart, where evil was born.

Where the purging began.

And Jack knew it was there where evil must be *cleansed*.

To get to the heart, Jack looked at the eyes of the soul. The eyes acted as the mirror to the heart. To study the eyes of a person was to actually peer into their heart and see what manifested there.

Years of betrayal and hurt could create the fertile ground where evil could begin to grow. But Jack wasn't naïve to judge that the cause of betrayal and hurt always led to the consequence of birth and growth of evil.

Sometimes there was no reason for evil to exist.

Sometimes, it just did.

Evil could simply creep in on its own, manifest itself, and one day reveal its shadowy face to the soul. If the soul allowed it, evil and the soul could unify and the results would be treacherous.

But only if the soul allowed it.

Many times, as Jack had witnessed, the soul wanted it.

It desired the evil like a lover longing for her betrothed to return safely to her arms.

For evil to live and grow, it must be cultivated and fed. The climate must be right. The food it needed must be precise. The souls it tasted must be readily available. Jack believed evil fed on an insatiable appetite that always craved more and its consequences on others never a consideration.

Evil, when living and breathing, wanted to consume as many in its path as possible. It all started in the heart.

The evil heart of man.

The *one* place Jack Angel knew all too well.

16

The basement was cold. The darkness, a black shroud. A reminder of the solitary silence Susan now existed in. Susan sat in her underwear on a thin dirty mattress smelling of mildew, past human waste, and blood. The damp, dirty air took Susan back to her grandfather's basement and she felt this basement was similar. Wooden stairs descending into a dirty dungeon with shallow ceilings. His basement had makeshift wooden floors to keep storage items off the compacted dirt floor. Three storage rooms existed, but only to keep old window and doorframes for later use…which never happened. Instead, years of dust and cobwebs collected on the abandoned housing treatments as they postured out of sight and mind for decades.

Never to be used.

Always forgotten.

This is how Susan felt. Just like the old window and doorframes.

Her hands were bound to a bar above her head with a dirty rag - tasting of mud, saliva, and a coppery hint of blood - wrapped around her mouth. Shivers of fear and the cold environment, shot through her body. Trying to keep her body warm, and without the help of her now-bound hands, she strained to pull her bare legs close to her chest.

She continued to plea, just above a whisper, for her mother, regretting having getting inside the Honda.

Why would he bring me here? What did I do to him?

The man had wrestled her into the abandoned house, finally subduing her when she began to resist and fight for her life.

"What are you going to do to me?" she cried through her tears while he tied her hands.

"Don't worry. I'm not going to touch you. I wish I could do many things to you, but I can't. I just did as I was asked."

Her pleas became stronger. "Please don't do this to me. I promise I won't say a word. Just let me go."

"You will stay here. He will come for you soon."

"Please don't. *Please.* I'm begging you."

After wrapping her mouth with the used rag, the man shut the door leaving Susan alone in the darkness with only her thoughts, prayers, tears, and regret.

An hour after he left, the door to her prison opened slowly. Susan saw her abductor walk into the room, but he refused to turn on the light. Instead, he shined a Maglite flashlight on her face observing the scratches on her arms and legs from her struggle.

Such a beautiful girl.

How sweet she must taste.

She continued to cry. The man bent down, keeping the light on her eyes so she couldn't see his face, and undid the rag in her mouth.

"What do you want from me?" she sobbed.

"Can I get you anything?" he asked, ignoring her question.

"I want my mom," she said quietly, already knowing what her captor's response would be before she spoke.

"Sorry, but that isn't going to happen."

Feeling defeated, Susan cried harder. "I want to go home."

"Again, that isn't going to happen."

"I'll do anything. Just please let me go. I wanna see my mom. Please, I'll do anything"

The man reached out and caressed Susan's cheek. "I was hoping you'd say that. But you don't have to worry about me. As much as I've thought about kissing your legs and lips, I'm not the one who wants you. Now that I've thought about it, you're not even my type."

"W-w-who wants me?"

"He'll be here later and he is anxious to meet you. You are everything he desires. Hair. Legs. Chest. Age. You have it all. You're the complete irresistible package. I bet the guys at your school talk about how they can't wait to get with you."

Susan cried harder. "I don't do that kind of stuff."

"Ah. You're a virgin?"

Susan nodded.

"That makes it even better." The man made a mental note to make sure he let his partner know. "Today's going to be your lucky day."

"Why?" she cried.

"You're going to experience what a *real* man feels like," he said smiling.

Susan, understanding that her innocence would soon be taken by force, screamed for God to help her.

"Sorry. God isn't here. I'm afraid it's just us. You get yourself plenty of rest. Trust me, you'll need all the strength you can get later on."

The man stood up and walked over to the other side of the room. He grabbed the tripod that was sitting unknown to Susan and set it up with the camera pointing at her and the mattress. He pulled out a DVD-R and hit the eject button on the camera. After he popped the disk in, he turned on the power along with the spotlight. He peered through the lens to get a clear focus on the half-naked Susan who was pulling against her restraints, twisting her body to break free, and screaming, her entire body shaking from the force of her anger and fear.

"Ah, you look beautiful hon. You're going to do just fine. Can't promise you won't get hurt though, being a virgin and all, but you'll get used to it."

He turned off the camera and exited the room, leaving Susan and her screams behind to think about the inevitable nightmare they were about to endure. Walking up the basement steps, he pulled out his cell phone and dialed. After the third ring, someone answered. "Yeah?"

"She's here."

"And?"

"She says she's a virgin. Honestly, it's hard to believe. The way she dresses and holds herself, you'd think she'd had a few guys in her."

"Fine. Don't touch her. I'll find out for myself. She's what I've always wanted."

"Don't worry. She's all yours."

"I'll be there in an hour."

The line went dead and the man went into the kitchen, grabbed himself a beer, and wondered to himself if the girl in the basement really was a virgin. He contemplated going back and sampling the goods to make certain she was after he finished his drink.

He chugged the beer, popped open another, and leaned against the counter with a smile. "I bet you're a liar," he said to himself thinking about the girl in the basement.

And there was nothing more he hated than liars.

Liars needed to be punished.

Liars needed to be purged.

Most of all, liars needed to be...

Cleansed

17

Monday. 10:30 PM EST.

Jack sat down on his couch after loading the DVD of Tom Sullivan's last sermon. Jack lit a cigarette and sat back to watch intently every action and word the late pastor had to say. Jack wanted to watch the video as if he were a member of the congregation, and then go back and study every movement and word as needed to help give answers to why Pastor Sullivan and the others killed themselves.

While watching as an observer, he wondered what it must have been like for the congregation and what they had to witness yesterday morning. They watched their pastor light himself on fire, feeling helpless in being able to stop him, and then enduring the screams as he died.

A horrific tragedy to say the least.

Jack watched the DVD as an observer four times.

Before the fifth viewing, Jack knew he wanted to study every frame, by pausing the DVD and replaying it, as if some revelation or clue would reveal the answers to what he and the others were seeking. Jack had a pen and paper handy to begin writing down questions he had while watching Pastor Sullivan.

He started the sermon again and watched as Pastor Sullivan approached the podium. Pastor Sullivan's face didn't look like someone who wanted to be there. His expression reminded Jack of similar faces he'd seen before.

Criminal trials.

His face looked just like the criminals he'd caught and were on trial.

He looked as if he felt he was being judged. Jack hit pause on the DVD player and scribbled down some notes.

Why did he feel judged? By whom? The congregation?

He unpaused the DVD player. Pastor Sullivan picked right up after staring at his congregation. Jack kept his pen and paper handy to jot down notes.

Voice seems shaky, not like he's been a pastor for years, but rather a newbie pastor.

Talks about the coming day that will burn like a furnace. Was he preparing them for what was to come that morning?

Pain of unrighteous. Final judgment.

Reads from Psalms. Upon the wicked…fire and brimstone.

Seems to reassure those who are good. Evildoers set on fire. Either you will be burned or walk over the fire into victory. Was he the "evildoer" he referred to?

Now he reaches for the jug of gasoline. People seem confused. Don't know what to think. Pours gas on himself. I can hear gasps from the crowd. No one tries to stop him. Why? Paralyzed with unbelief?

Makes another reference to fire and how the devil being cast into that the fire. He is definitely talking about himself. Talks about Abraham and Isaac. Abraham slays his son on the altar in obedience to God.

Now he reaches for his own lighter inside his sport coat. Was this what he meant by his reference of Abraham slaying his son? A burnt sacrifice?

Screams heard all over the church.

The unbelieving.

Murderers.

Whoremongers.

Liars.

All will have their part in the lake of fire.

Second death.

This must be his second death too.

Lights himself on fire. More screams erupt. He continues to preach even though he is on fire. He is shouting.

Beast coming from a pit.

To make war.

To overcome.

The Cleansing: A Thriller

And to kill.
He screams something unintelligible — Leon? Theon? Neon?
Pastor Sullivan falls to the floor.
People surround him. Try to put the flames out. Try to save him. It's
too late. He dies in front of his congregation.

Jack stops the DVD and writes down some final thoughts.

Sermon was a message he sent to his church. His judgment was fire.
His death was to be by fire. What was he guilty of? Lying? Murdering?
Whoremongering? Unbelief? Who is this beast he talks about? Is there
someone else? Is it just a symbol? Figure of speech? A person?

If it is someone, then who? What do they want?

Jack lit another cigarette and reviewed his notes. When he
felt as if he captured all of his thoughts and understood the
message he wrote a few final sentences.

Were all the pastors who killed themselves guilty of the same act? If
so, what did they do? If he meant that someone was the coming beast, who
is it? Most important, what does this have to do with Ainslie?

59

TUESDAY

18

Tuesday. 7:45 AM EST.

Jack stirred from sleep from his phone ringing off the hook. He ignored the first set of rings wishing the caller to go to voicemail, but when the phone started again, he angrily answered it.

"What?!?!"

"Jack it's Frank. Sorry to wake you, but this is important."

"Dammit Frank I'm trying to sleep a hangover off man!"

"Well, you're needed at a crime scene."

"What the hell for? Another dead pastor?"

"No. Prostitute this time."

"Frank? You know I'm not here to help out with prostitutes getting axed by some John or methed up pimp."

Frank looked over to where the body was laying and the officers roping off the crime scene. "I don't think either of those are the case here."

"Then what is it?"

"I don't know for certain, but I believe this might have a connection to our current investigation with the pastors."

"Why? What makes you think that?"

"Can't get into it right now. Just hurry up and get down here."

"Got it. Let me get ready and I'll be there. Where ya at?"

"I'm at the Great Miami River. Down by the art institute."

"I'll be there. Do I need to bring anything?"

"Yeah, a Bible. Do you have one?"

"Possibly, but I don't know. Haven't had a reason to read one to be honest with you. But there might be one laying around here somewhere. I'll take a look."

"See you in a few."

Frank hung up the phone.

Jack sat on the edge of his bed and fished for a cigarette in his nightstand. He saw his near- empty bourbon bottle standing at attention without its cap, encouraging Jack to take a quick drink. Since Jack wasn't one to disappoint he poured himself a quick shot and then got dressed. As he stared at himself in the mirror fixing his hair, he repeated one of his favorite lines from a Humphrey Bogart movie, "Here's looking at you kid."

Jack headed towards his car, but not before rummaging around the house looking for a Bible. After fifteen minutes of fruitless searching, he remembered where he saw one months ago on the living room book shelf. He looked up and down the bookshelf, quickly scanning each level. Finally, he saw what he was looking for and grabbed the Gideon Bible, the same one he swiped from the hotel he stayed at when Dani and he fought. It was their final fight before she finally kicked Jack out for good.

To Jack, it was the final nail. A nail that sealed him in his lonely world void of emotion and the urge to do anything productive outside of the occasional private investigation jobs.

He arrived at the Great Miami River within thirty minutes of his conversation with Frank. He got out of his car and saw all the cops and bystanders swarming the crime scene. He scanned the crowd looking for Frank and finally caught him standing by the Lieutenant.

"Okay I'm here," Jack said walking over to Frank and the Lou. "So what's this about?"

Frank put his arm around Jack and started walking him towards the body with the Lou following behind. "About a week ago a prostitute named Hollywood, real name's Julie Schans, came into the station saying her friend, Bambi, another prostitute..."

"Oh Bambi's a prostitute too?" Jack asked sarcastically. "What made you think that? The name?"

"Her real name's Sonja Ericson. Anyway, Hollywood said Bambi went off with one of her regulars. Hollywood always thought the John looked a little scary. He made her feel uncomfortable, but she didn't give it a second thought. Until she hadn't heard from Bambi in like 5 hours. Therefore, she came in and reported it. We said give it twenty-four hours before we call it a missing persons."

"And?"

"She did. She came back night after night. We said we hadn't heard anything."

"So let me guess. That's Bambi over there?"

Frank nodded. "Actually a jogger found her. He was running by here this morning and thought he saw what looked like a hand sticking up from the muck on the riverbank and so he went to take a look. We got the call, responded, and had one of our patrols who knew Bambi positively ID the body."

"Okay, so why am I here with a Bible?"

"I want to show you something." Frank and Jack lifted the crime tape and walked underneath it towards the body. They each took a position with one on her right and one on her left. Bambi was facing up looking blue and lifeless. Her lifeless eyes stared past them as if she were still looking up at her killer. Old wadded fishing line, a few Styrofoam pieces, twigs, and mud from the river had collected in her mouth, hair, around her legs, and in her fingernails. Jack and Frank both covered their mouths and noses from the smell of death and rotten fish.

"I wanted you to see this." Frank pointed to cuts on Bambi's stomach. They started from the right side of her abdomen and continued to the left. At first Jack couldn't tell what the cuts were, but after staring at it intently, letters and numbers came to focus. "What does that say to you?"

"Looks like the word *Rev*. An abbreviation? Maybe for Reverend?"

"Possibly. What else do you see?"

"The number 21, and the number 8." Jack said.

"What do you think that means?"

"It could be reverend, but the 21 and 8 wouldn't make too much sense. Unless that was a day and month like 21 for the day and August for the eighth month. But again, that doesn't make sense."

"That's why I asked you to bring a Bible. Look up Revelation chapter twenty-one verse eight. What's it say?"

Jack looked at the table of contents for the book of Revelation and flipped through his Gideon Bible until he located the book and the kept turning the thin pages until he found the right chapter and verse.

"Here it is."

"Read it. Out loud."

Jack cleared his throat. "But the fearful, and unbelieving, and the abominable, and murderers, and whoremongers," Jack paused. It was the same passage he heard Pastor Tom Sullivan use on the DVD in his sermon before he killed himself. He stared at Frank.

"Continue," Frank commanded.

"...and sorcerers, and idolaters, and all liars, shall have their part in the lake which burneth with fire and brimstone: which is the second death."

Jack couldn't believe what he was reading. What connection to the pastor suicides did she have? Who killed her? Why? What did she know?

"Jack? You okay?" Frank asked bringing Jack out of his thought stream.

Something clicked inside Jack. It was the hidden truth, which blinded him for two years. The beginning truth behind Bambi and Ainslie. "She trusted him Frank."

"You talkin' about Bambi?"

"Ainslie. Bambi. Both of them," Jack said emotionless. "That's why they went willingly. They knew their abductor."

Frank put his hand on Jack's shoulder. "You okay? If this is too much, I understand."

"Don't you get it Frank? That's why no one heard a little girl screaming in the park that day. She went willingly! She

The Cleansing: A Thriller

trusted the man who took her! Just like Bambi trusted her John."

"Jack don't do this to yourself."

Jack stared coldly at Frank. "Frank, I'm beginning to understand more. I need this. If I'm ever going to find Ainslie's killer and have closure, I need to commit."

"Fair enough," Frank nodded. "You do realize, if there's a connection, what we have here today just made those suicides from Sunday a lot more than two people offing themselves. This runs a lot deeper and I have a feeling this isn't going to be the first body that shows up."

"I think you're right. There is something a lot bigger that we aren't seeing. At least not yet. We need to get some answers and fast."

Jack turned away and walked towards his car.

"Where you going?" Frank hollered.

"Where do you think? I'm gonna pay a visit to our friend Reverend Ray. I'm going to shake that bastard until he starts speaking and not in Biblical verse!"

"Hold up," Frank yelled again while catching up to Jack. "I'm coming too. Someone needs to let you in to his room and Reverend Ray needs someone sane."

"Forget sanity! It's overrated," Jack said opening his car door. Frank shook his head and laughed, getting inside the car to go and pay a visit to Reverend Ray Stevens.

67

19

One Week Ago. Tuesday. 11:30 PM EST.

Bambi followed her John into the decrepit house. She didn't give it a second thought as she has been in worse places than this to turn a trick. The man had paid her $100 in advance and said he would like to video record her so he can watch it later. She didn't care and said she's done that before. Johns always wanted something different from her to fulfill some shitty fantasy they had. No matter the fantasy, the money all worked and spent the same and Bambi didn't care.

When they entered the house Bambi sat on the dirty ripped couch. She looked around and saw the limited mismatched furniture the house offered. One couch, an old broken vinyl armchair, a card table used as a dining table, and a plastic coffee table. The foul and unclean house, long ignored for years. Stale cigarette smoke and spoiled food permeated the air. She knew better than to ask to use the bathroom because she could only imagine how that looked and smelled or if there were any running water at all.

"Who lives in this shithole?" she asked crossing her legs and lighting a cigarette.

"No one. Some of just like to hang out here and get away for a bit," the man said lighting a Coleman lantern to dispel the dark void of the house.

"So what do you want to do this time? I'm all yours for an hour and you know I do anything and everything."

"Yes, I remember quite well." the man responded feeling aroused.

68

The Cleansing: A Thriller

"So what's your pleasure? What can Bambi do for you?" she asked running her hands up her legs exposing more of her meaty thighs and across her breasts.

"What do you desire the most? What haven't you done yet?"

"Oh, I've done everything. You know that. I've taken it in all places; ass, mouth, and everywhere in between."

"Well let's try something new tonight. I want to record us. Let me get the camera set up okay?"

"Whatever makes your shit float. It's fine with me, but I don't have all damn night okay?"

The man nodded and exited down the hall to grab the video camera. When he returned, Bambi was sitting on the couch already topless. She smiled at him when he returned and began rubbing her hands on her tiny breasts.

"Very nice," the man said. "Keep doing that while I record you. That is some hot shit you're doing there."

Bambi started acting as if she were on an adult video and got more into her masturbation.

"Yeah! Keep doing that. That's great! Nice!"

"You mean like this?" she asked and turned around and bent over for the camera.

With her back to the kitchen, Bambi didn't see the other man who was wearing a burlap bag over his face, enter from behind. Bambi, already bent over, concentrating on her porno acting skills, failed to see the coming pounding from the man's fist to the back of her head. She let out a scream and fell to the floor shielding her head from another blow. The man operating the camera kept recording.

He zoomed in on the assault.

The other man jumped on the now weakened Bambi and started raining fists to her face and body. Blood quickly spread across her busted mouth.

"*WHORE!* VILE *SLUT!* You're all sluts and whores!"

Bambi screamed and tried to fight back, but felt her strength expel with each blow that landed on her. She could taste the coppery blood on her tongue and felt a couple of her teeth fall to the back of her throat.

The cameraman zoomed in closer.

The man on top of Bambi pulled out a knife.

Bambi saw the blade through the foggy haze of her beating. "Please don't," she slurred.

But it was too late. The man started carving on her stomach the word REV followed by the numbers 21 and 8. With each sharp slice into her flesh, the final grains of life trickled through her hourglass and what little hope of seeing a brand new tomorrow finally exited.

Bambi's killer stood up and looked at the cameraman who had zoomed in on the killer's burlap mask. "Dump the whore. Let the river of life cleanse her of her filth."

The cameraman turned off the camera and picked up Bambi's naked lifeless body. After placing her in the trunk, he drove her to the river and dumped her body. He didn't care if somebody found her or not. She was whore-trash. It wasn't for him to worry about. He came for one purpose, bring the whore, record the event, and dispose the trash. That's what he was asked to do and that's what he did.

Nothing more.

He'd been paid handsomely so he'd keep quiet and didn't care if he ever felt guilty or not. Any guilt associated afterwards wasn't an option. If any guilt tried to creep in, he would expunge it immediately. After he dumped the body, he had another job to attend to that evening. A job he was certain could line his bank account even more. There was a market for what he would do with tonight's recording. Make copies of the sexploits and sell it on the Internet.

This was his business.

And business was good.

20

Tuesday. 10:45 AM EST.

Jack and Frank walked into Miami Valley Hospital. Frank reminded Jack that the hospital admitted Ray for a psyche eval. They walked to the information desk and asked where to find Ray Stevens. After getting his room number, they entered the elevator and took it to the twelfth floor. When the doors opened, they flashed their badges to the charge nurse to let them onto the floor. Once she buzzed them in, they entered the floor, walking briskly by the charge nurse desk as if they'd been paged over the loudspeaker to respond to an emergency.

"Gentleman? Can I help?" the charge nurse asked.

"No," Jack answered as he and Frank walked by the desk, ignoring her request. When they found Ray's room, they tried to open his door with zero success.

"It's locked," Jack said.

"We're on the psyche floor. We need someone to let us in." They both turned and looked back at the charge nurse who was already on the phone calling security. Wanting to defuse the situation from getting out of hand, Frank ran back to the nurse's station to explain the importance of getting into Ray's room. After a few minutes, Frank returned and the nurse buzzed them into Reverend Ray's room. Jack turned the knob, barging inside, startling Ray who was watching TV.

"What the-"

"Good morning Ray," Jack interrupted. "You've got some questions to answer and not in verse."

"And if I don't?"

71

"How about we arrest you here and now for first degree murder?" Frank asked.

"What're you talking about? I didn't kill anyone!"

"Good," Jack said leaning into Ray's face. "Then you'll have no problem telling us why we found a dead hooker in the river."

"I don't know what the hell you're talking about. I never touched a hooker."

Frank pulled a chair and placed it in front of Ray's door preventing anyone from coming in. Grinning, he grabbed a magazine from the table, sat back, and let Jack take control of the situation. It was a good feeling to see his old partner back at it again. He missed this.

"I disagree," Jack said walking to Ray's bedside. "I think it has to do with what you and the Flaming Two did on Sunday." Jack motioned to Frank to toss his gun to him. Frank tossed his Beretta and Jack immediately pointed the gun at Ray's head while Frank returned to his magazine. "Do you know what nickname I earned while on the force?" Jack asked, briefly changing the subject.

Ray, eye-balling the door hoping for his nurse to come in for her rounds to rescue him, shook his head.

"You see I had this uncanny ability to get the information I needed. I didn't care how I got it, as long as I got the details and it was credible."

Jack flipped the Beretta around holding the gun by its muzzle and then slammed the butt of the gun into Ray's kneecap. Anticipating a scream, Jack covered Ray's mouth with his hand while the reverend screamed and arched his back, holding his knee as the pain shot through his leg like a thousand needles.

"They called me Death Angel."

Ray was rolling from side to side holding on to his injured knee.

Jack continued. "At first it started as a joke, but then many people came to believe it as true. And you know what? So did I."

The Cleansing: A Thriller

Jack let his words register with Ray.

"This is how it's going to work dipshit. I'm going to ask you a question. If I get a memory verse, I break your knee. If I get some cryptic message, I break your knee. If you decide you're not going to answer any questions, I put a bullet into your shit ugly fat face."

Jack removed his hand from Ray's mouth.

"You can't do that!" Ray shouted, still holding his knee.

"I can't do that? Watch me! I have nothing to live for anymore. You should know that by now." Jack turned to Frank. "Frank will I do it?"

"Absolutely!" Frank replied, not looking up and flipping pages in his magazine as if reciting pre-canned rehearsed lines. "You have nothing to live for. Nothing at all."

Jack turned to Ray, "So are you in or out? I don't have all day."

"You're a nut job!"

"Mmmmm, that's not an answer. Sucks to be you." Jack covered Ray's mouth again, held the gun up in the air, and flinched as if he was going to hit Ray's knee again.

"Okay! Okay! STOP!" Ray screamed, realizing Jack was serious.

Jack hesitated and removed his hand.

"I'm in! I'm in! Just don't hit me again!"

"Now we're talking. Why don't you begin by telling me why you and two other pastors tried to kill yourselves?"

Crying, Ray closed his weary blood-shot eyes and started revealing what he knew.

73

21

"Two months ago I was having breakfast with Pastor David Stout."

"He was one of the two who killed himself." Jack stated as if for the record.

Ray nodded. "I shared with him I'd been struggling with an addiction I had."

"Which was?"

"Homosexual porn."

"I'm sure your wife appreciated that."

Ray ignored Jack and continued. "I told David as much as I struggled and wanted to stop, I couldn't help it. I would look at online gay porn sites, but that was it. I never acted on my desires with anyone. After awhile I wondered what it might be like to try it once. Just once. That's all I wanted to do. He said he knew of a guy who could set it up for me to act out my curiosity. He assured me it would be discreet, but of course would cost me about a thousand dollars."

"So how long until David Stout called you back?"

"That afternoon. He said if I could pay the thousand the guy could be ready that night. I didn't want to lose this chance, so I jumped at the opportunity. Plus it was discreet."

"So what happened?"

"I met David at the county park. He said he needed to blindfold me and took me to a house about twenty minutes away."

"Do you remember the location of the house?"

Ray shook his head. "All I know is that it was out in the woods in the middle of nowhere."

"And what happened when you got there?"

"I went inside a guy I never met before asked to put a burlap bag over my face."

"A burlap bag? Was that supposed to be the discretion?"

"I think so. Holes were cut into it for eyes and a mouth."

"The person who asked you to put on the bag, was he the one you were supposed to meet?"

"No."

Jack nodded and looked over at Frank who was writing furiously, taking down the information.

"After a few minutes I met my partner. It was a kid in his early twenties. He came into the room and asked if I wanted to shoot up. I told him no, but watched as he found his vein and shot up his arm. After he was done he came over and performed oral on me. The same guy who gave me my mask was recording everything."

"Did you see this guy's face who gave you the mask?"

"No. He was wearing one too."

"Why was he recording it? I thought you were looking for discretion."

"I was. But I didn't care. I wanted this moment. I was willing to let it go."

"So that was it?"

"For *that* day. I felt guilty at first, but wanted to do it more and more. So I kept contacting David who kept setting up these sessions."

"Same kid each time?"

"Yeah."

"Recorded each time?"

Ray nodded.

"Same person videoing you?"

"I guess. He wore a mask each time. Had the same voice though. I'm sure it was him."

"When was the last time you were there?"

"A few weeks ago." Ray began to break down and sob.

"What happened when you were there Ray? Keep talking!"

Ray tried to collect himself, but continued to weep through his words. "Everything went like all the times before, instead on this day, when the kid wanted to shoot up, the cameraman offered him some different heroin that he had. The kid accepted, but before he shot it up, the cameraman suggested *I* shoot it into the arm of the kid. I nodded and while I was shooting that evil poison into his arm, I saw the kid's eyes begin to roll back into his head. He turned blue and started shaking violently. Blood poured from his mouth and nose. I got scared and tried to do CPR on him. I kept doing chest compressions, but nothing was working. He just kept seizing uncontrollably. I was screaming that he was dying and that I killed him. I KILLED HIM!"

"What was the cameraman doing?"

"That sick bastard kept filming. I pulled off my mask and screamed at him to help. He just continued to record my anger and fear and the death of that kid." Ray's eyes closed as the horrific memory stitched itself once again from the past and into the present.

"And you have no idea who this cameraman was?"

"None. I wish I did because I would've killed him myself."

"So bring us now to this past Sunday."

"A couple days after this happened I was in my office working late and this guy who I'd never seen before came in. I was alone and could've sworn the doors were locked, but somehow he was able to walk in."

"Can you describe him?"

"His demeanor frightened me. I felt my heart thundering in my chest while he stood in front of me. He looked like walking death. Pale gray with greasy gray hair tied in a ponytail. Appeared old and emaciated, but I could tell behind it all he was strong. *Very* strong. He seemed like he was on the verge of insanity and wouldn't think twice about killing me."

"Did he have a name?"

"No. I didn't dare ask either. I do remember he had tattoos. One said Revelation and that was on his right forearm.

The other arm had a couple numbers. I don't remember what they were though."

"What did he say to you?"

Ray started to shake in fear as tears flooded his eyes. With eyes closed, he saw once again the strange man who came to his office that day. He remembered hearing the man talk of the punishment he and the others were to receive for their acts of evil and how they must account for their sins.

It was while he was remembering, Ray's body stiffened. His head started thumping back and forth on the mattress with the rest of his body seizing. Frank jumped up and opened the door and yelled for a nurse to come quickly.

Jack tried to move objects out of the way so Ray couldn't hurt himself. They waited for the nurses and additional medical staff to respond, who were there within seconds.

As Jack stood back to let the team take care of Ray, he leaned over to Frank and said, "We need to find this guy who visited Ray and soon."

"And apparently a cinematographer who is into some sick voyeurism."

After placing their business cards on the table, Jack and Frank left the hospital hoping Ray would recover soon. There was more they needed from him and hoped he would call them when he was feeling better. It became increasingly clear after talking to Ray that he held clues that would be crucial in unlocking the door to the room of mysteries. A room that now held two new suspects that needed to be located and questioned before any more blood was shed.

22

"So where are you going?" Frank finally asked Jack. They had been silent since they left the hospital and Jack's driving had been fast at times.

"We're going to talk to Pastor David Stout's Associate Pastor and see if he can shed any light on this. We need to get to him ASAP."

"And after that we need to find Bambi's friend Hollywood. She isn't safe."

"She left a contact number right?"

Frank nodded. "We can get it and give her a buzz."

"We need to find her and fast. When the news hits the airwaves with the story from this morning, about the body at the river, Hollywood may not even talk to us. I wouldn't blame her if she didn't. She's probably scared as hell."

"It's possible, but I think we need to try her no matter what."

Jack nodded in agreement. Frank looked at his longtime friend. He'd wanted to talk with Jack about his intuitive skills ever since he brought him in to help with the case.

"I need to ask you something."

"Shoot," Jack replied changing lanes on the highway.

"Your ability."

"What about it?"

"Have you been able to get a sense from the pastors' viewpoint yet or anything at all?"

Jack didn't blink an eye. He continued to stare at the line of cars in front of him, *Come on! Speed up or move over ass wipe*, he thought to himself. *This traffic is unreal.*

The Cleansing: A Thriller

"Jack? Did you hear me?"

"Yeah I heard you."

"Well?"

Jack recklessly sped around the slow car in front of him. Frank's hands went to the roof of the car to brace himself as he said a quick prayer. Instead of taking the Interstate 675 north onramp, Jack continued on State Route 35 east towards Xenia.

"I'll answer your question. Just give me a damn minute," he snapped.

"Where are you going Jack? We need to visit David Stout's church," Frank urged.

"We'll get there, but you asked me a serious question which deserves a serious response. You want to know how I am right now investigating this situation?"

Frank nodded.

"Then I'm going to answer you and when I'm done, please don't ever ask me again."

Frank sighed and looked out his window, not saying a word. He watched as the cars passed by. *What's going on with you Jack?* He thought to himself. *I know losing Ainslie and divorcing Dani changed you my friend, but will you ever be the same again?*

After fifteen minutes riding in silence, Jack pulled the car onto the long gravel driveway at Byron Cemetery. He brought the car to a stop and threw it into park, not shutting off the engine. "Get out...," he said not waiting to hear an objection. "...and follow me."

After pausing for a moment, Frank complied and followed Jack through the garden of stones. The final resting place of Ainslie Grace Angel.

23

Jack stood at the final resting place of his daughter. It was here, he and Dani, watched her buried two years ago. He stared at her black granite headstone, running his fingers across her inscribed birth date followed by her date of death. Along the front right and left sides of the marker were angels and birds to represent her peaceful soul. In the upper right portion was her most recent school picture etched into the stone. To Jack, it was as if her spirit would forever be captured within the headstone and always be smiling at him or anyone who wanted to visit.

Why you Ainslie? Someone took you from us at such a young age. You had so much to give, so much life. Why not me instead? Oh what I would do to trade places with you. The world needs your spirit and life. The world doesn't need me. It would be a better place if you were in it. A happier place that would replace sorrow with your continued joy.

A salty trail of tears started trickling down Jack's face. He closed his eyes and remembered Ainslie at her happiest. Riding her bike and feeling as if she were the wind.

This was the essence of being a kid.

She had so much to give to the world. And the world would've been better for it.

Her precious tiny hands were there to hold Jack's hand when he was walking their dog Decker. She always seemed to find the precise word of encouragement for Dani when her mommy felt weary.

The Cleansing: A Thriller

But now, ripped from their hearts and life, Ainslie was gone.

This is where she was now.

This is one man's evil on my daughter and the day is coming when I will have my retribution.

Frank stared at Jack waiting on him to explain why they were here. He wanted to be sensitive to Jack and give him enough time to collect himself and open up. He placed his hand on his grieving friend's back, reassuring him that he didn't have to trod through the pain alone.

"Two years ago I buried my daughter here in this cemetery. If you took time to look around at all the graves you'd realize she and other children are in the small percentage of people that are buried by their parents. Don't worry about doing it. I already have and I can assure you I'm right about this." A single tear dropped from Jack's eye. It wasn't just a tear for Ainslie, but the other buried children around her. "Ever since we saw her broken body, I've vowed to find her killer. Not to bring him in and prosecuted, but to punish him like he did Ainslie. Because of this burning determination, I've lost my marriage and every bit of who I used to be. Something happened to me and for reasons I can't explain, I can't seem to get inside my daughter's mind or her killer's mind to get a feel for who he is or where he might be."

Frank's eyes locked in on Ainslie's grave. He studied the dates written across the top along with the pictures etched in stone. He couldn't help to stare at the dash that joined her date of birth to her date of death.

What a short life you had sweetheart.

He chewed on the inside of his lips replaying the words Jack shared, wanting to respond carefully.

"I know this has been hard on you and Dani. I've watched you retreat inside yourself and I know you haven't been the same. Please know I've been doing everything possible to find this guy and help you bring closure. This isn't a cold case yet and I'll be damned if I ever let it go that way."

81

"Frank, didn't you hear a word I said? I don't want him found and arrested. I want this asshole to stare into my eyes and know that I am going to make him suffer, make him experience all the pain I am feeling, and know he is going to die!"

"I know Jack," Frank said gently. "Trust me, there's a part of me that wants to see that too, but maybe this rage you have is clouding everything else. Not just clouding your life, but your ability too."

Jack couldn't help but laugh cynically, "You don't get it Frank. You never went through anything like this. This man didn't just take my daughter from me, but he took my entire life as well."

"What can I do to help?" Frank asked feeling exasperated and angry himself. "What do you need from me?"

Jack pulled a cigarette from his front shirt pocket, lit it, and inhaled the menthol smoke deep into his lungs. "I need your understanding and not trying to lecture me on my attitude or drinking. I'm handling this best way I know how."

Frank reached into his back pocket and pulled out his wallet. He flipped through some of his credit and business cards. He retrieved what he was looking for and handed it to Jack. "When you're ready, I want you to give this lady a call."

Jack reluctantly took the card from Frank and read the name on the front, Rebecca McNeil M.S., L.P.C. *Specializing in Individual, Marriage, Family, Parenting, and Grief.* "I appreciate your concern Frank. Really. I do. Please understand, right now, as much as I may want to, I can't make any promises."

"I *do* understand. I just wanted you to have a way to sort through it all if you were ever looking."

Jack filed the card in his wallet then flicked his half-burned cigarette onto the blacktop. Frank followed him to the car and wondered if his friend was really going to make the call. The Jack he knew before would have, but this wasn't the same Jack and he wondered if this was just an exercise in futility.

24

Ray Stevens was sitting up in his bed, eyes closed and resting, following his seizure. The doctor ordered an EEG to identify background epileptogenic activity to help identify particular causes of Ray's seizure.

An exhausted Ray was still asleep when the door to his room opened. The Gray Man walked over to Ray's bedside and placed his skeletal hand on Ray's arm. The icy touch to his arm startled him awake. He strained to open his eyes and clear the fog from his mind, hoping it was his nurse bringing him more ice chips to chew on. The heart rate beeps quickened on the monitor when he realized who had caused him to wake.

The Gray Man held his index finger to his own mouth, "Shhhh," the Gray Man hissed just above a whisper. "I don't want you to talk. I want you to listen and answer any questions I have for you. Do you understand me Ray?"

His tone had such authority Ray was compelled to obey. The reverend nodded his head slowly in fear, looking at the Revelation tattoo on the Gray Man's arm, knowing what would happen if he didn't comply.

"Good." The Gray Man said. "Let's begin with you and your suicide companions."

The Gray Man allowed a natural pause to see if Ray would object. Knowing he had Ray's attention he continued.

"I understand that two died on Sunday. Is that what you understand as well?"

Ray nodded.

"Including you, there should have been four cleansings, but there wasn't was there?" The smoothness of the Gray

83

Man's voice sent chills through Ray Stevens's body. Again, the monitor picked up a faster heart rate rhythm.

Ray shook his head acknowledging this fact.

"There were only two. You were a lucky one. Your congregation actually wanted you to live another day. Too bad they don't know your soul like I do. You thought you could continue and inflict damage on another soul. Is that a fair assessment?"

Ray didn't move.

"I asked you a question Ray," the Gray Man demanded. "Don't make me repeat myself."

Slowly, Ray nodded.

"We both know who didn't cleanse himself don't we?"

Again, Ray acknowledged the question with a nod.

"It's a shame he didn't take his own life. I think you and I both know what's going to happen to him. His cleansing won't be as quick as the others. He'll beg for an end, but his suffering will be infinite. To quote Matthew twenty-four, 'There will be weeping and gnashing of teeth.'"

"I don't think he's ready," Ray replied, trying to theorize. "He wants to do more. He's compelled to do more. To finish what he started."

"I'm aware. I'm very aware. He has taken a girl. Her name is Susan Cleavenger."

Ray closed his eyes as if the act would somehow make the horror go away. "I didn't know."

"That's not your concern. You are right though. He thinks he needs to continue to purge the sins from others. Make them atone. Unfortunately he will fail and his punishment will be far greater than yours."

Ray trembled, fearing what punishment would come to him. "And what about me?" he asked, voice shaking. "I tried to obey you. I tried to purify myself with fire."

"I know you did, but you haven't given penance yet for your wicked sins have you?"

"I tried," Ray pleaded through tears. "But they were blind to me and stopped me before I could cleanse myself. It was my congregation's fault! *They* were the ones who stopped me. I tried to do what you asked."

The Gray Man held the same index finger as before to his lips. "Shhh Ray. Don't worry. Your day will come, but not yet. Not yet."

"Then when?"

"Don't worry. You'll know when your time has come, but I can use you."

"What is it?" Feeling relieved his execution had been stayed for at least a short while. "Anything. I'll do anything."

"The man who visited you earlier."

"His name's Jack Angel," Ray said quickly trying to show his allegiance.

"I know that Ray. Don't interrupt me again. I just want you to listen. Listen to every word I have to say to you."

"Okay. I'm sorry. I'm so sorry. I'm listening to you."

"He's on a journey that will take him to the darkest regions of man's forsaken soul. You don't need to guide him by answering his questions. He must find out the evil and wickedness that has occurred on his own. He must seek that which he questions on his own. If he needs any guidance into the dark soul of man, it will be by me. Not you. Am I clear?"

"Yes."

"I must go now. I have a fourth man that must atone for his sins. Do you have any questions for me?"

Ray nodded cautiously.

"Ask."

"What if Jack Angel comes back and presses me. His heart is determined. He is driven by rage and retribution."

"Rage is good. Rage will be the dark path he needs to follow to fully experience man's evil doings. And I know you struggle with defying what I asked you to do."

"I do. I really do."

"Then I shall take care of that right now." The Gray Man took his right hand and placed it over Ray's mouth. He squeezed Ray's face, flexing his forearm, his tattoo undulating with the tightening grip, and then pushed Ray's head down into the pillow, almost crushing Ray's skull. Ray tried to scream, but the Gray Man's fingers continued to dig deep in his leathery face, silencing his voice.

Under the full, punishing weight, Ray used both hands and grabbed on to the Gray Man's arm and tried to pry it from his face. *He's killing you*, Ray's instinct told him. *He's going to smother you.*

But Ray was unsuccessful in his efforts.

Ray was certain he was going to die.

But in that moment, as fast as it started, it was over. The Gray Man released Ray's face when he knew what little life he had left remained. Ray coughed, gagged, and sputtered, inhaling and exhaling, trying to breathe life deep into his lungs.

The Gray Man towered over him. "Speak to me Ray."

Ray tried to formulate words in his mouth, but was unable. His brain was working, sending the words he wanted to say to his mouth, but his tongue refused to touch the appropriate parts on his mouth's inside. Ray grunted, but no words came out, only unintelligible sounds. For a moment, he thought his tongue had been ripped from his mouth. He placed his fingers inside to make sure his tongue was intact.

It was.

But he still couldn't speak. He tried again, but nothing. Instead, just a low gurgling-gag sound.

"Now you don't have to worry about saying a thing to Mr. Jack Angel. Leave him to me and get your rest. You'll need it."

The Gray Man exited the room. Ray closed his tear filled eyes wishing desperately he'd succeeded in taking his life like the others.

25

Jack and Frank pulled onto the Interstate when Frank's cell phone chirped at him. He looked at the caller I.D. and recognized the police station's phone number. Thinking it may have something to do with the discovery of this morning's body he answered his cell.

"This is Frank."

"Frank, it's Sergeant Rand. Sorry to bother you."

"You're fine," Frank said watching Jack light up another menthol.

"I've got a woman here at the station. Name's Linda Cleavenger. She said she wanted to talk to somebody about her daughter. She claims she hadn't seen her daughter all morning and apparently she never came home from school."

"Has it been twenty-four hours? You know we can't do anything until then."

Frank heard Sergeant Rand cover the mouth piece with his hand as he asked Linda Cleavenger how long it's been. When Sergeant Rand returned Frank could hear her crying in the background.

"Says she went to school yesterday, but that was the last time she saw her. She thought maybe her daughter went over to her friend Chrissie's, but when she called Chrissie's mom and dad, they said they hadn't seen Susan at all. Chrissie told them she saw Susan walking home and that was it. Nothing else."

Frank exhaled in frustration, *One more distraction*, he thought to himself. "Okay. I'll be down there. Just help her relax and I'll get there as quick as I can." Frank punched off his cell phone. "Shit."

87

"What the hell was that about?"

"Looks like a runaway and so the mom is there at the station to report her missing daughter. For whatever reason Rand thinks to call me and not to give this to someone else."

Jack chuckled. "Because he knows you're good with these missing person things. You and I both know within a few minutes of talking to the parents you can tell if it's a runaway or something else."

Frank scrunched his eyes and scowled at Jack. "What've you been smoking?"

Jack took his eyes off the road and glanced at Frank who was still scowling at him. The bitter-beer-face look on Frank was too much. "It's true," Jack cackled. "You know it is. Two words. Ashley Zumberger."

Ashley Zumberger was a sixteen year old who decided to run away one night after she got into a heated argument with her stepdad. She called her boyfriend to come and get her and the two drove off in the middle of the night. Her mom came into the station in hysterics thinking someone broke into the house and abducted her daughter. Frank asked if there had been an argument earlier in the evening. A connection between teens running away and arguing with their parents or stepparents was not unheard of.

Feeling somehow responsible, the mom nodded her head. After getting a little more information, Frank placed his hand on the mom's knee and reassured her chances were good Ashley would be home within the next twenty-four to forty-eight hours. After she collected herself, Frank looked at the stepdad and reminded him how important it was for him to be a father to Ashley and not act like a stepdad.

Twenty-four hours later, Ashley was home.

Frank would check up on them every once in awhile and was glad to see the family dynamics improve for Ashley.

"Look," Frank said responding to Jack. "Anyone would have said that and you know it."

"Sure, anyone would have, but it was the personal touch you added afterwards. You let'em know you cared."

The Cleansing: A Thriller

"I did my job."

"And that's why Rand called you. You do it better than anyone else."

"Well thanks. Why don't you go ahead and drop me off at the station and go see the Associate Pastor to David Stout on your own. I'll meet up with you after awhile. You may be finishing up by the time I'm done."

"Call me when you're done. I'll give you the details of what I learn."

"Sounds good."

After he dropped Frank off, Jack continued to maneuver through traffic, zigzagging in and out of cars. For the first time since Monday morning he started to feel like he was starting to get back into the police procedural zone again.

It felt great.

He felt alive.

This is what he did. He investigated crimes and Jack knew no one did this superior than himself.

He'd forgotten how much he enjoyed the job and started to wonder what he'd do when the investigation came to an end. For now, his biggest concern was whether or not he'd be able to get inside the head of these pastors and the killer or killers that were still at large.

26

"Hi Mrs. Cleavenger. I'm detective Frank Madiolie," Frank said extending his hand. Linda Cleavenger stood up and returned the gesture. She took the Kleenex in her hand and dabbed at her red eyes and moist face while taking a seat in Frank's office.

"Thank you for taking the time and coming here to see me."

"You're welcome Mrs. Cleavenger. Can I get you something to drink?"

"No thank you. I'm fine. By the way, you can call me Linda. Please, no missus."

The unknown whereabouts of her daughter blanketed her body language. Her worry-filled eyes were coupled with vulnerability and pleas for help in finding her daughter. The damp tissue in her hands acted as a testimony to the hours of crying and panic from unsuccessful leads. Frank made mental notes to himself; *No missus? No husband? This is probably a family that cares for one another. Very close. Daughter is all she has.*

"Why don't you tell me what's going on."

Linda collected her emotions. "I came home from work late last night. I was tired and decided to turn in and go to bed. Which was probably a mistake."

"Why do you say that?"

"I usually check on Susan and didn't this time."

"Why's that?"

"Lights were off in the house and I figured she was in bed already. I didn't want to bother her and so I left her alone."

"Okay. Then what happened?"

The Cleansing: A Thriller

"This morning, when I woke up to make Susan breakfast," Linda tried to hold back tears, but recalling the events became too much. "I'm sorry. This just has me worried and sick to my stomach."

"It's okay. Take your time."

Linda dried her eyes and started again. "So this morning I finished making breakfast. Susan is usually at the table by the time I am done, but this morning she wasn't. I went to check on her to see if she overslept and when I went into her room, I saw her bed was as she left it yesterday. It hadn't been slept in all night." Tears came again.

"Could she have stayed the night with a friend?"

"I thought about that. Sometimes when I work late she goes to a friend's house to study or do homework, but she typically calls me to let me know."

"And did she?"

Linda shook her head.

"Has she forgotten to call you before?"

"Yes, and that's why I didn't think much of it."

"So when did you start to call around to find out where she was?"

"Right after I went into her room."

"Who did you call?"

"The only friend she ever goes over to, Chrissie Imfeld. Her parents asked if she'd seen Susan and she said not since school let out."

"Does she have a boyfriend?"

"No. Not that I'm aware of."

"How about a cell phone? Does she have one? Have you tried to call it?"

"Yes," Linda said feeling as if any hope to finding Susan was fleeting. "But no answer."

"Okay, we'll want to secure a record of all incoming and outgoing calls on that. Try and see if anything pops up. Do you all have a computer?"

"Yes. It's in the living room."

91

"Okay, do you know if she had an online email account, Internet community, or Facebook?"

"She did, but I don't know her passwords. I let her have her privacy. Was that wrong?"

"Probably not the wisest, but I understand. Any recent fights between you two? Sometimes teens runaway after a huge fight."

"No, none at all. Susan and I rarely fight. I can't think of the last one we had. Are you thinking she ran away? Please understand that's just not like her. Susan wouldn't do that."

Frank reached out and touched her hand. "It's okay. You'd be surprised. Things at home can seem fine to the parents, but something else is going on that you don't see. That's why I want to have the detectives secure the computer and look at postings or emails and see if we can find anything. A lot of times kids open up more to their friends than their parents on those websites. We just want to review it. Keep in mind, computers and cell phones will have evidence like detailed emails, text messages, pictures, and caller ID. All these things can be recovered by a technical examination, but not unless the devices are secured. If she planned this, we will find it."

"You just don't know Susan. This isn't like her. I just want her home. Please help me find my daughter."

Frank continued to place a comforting hand on Linda. "We're going to okay? We'll interview Susan's friends and the friends of friends. We'll also locate emails and trace the communication link and figure who received them. Usually in the first week, if she ran away, she'll stay with friends. She may try and contact people on her web community or Facebook list, so we'll monitor those. Our detectives will contact the people on her personal ads, if she has any, to see if they know anything. The good news is this, kids that run away will have little to no resources so they'll eventually try and rely on their parents. They'll use the family cell phone and email accounts and we can trace this activity. We'll do everything we can to find her. I can assure you that."

"What do I do in the meantime?"

The Cleansing: A Thriller

"Call around. Send her emails. She may be checking her email still. Try and establish communication. Post on her Facebook page to see if her friends have seen her and ask for their help. We will work our end and scour all over."

Linda nodded. "I already made a missing flyer for her. Can I give this to you?"

"Absolutely. We will fill out a missing person's report and do everything we can to locate your daughter. Okay?"

Linda attempted a smile. "Thank you for your time," she said drying her eyes and standing up.

Frank stood up with Linda. "We'll let you know as soon as we find anything. I promise you."

"Do you mind if I call each day, you know, just to see?"

Frank smiled and nodded knowing how hard this must be on Linda. "You can call as often as you like. We want her home as much as you do."

Linda smiled and couldn't help herself from hugging Frank for giving her his number. "Thanks detective. You have no idea how much this means to me."

Frank returned the hug letting her know it wasn't a problem. Linda grabbed her black Liz Claiborne purse and gently laid the strap on her shoulder. Frank continued to stand as she headed towards his office door. As she crossed into the hallway, she paused and turned back to Frank. One question she feared most continued to weigh her emotions. Linda feared if she spoke the words then the question would come to fruition. Her conscious pled with her to disregard it. *If you ignore asking the detective, then all she'll ever be is just a runaway and she'll eventually come home.* But Linda paid no attention to the small voice. She had to know.

"Detective Madiolie?"

"Yes?"

"What if she was taken? Like I said, this isn't like Susan to just leave. I'm afraid something horrible may have happened and I'm so afraid," Linda sobbed through her words. Her face collapsed in her hands wanting all this to go away.

93

"I know this is hard," Frank said comfortingly. "Let's focus first and see if someone knows something. If we don't get anywhere, we'll redirect our efforts okay? And please, try and stay positive."

Linda nodded as if expecting to hear that answer.

"Do you have friends or family you can stay with to help you?"

"I have some friends I can call. I'll stay with them."

Frank reached for a business card and handed the card and a pen to Linda. "Write down their number just in case so I can reach you."

Linda jotted down the number along with a few others annotating what each number was for. Frank took the card from her and watched as she exited the station. He placed a few phone calls to set up times to go over to the Cleavenger's home to pick up any computers and phone records. He placed the phone back on the cradle and leaned his chair back, interlaced his fingers behind his head, and stared at the ceiling.

"For this mother's sake, let this just be a runaway," he said to the ceiling as if it took requests. "I don't think she could handle anything worse."

27

The cold basement room which held Susan Cleavenger smelled of blood and sex. Susan laid curled in a fetal position on the dirty mattress crying and praying silently for an end to the evil and sick madness she was experiencing from the man who wore the burlap mask.

Hitting.

Slapping.

His justification for the continued rape of her body.

Constantly forcing himself inside her.

"I always find it interesting," the Burlap Man said standing up and zipping his pants. "That no matter how many times I'm with a young woman like you, I never get tired of it. You all remind me of a summer peach. You're soft, sweet, very juicy, and always fuzzy."

The Burlap Man laughed at his own joke as he lay back down beside Susan, running his fingers up and down her arm gently. With her head turned away and laying in a stupor, she stared blankly at the cement block wall. He rubbed her back like a lover would their partner after sharing a romantic time of making love. Susan's muscles tightened in her back hoping to suppress any feeling his touch sent through her nerves and then to her brain.

"I know it's hard for you. You didn't think your first, second, or even third time would be with an older man. I bet you were even trying to save yourself for your future husband. Or, maybe you were waiting for the first guy you fell in love with. Perhaps, and I believe *this* to be the case, you would've given yourself to the first *real* guy who said he loved you. Yeah, I bet that's it. So you can rest assured, *I* love you."

He bent over and started kissing her neck and ear. Susan tried to inch away from his advances, fearing he might want to violate her innocence again.

"I can honestly say out of all the bitches I've been with, you're the prettiest. Actually, you're the sexiest. There's never been one that could make me go as quick as you did."

Silence

"You must understand something. Before you can be given, you must first be purged of the ugliness. The black tar of sin has corrupted you and because I love you, I will purge you. That's right. Like I said, I *do* love you."

"How can you call what you did to me love?" Susan asked fearfully, seeking an opportunity to possibly use his feelings for her as leverage to escape.

The man's eyebrows raised, surprised she spoke to him. "What a pretty voice you have. You know, you should use it more often."

He paused to let Susan respond, but wasn't surprised when she didn't.

"Do you want to know what love is?" he asked. "I remember a rock group, maybe *Journey*, who sang a song demanding to know what love is."

"*Foreigner*," she responded softly.

"I'm sorry?"

"The band's name is *Foreigner*."

The Burlap Man laughed at his ignorance. "I didn't know that. I might have to pick up the CD and play it for us some time. Anyway, I'll not only tell you what love *is*, but I'll tell you what it *isn't*. First, love is the act of doing something for someone no matter the risk or loss he may experience in the end. What love *isn't* is someone acting ungrateful for what the other person did for them. That's not love. Plain and simple. You can even use that as a quote one day if you'd like."

"That's okay. You can keep it."

The Burlap Man started running his fingers tenderly along her neck, kissing her earlobes with each pass of his hand. "Are you grateful?" he asked with a kiss to her ear, slowly untying her hands and feet, as if slipping her out of lingeri. "Or are you ungrateful?" he asked with another kiss to her neck.

Susan felt him press his hardened groin to her back. She knew no matter how she answered what the end result would be and she knew she couldn't stomach another encounter with him. Her mind raced with what she could do. Hit him? Bite him? Find something sharp and stab him to death or just somehow take her life instead? As if her subconscious came to rescue her, she knew what to do.

Use his words.

Make them your own.

Use them against him.

Buy yourself some time.

"I'm grateful," she struggled to say, almost vomiting forth the words. "But if you love me the way you say you do, can you let me rest? I want to love you too. I just need my rest."

Feeling slightly rejected, but more ashamed of himself for not realizing she did love him, he complied. He stood up and walked towards the door.

"Thank you Susan. Thank you for wanting to love me. I am planning something big for you and myself. This Sunday, everyone will know about our everlasting love."

Susan trembled from his words. *Dear God, what is he planning?*

"Don't worry your pretty head. Just get your rest. I'll be upstairs planning our announcement. Your gratefulness will be rewarded tenfold."

The door shut, soon followed by a locking click. Susan lay in the darkness, untied, weeping for her mother and praying it all to end soon.

28

Barry Spencer, the Associate Pastor of the River of Life Community Church, ushered Jack Angel down the sanctuary aisle. While walking behind Barry, Jack studied the layout. To him, it didn't seem as grand like some of the churches he'd seen saw on TV. The construction of the sanctuary seating divided the congregation into three sections of pews with an aisle on each side and a balcony above, extending over a third of the pews. The choir stood behind the pastor's pulpit with a glossy jet black Steinway grand piano to the right of the Pastor David Stout as he preached and band instruments directly behind him.

Before Pastor David Stout delivers the message on Sunday mornings, the choir and instrumentalists leave the choir loft, followed by the Minister of Music.

Barry stood by the section of pews furthest to the right of David Stout when he set himself on fire. "I was sitting right here when it happened. At first we all thought it was part of his sermon, like he was trying to make a point."

"How soon did you realize what he was going to do to himself?"

"I think when he pulled out the lighter." He paused to recollect. "Yeah. That was it. That's when I knew."

"And what did you do?"

Surprised by the question, Barry jerked his head back. "What any sane person would've done. I jumped up to try and stop him. It was too late. He was fully engulfed." Barry thought for a moment. "I could hear his skin sizzling. And the smell.

Oh God it was awful. *Burning flesh.* Just like the burning flesh he was preaching about."

"Listen," Jack said. "Do you remember any attitude change in him that week at all?"

Barry thought about the question. It was something he'd thought about as well since David's suicide.

"You know, looking back, I guess I did, but I just ignored it."

"Like what?"

"He seemed distant. He wasn't himself."

"In what ways?"

"Well, it wasn't in "ways"," he said making quotes with his hands. "It was just in one way."

"And what was that?"

"Looking back, I think he knew what he was going to do Sunday, as if he'd been planning it."

"Did he talk about any strange dealings that week? With anyone at all?"

Barry shook his head. "No. Why? Are you implying someone wanted him to do this?"

Jack thought about his conversation with Ray Stevens. He didn't know if he should reveal what he knew about David Stout and his association with Ray Stevens. Instead, he chose only to give the same information the news media had on the tragic deaths. "I don't know. But doesn't it seem odd that two pastors kill themselves by fire in front of their congregation?"

"I've thought the same thing."

"So this is what I'm dealing with, one person killing themselves, it's an isolated suicide. But two people? Same method? Not so isolated. And now throw in a third person who was unsuccessful. In my book, that's a little more calculated, and something's behind this. And I want to know what! So, if you're trying to protect his legacy in some way, forget it. I need to know everything you do."

"I told you what I know. He did seem like something was bothering him during the week. I didn't think anything of it because we all have hard weeks."

"Sure."

"But when he set himself on fire, well, I was confused. I didn't know why he did that. I didn't know why he just didn't talk to me before and tell me what was wrong with him. The entire congregation is still in shock over it."

"I can imagine. Did he talk about anything odd leading up to Sunday that might've hinted he was going to do this?"

"In what way?"

"Did somebody coerce him?"

Barry seemed taken aback by the question. "No! We all have bad weeks and I just thought that's what he was having."

"Knowing that two people did the same thing, doesn't this seem a little more than coincidental?"

"You think this was an orchestrated matter?"

"I don't just think it. I believe it. If you don't, you're only fooling yourself."

"Okay," Barry replied. "What do you want from me?"

"Do you have a copy of Sunday's sermon I could watch?"

"Absolutely! Let me go and burn a copy for you. Wait here. I'll be right back."

Jack walked up onto the charred stage where David Stout stood and burned himself in front of his congregation. The area he stood in still had the sweet residual smell of pungent gasoline. Jack bent down and touched the scorched carpet.

"What was going on in your mind?" he asked the blackened spot. "Who made you decide to do this?"

Jack closed his eyes as if he would receive some radio transmission that would answer his question.

"C'mon David, talk to me."

Jack began to feel a slow burning in his eyes. He received quick flashes, like a bulb on a camera, but nothing tangent. He continued to ask questions.

"How did you see them? How did you see yourself?"

More quick flashes.

But nothing.

Jack walked around, hoping at any moment it would become clear.

Visible.

What the hell? he thought to himself. *Why can't I get a read on this?*

"Here you go detective," Barry said abruptly interrupting Jack's process. "We already had a copy made."

Jack stood and met Barry in the aisle where they stood previously.

"Thanks," Jack said taking the DVD from Barry.

"I hope it helps. Please let me know if there's anything else I can do to help."

Jack nodded and headed up the aisle to exit the church, concerned if his ability was going to come back or if it had left him permanently.

"Detective?" Barry shouted. Jack turned to face the Associate Pastor. "If you find anything, can you please let me know?"

Jack nodded and turned for the doors. He started to doubt if he was going to be able to discern for himself anything these pastors did and why they did it.

Only time would tell.

But Jack started to feel, time was running out.

Something bigger was going to happen.

But what?

29

Jack poured himself a second shot of bourbon while watching the video of David Stout's sermon. Jack focused on David's demeanor prior to the pastor standing up to deliver the morning's sermon and throughout his message. While watching, Jack recalled Tom Sullivan using the same verses David Stout was currently speaking. Watching the video confirmed the rumor he'd heard and the one he shared with William Brookings, Tom Sullivan's Associate Pastor. But the video Jack was watching revealed something more. Something no one had known previous. David Stout wasn't simply delivering the same message subject and quoting from the same Bible verses, David Stout was reciting Tom Sullivan's message word for word.

The spoken message and the verses used were the *exact* same as if memorized from a script.

A script?

A rehearsed script complete with actor and director notes. Notes on where to move, what to say, and what actions to deliver in front of the audience.

His words were eerily similar to Tom Sullivan's in their inflection, tone, and voice. He even pulled the jug of gasoline out at the same moment pastor Sullivan had and lit himself on fire at the precise pre-defined moment as well.

Did the other pastor, Reverend Ray, say the same words as well? Did he attempt to light himself on fire after reciting these apocalyptic words from the same script?

Jack made a note making sure to collect the video from Reverend Ray Stevens so he could verify.

As he was jotting his notes he heard David shout a single word. Jack snapped his head up and looked at the TV. It was the same unintelligible word Tom had shouted during his fiery death. The one word Jack couldn't discern from Tom's sermon. Now he was hearing David shouting it too.

Neon?

Leon?

Eon?

Jack played the shouts. Rewound the video. Played it again. Rewound it. And played it again. With eyes squinting, he leaned his head in as if this would make the word clearer.

Theon?

Is he saying Theon?

"That makes no damn sense! What the hell is Theon?"

Jack booted up his laptop and after logging in he quickly jumped on the Internet and Googled the word *Theon* to see what search results he'd get.

In less than one second, Google returned 124,000 results. The first page displayed information on a Greek mathematician by the name of Theon of Alexandria, but after clicking on the links and reading the information on Theon of Alexandria, he wondered if his spelling of Theon was accurate. *Could there be other possibilities on the spelling?* Jack grabbed his notepad and added the word *Theon* to the growing list of possible words David was saying and added a comment to check different spellings.

Jack turned and saw his bourbon bottle beckoning him from across the room. He stood up and crossed the room when his telephone rang, interrupting his thoughts. He looked at his caller ID, debated on answering the phone, but decided to give in to the ring.

"Hey Dani."

"Hi Jack," Dani said in a cautious, but soothing voice, not wanting to upset her estranged husband.

"What can I do for you?"

"Did I catch you at a bad time?"

"Not really. Just helping Frank out with an investigation and hit a dead end on some word. You're fine."

"Well I'm glad you're doing something you enjoy."

"I think that's why Frank called me. I think he was worried."

"He cares about you Jack."

"I know he does. So what can I do for you?" Jack asked quickly changing the subject.

"Well a woman at my work asked if I knew any good private investigators she might want to hire."

"Why? Cheating husband?"

"Yeah, I think so."

"So why'd you call *me*?"

"Because I've been concerned about you and thought this could be something that gets you out of the house."

"Well, I'm already up to asses and elbows in this thing with Frank."

"Okay, I'll tell her you're too busy. I'm at least glad you're doing something other than drinking."

Jack looked over at the bourbon and thought, *Well, not exactly.*

Jack rolled around the idea of following this woman's husband for a moment. "How much and how long?" he finally asked through a sigh.

"She says she only has about a thousand to pay. I know that's low, but she seems really distraught about it all."

"Is she a friend of yours?"

"We're good friends here at work, but haven't done too much outside of here."

Again, Jack toyed with the idea of adding something else to do with his time. He enjoyed getting back into investigative work and had followed cheating spouses in the past. He typically got the information needed within a short amount of time and so the money was quick and good.

"What the hell. I'll do it."

"You will?" Dani asked excitedly. She'd expected Jack to turn her down.

"Yeah."

"Jack I can't thank you enough."

"Actually Dani, I'm the one who can't thank *you* enough." Jack paused a beat. "I mean that."

"I know you do. Thanks again for being willing to meet with her. It means a lot to me."

"You're welcome. Tell her to meet me at Crisper's tomorrow at noon for lunch. We'll talk and I'll get all the info I need."

"I will. Her name's Beverly Cooper."

"Okay. Give her my number so she can reach me if anything changes on her end."

"Absolutely. Thanks again Jack," Dani said quickly and hanging up before her estranged husband changed his mind

"No problem." Jack replied pressing the off button. When he saw there was no more connection, he mouthed, "I love you Dani."

Jack walked across the room and grabbed the bourbon bottle and instead of pouring a third glass, he screwed back on the cap and returned the bottle to its cabinet.

While fishing out a cigarette, he grabbed the last family picture all them had taken and went and sat on the couch. He tenderly ran his forefinger across Dani and Ainslie's smiling faces. Tears filled his eyes as he reflected back on the time when they were a family.

"I don't care how long it takes me Ainslie, but I will find the one who hurt you. I swear to you. Your daddy will get the man who took you away from us."

Jack leaned back on the couch, embracing the picture close to his chest and stared at the ceiling while precious memories fell from his eyes and moistened his cheeks.

30

Associate Pastor William Brookings finished packing the last box of Tom Sullivan's belongings. He placed a call to his wife Jana to let her know he was leaving shortly. After promising to pick her up a café mocha, he hung up and double checked to make sure he had packed everything.

As he scanned the office one last time, he noticed a black leather satchel laying beside one of the enormous book cases. After questioning why he didn't notice it before, he walked over and grabbed it to add to his box.

He placed the leather bag on top of the box and paused while staring at it. Curiosity from his earlier conversation with Jack started to consume his heart. He unzipped the bag and fished through its contents. Nothing seemed out of the ordinary until he started zipping the bag. William's hand bumped against something hard on the inside pocket. He opened the pocket and pulled out a videotape. Written on the white label with a black Sharpie were two words:

William Brookings.

Confused about the label and the tape, William decided to power up the TV and VCR in Tom's office to watch the tape. The TV's blue screen came alive and William sat down in the leather high back chair. He grabbed the remote control and pressed play. After a few seconds of snow the video revealed the same office he was sitting in.

Pastor Tom Sullivan's office.

The camera, pointing directly at Tom's desk and empty chair, waited for its operator to appear. Within a few seconds a man sat down in Tom's chair.

The same chair William was sitting in.

The man was wearing Khaki pants, a blue sport coat, and white collar shirt with no tie. What chilled William was what the man was wearing over his face.

A burlap bag with holes cut in it for eyes and a mouth.

"Tom? Is that you?" William asked the television set.

As if the man could hear William's question, he spoke to the camera.

"Hello William," the voice sounded distraught. "If you're watching this tape, you know I've taken my life."

William couldn't help but notice his hands shook while hearing Tom speak to him.

"I sit before you ashamed for the evil I've caused. By now you may already know what I've done. What I've become. You must know, I've raped the innocent. I've killed for evil's sake to cover up the pain I've caused. I've heard the demands of victims to spare their life and then moments later watched as their insistent pleas were replaced with violence and drowned out by their screams. I'm not the man I used to be. I've fallen into the talons of evil. My heart pierced with the darkness I tasted and fellowshipped in. How did I let it get this far? Why did I fall into the temptation of madness? These are questions you and many others will ask for years to come. I don't have the answers you and many others will seek. I've covered my face in shame, but this isn't the first time I wore this hideous mask. Every victim I encountered saw what you see sitting before you now. Me and the others, and yes, there are more. Four of us in all.

"Understand this...because of our sins...we will meet our fate this Sunday. It is a sentence of death we rightly deserve.

"But, woe to the man who doesn't follow through with his duty, for by reason of transgression, cometh fall, which fall bringeth death.

"A man whose work is his own has visited me. Whether he is a messenger of dark or light is not for me to decide, but know this, I've seen the face of Death. His tattoos spoke for themselves. This man...*this man*...he's not human. He can't possibly have a soul. I can't see how.

"We call him the Gray Man. I pray you or no one else will meet him. I know why he came to me. I accept what I must do to cleanse myself of the unrighteous deeds I have done. Don't weep or mourn for me. Weep for the innocent whose lives I've taken. Weep for the family and friends whom I robbed of those they loved.

"But do not weep for the one who does not go through with his duty. *His cleansing.* If that should happen, and I pray it doesn't, he will experience anguish and pain seventy times more than the fire we used to cleanse our sins. I would ask you to forgive me, but I fear it is too late. May the hand of God keep you safe."

Tom Sullivan stood up, walked towards the camera, and shut it off. The snow returned to the TV as William continued to sit in numbed silence caused by the message he just heard.

He quickly pulled out his wallet and grabbed the number Jack Angel left for him. After the fourth ring, the phone went to voicemail.

"Mr. Angel, this is William Brookings, you came by and spoke to me earlier. You asked if I found anything to let you know. Well, I just watched a disturbing video message from Tom that you must watch for yourself. Tonight if at all possible. Please call my house at 937...555...1482. Call me at any time tonight. I don't care how late. This is important. I must see you. You need to see this tape. I'm sorry, I'm shaking so bad right now.

"Listen to me carefully. This is important. Tom said there were supposed to be four suicides. Four pastors total. I only know of two that were successful, plus the one pastor who was saved by his congregation. That makes three. Mr. Angel, that means there is another out there. A fourth person. Tom stressed on this tape, woe to the man who doesn't follow through with his duty that something far greater would happen to him.

"He also talked about a gray man. He didn't know if this man was a messenger of light or darkness. I have no idea who this person is, but this man has a connection somehow. Please, we need to meet. Call me as soon as you get this."

William stood up and ejected the tape from the VCR. He gathered his belongings along with the tape and turned to leave.

Standing in the doorway and not moving, but just staring and pointing a gun, was a man William did not immediately recognize.

"You and I need to talk Mr. Brookings," the man commanded with finality. "Let's go for a ride."

He motioned with his gun for William to lead them out. "Don't forget the videotape. We'll need that too."

William grabbed the recording of Tom's message and walked out the door. His heart rate quickened as he feared what possibly would happen to him and wondering if he'd see his wife and children ever again.

This is about what happened on Sunday and the events leading up to it, William surmised.

It became clear to William if Tom's confession was true then the man standing before him was a part of it. William started to feel the fragility of his mortality and the time spent with his kids at breakfast that morning was the last time they would ever see their father again.

31

William got in the front seat as his captor entered the passenger side still pointing the gun at William. William started the engine and turned off the radio.

"Where are we going?"

"Just start driving. I'll tell you where to turn. Just keep going straight unless I say otherwise. Are we clear?"

"Yes," William said shakily nodding his head. He put the car in gear and pulled forward.

"When you get to the end of the parking lot, turn left."

William did exactly as instructed.

"What do you want from me?" William asked trying not to sound terrified.

"I despise that question. Completely despise it. Understand for me if you will, sometimes things happen because they need to happen. It's not always about *wanting* something from somebody. Take a right turn here and then at the second light, go left."

William nodded letting the man know he understood.

"I'm sure you have many questions after watching that tape. Am I right?"

William nodded.

"I thought you may, but you'll never understand by being an outsider looking in. That's because there's a deeper issue. Its complexity is blind to those who don't understand its meaning."

"You're talking about why Tom and the others killed themselves?"

The Cleansing: A Thriller

"I am," the man paused a beat and then continued. "So, instead of wasting our time talking about something you'll never understand, let's talk about *you*."

William felt a wave of fear crest through his body. "What do you want to know?"

"Before this past Sunday, had you ever watched somebody die? I mean *intently* watch the life drain away from their eyes as it escapes their body?"

William shook his head.

"I didn't think so. You see, I have. I've seen a lot of death over the years. I watched people - kneeling - pleading their case why they should live. Then ultimately watch their face change as they accept their cries had fallen on deaf ears. I've witnessed innocent children die at the hands of the wicked. You see William, the wicked know how to steal, but they don't know how to give."

"But I've never done that. I'm not wicked."

The man quickly struck William, slapping him in the face. "You need not merely hear my words, but instead, *understand* my words."

William nodded, still feeling the sting of the slap.

"You see, I believe the moment a baby is born that baby is dying. It may take it seventy, twenty, or even five years to do so. Rest assured that baby *will* die. We all will. It's just a matter of how and when. You see, I believe in natural death, which is the path a normal person walks and experiences late in life. Of course, some will experience unnatural death as well. We can't have one without the other now can we?"

William shook his head in agreement. He feared where the conversation was going.

"Turn left up here. I want you to take the dirt road beyond the mailbox."

William continued to follow the man's instructions wondering where they were going and still contemplating how he was going to get out of this situation. He knew as long as he acted calm and relaxed, he may have a better chance in surviving the ordeal rather than trying to flee and getting shot.

"To me, unnatural death is the wickedest kind. You've seen the worst in man when you see a child lying in his bed where he'd been sleeping, only to see his blood-soaked pillow from a pointblank gunshot to the back of his skull. The father, who was insanely mad at his wife for wanting to divorce him, decided he was going to kill every innocent person in that house. Of course the bastard ate a bullet too. No one mourned what he did to himself, but people mourned the loss of the innocent. You can stop the car right here."

William obeyed the command. He placed the car in park and shut off the engine. The man turned and pointed the gun at William. William stared down the barrel wondering if he was about to experience the unnatural death the man had been describing.

"I am one who thinks those who bring unnatural wickedness and death to the innocent can taint those around them. It's like a disease. It enters the person like a parasite and festers until one day it decides to eat away at the insides and consume the heart. Eventually, that person becomes just as evil. They try to deny it at first and may want to fight it. But each day thereafter, they become what they hated. They become what they fought. They become evil and want to hurt the innocent."

The man cocked back the hammer of his gun.

"Have you been tainted?" he asked William.

"No. I haven't. I promise." William's voice shook.

"I don't believe you. I think the parasite has entered you too. Problem is, you have shit for brains to realize it! People like you prey upon the innocent. You rape them with your words and phantom kindness. You confuse them with your prayers and make them feel unclean. You tell them they are dying and offer them a remedy, but if they don't drink the blood or eat the flesh of Christ, they burn eternally in Hell. Yes, the infection *has* entered you heart. You don't realize it, but you're a bringer of unnatural death just like your pastor."

"I'm not like him," William pleaded.

The man laughed. "You're a damn fool. At least he knew what he was and took his life to end his reign of evil. But you're too blind to see your sickly heart. You and others like you need to be cured."

William's hands shook, he looked outside the car windows to see if anyone might be around that he could honk the horn to get their attention.

Blackness of night.

That's all there was.

William saw the man's directions took them into a desolate area of the woods. There was no sign of life to give William the hope he needed. It was just him and his captor.

Soon, his captor would become his executioner.

The man reached into his pocket and pulled out a small tin can. The kind someone might put oil in to eliminate the sound of squeaky doors. Along with the can, he also pulled out a pair of zip strips.

"Bind yourself to your steering wheel," he said tossing the plastic strips to William.

William didn't move.

"Do it now! Or I'll kill you right here and then go put a bullet in your entire family, starting with your children."

"Please don't hurt them."

"Tie yourself...*now!*"

William obeyed the harsh instructions, hoping his compliance would save his wife and children.

"Very good. Now where's your phone?"

"In my front right pocket."

The man reached for the phone and searched for William's home number.

"Is this it?"

William nodded.

The man pressed the call button. "When your wife answers tell her you're unclean and must atone for sins you've caused and those you've yet to cause."

William sobbed.

On the third ring, Jana answered.

113

"William where are you? I'm getting worried."

"J-J-Jana," William stuttered.

"Honey what's wrong?"

"Say it," the man said. "You're a sinner. Say it!"

"Jana, I'm a sinner."

"What? What do you mean, you're a sinner?" Jana asked. "Who's that with you?"

"You're a sinner who must atone."

"I'm a sinner and must atone for what I've done and what I've yet to do."

"Sweetheart what are you talking about? Who's that talking in the background?"

His executioner started squirting gasoline from the small tin can all over William's face, arms, hands, and legs.

"William, where are you? You're not making any sense!" Jana started to cry. Her voice, shaking with fear.

"Your time has come William...say it."

"My time has come. Tell the children I love them. I love you too my dearest."

"William please! You're not making any sense. Where are you? I'll come get you!"

"The road of life which leads out of here is dark and desolate. If you follow it, you will find only death-"

The man snatched the phone from William before Jana could respond and turned it off. He stepped outside of the car and looked in on William.

"You must be cleansed of the evil unnatural death you brought into this world!" The man pulled out a book of matches and lit them all. "Burn in Hell you bastard!"

He threw the flaming book onto William's lap who howled in pain. The fire quickly engulfed his body and singed his hair. The smell of burning flesh filled the nostrils of William's executioner. Satisfied by his deed, he turned and walked away leaving William screaming for God to save him.

God's not going to save you today, the man thought. *Not while I'm here cleaning up His mess.*

As he turned off the hidden road and walked back to town, he looked back to see the enormous orange glow of William's car fully ablaze. A thunderous explosion, ending the life and ministry of Associate Pastor William Brookings, soon followed.

WEDNESDAY

32

Jack Angel lifted the crime scene tape and b-lined straight for Frank Madiolie who was standing by the burned out car owned by William Brookings.

"What the hell happened here Frank?"

"Looks like he was kidnapped last night, brought here, and then killed."

The charred body of William Brookings was still sitting in the car with his hands zip-stripped to the steering wheel. Wisps of smoke continued to snake into the air as crime scene investigators walked around taking pictures and collecting evidence.

"Any idea who's responsible?"

"No. The station received a few phone calls last night about the fire plus one from a frantic Jana Brookings."

"What did she say?"

"Our pastor friend was packing up Sullivan's office and was supposed to stop off for some coffee on the way home. He was running late, but she didn't start to worry until he called."

"He called her?"

Frank nodded. "Apparently his abductor had him place a call to Jana to tell her he was going to have to pay for past sins and sins to come."

"I'm sure he was bound the entire time."

"Looks that way."

"Anything else?" Jack asked while peeking his head through the charred driver's side window.

"Apparently he was doused with gasoline and lit on fire."

119

"What the hell is going on here? What sins was he talking about?"

"I don't know."

"I just talked to him on Monday. I'm telling you, William Brookings isn't connected in any way to what the other pastors did."

"I agree. I don't think he is either. What are your thoughts?"

"I think he may have found something out," Jack immediately clamped his hand over his mouth. "Holy shit!"

"What?"

"I told him to call me if he found anything out."

"Yeah? So?"

"I put my cell on silent last night because I was thinking about Dani and Ainslie and didn't check it before I went to bed. Then you called me this morning, but you called my house. Not my cell."

Jack flipped his phone open and saw a new voicemail message notification displayed on the screen. Jack pressed the button to call his voicemail and stood while horror spread across his face as he realized William had called him. He rubbed his forehead feeling defeated while listening to the frantic message left by William Brookings.

"Dear God I was afraid of that. I should've answered this last night!"

"Why? What did he say?"

"So far our investigation shows there were two suicides, plus Reverend Ray's attempt."

"Yeah. Three in all."

"Wrong!"

"What does the message say Jack?"

"He found a videotape by Pastor Tom. It was a message to William. Tom didn't confess to what he'd done, but he did say there were supposed to be four suicides in all!"

"Four?!?!"

"Yes! But we only knew of two Frank! Reverend Ray would've been the third, and we know he was stopped by his congregation."

"So who was the fourth?"

"William didn't say. I don't think he knew, but he did add something else."

"Yeah?"

"Here, listen." Jack put his phone on speaker and played the message again, skipping ahead to the final part of the desperate message. It was eerie hearing William's voice knowing what happened to him after he called Jack. It was hard not for Jack to look over at the burned out car and watch the coroner take William's charred corpse away.

"Here. This is the part you need to hear."

The fear in William's voice seeped from the cell phone, "Tom stressed on this tape, woe to the man who doesn't follow through with his duty that something far greater would happen to him. He also talked about a gray man. He didn't know if this man was a messenger of light or darkness. I have no idea who this person is, but this man has a connection somehow. Please, we need to meet. Call me as soon as you get this.."

Jack turned off his phone.

"So who is this Gray Man he's talking about?" Frank asked.

Jack shook his head. "No clue, but we need to put him on the top of our list as a person of interest to talk to about who this fourth pastor is."

"Woe to the man who doesn't follow through with his duty-"

"Something far greater would happen to him," Jack finished for him. "You heard what William said. This man, he's connected somehow. We need to find this videotape William watched."

"I think we already did."

"Where?" Jack asked with a sense of hope.

"We found what looks to be a melted VHS tape on the front passenger seat. It's gone. We won't be able to retrieve anything from it."

"SHIT!"

"If we have someone out there seeking retribution, we need to get to the other associate pastors."

"Meaning we sequester them?"

Frank shook his head. "Not yet. That might be a little premature, but I do think they need to be told and let them know we are going to put them under surveillance."

"That's a good idea. If this fourth pastor, whoever he is, is starting to murder the associates, we need to find him."

"Or if it's this gray man William talked about."

"Exactly." Jack pondered for a moment. "We also need to check if any of the other pastors may have left a video or note of some sort like Tom did. That could help break this case."

"Good idea. I'll get a team together to start scouring their offices and homes. Maybe we'll find something."

"Talk to the wives too."

Frank nodded. "Where can I find you?"

"I've got to meet someone for lunch. Talk about following her husband. She thinks he's having an affair."

"Okay, but Jack, I would like you to keep this case your priority. Will you do that for me?"

"You know I will."

Jack turned and walked towards the burned out car. He strolled around as if he was investigating the scene. Crime scene investigators were gathering evidence and continuing to take pictures. Jack looked on the front passenger seat and saw the videotape bagged and tagged as evidence. When no one was looking he grabbed the bag and placed it under his shirt. He walked swiftly away from the crime scene leaving Frank and the others behind. When he got to his car he placed the bag on the seat beside him hoping later on he could focus on it and try to get inside the head of William Brookings killer.

33

The Gray Man stood just out of sight watching Jack Angel and his former partner, Frank Madiolie, talking about the crime scene. He watched intently as Jack went inside the car and scrounged around for something, then place it in his shirt, and leave the scene.

"This is for you Jack Angel. This is your time to grow. This is your time to become what you never could, or too afraid to do so on your own."

The Gray Man lit a cigarette and took an excessively long drag and then exhaled through his nose. He watched as the coroner bagged William Brookings and drove off to the morgue.

"You could've stopped this Jack. You don't realize it, but you had it within your heart to do so. The abduction and death of William Brookings was not in my plan, but you could've prevented this if you hadn't been so self-defeated over the last few years. But you're a selfish individual. You only want what you can get for your own good."

The Gray Man stared while the tow truck hoisted the blackened car off its front wheels and pull it onto the back of its flatbed. He began smiling to himself.

"None of you even know what you're about to delve into. You have no idea the measure of evil soon to rain down on your souls. It will devour you. It wants to feast on your flesh and then spew you from its bowels."

He took another drag of his cigarette and exhaled the same as he did before.

"You've yet to realize the entire picture - the connection of souls being taken. This is greater than you can imagine. Why these events are happening. The sooner you do, the more you will save. The longer it takes, the more there will be that sit at evil's table, staring into the abyss of Death. And while they are sitting, staring at Death, Death and its minions will feast upon every last one of them."

The Gray Man turned and walked away from the scene unnoticed by all the activity surrounding the area.

As he walked back into town he knew it was time to pay a visit to Jack Angel. He refused to give Jack the answers he sought, but he knew that Jack needed to look inside himself to seek that which he needed.

How to become.

Becoming.

A killer.

It was right there. He only needed to be convinced to go there. The one place Jack feared the most. The reason why so many referred to him as Jack "Death" Angel.

The Gray Man remembered a quote from Friedrich Nietzsche, *"Battle not with monsters lest ye become a monster; and if you gaze into the abyss the abyss gazes into you."*

Yes, it was time.

34

Jack walked into *Crisper's* looking for his soon-to-be new client, Beverly Cooper. The restaurant was starting to fill up with the day's lunch crowd, but Jack was relieved to see a lone woman sitting by herself in a booth. Figuring it was her, he walked over to introduce himself. "Beverly Cooper?" Jack asked. She nodded her confirmation. "I'm Jack Angel," he said sitting himself across from Beverly in the booth. "My ex-wife called me about you."

"Thank you for taking the time to meet with me."

"Not a problem." Jack motioned for the waitress and when she came over he ordered a barbeque bacon burger and a beer. "Do you want anything?" he asked Beverly.

"Maybe just a water."

"Go ahead and bring her a water."

"With lemon please," she added before the waitress retreated to the kitchen.

The waitress nodded and left to go place the order. Jack turned back to Beverly and started to study her. Her body's frame was a dead giveaway that her self-confidence was low. Her swollen lost puppy dog eyes were a result from endless hours of crying. She continued staring at the table, not once looking at Jack.

"Why don't you tell me what's going on. You think your husband is having an affair?"

She nodded. "Yes I do."

"His name?"

"Stefan."

"Okay, why do you think he's cheating?"

125

"For one he seems to have lost interest in being around me. Never wants to have sex with me anymore. Now he is always angry with me. Constantly yelling at me. Has no tolerance being around me. He was never like that before Mr. Angel."

"It's okay. You can call me Jack."

Beverly smiled and nodded a *Thank you*, "I guess what finally got me thinking he's having an affair is that he's constantly leaving the house at odd hours saying he forgot to do stuff at the office. He'll leave and won't return for a few hours."

"Have you tried to call his desk?"

"Yes, but no answer. When I ask Stefan why he didn't answer he comes up with an excuse. And then we get into an argument. I know he's lying to me. I can tell. He always has a certain look about himself. And when I ask him, he gives me that look."

"What else?"

"He now has his login name on our home computer password protected. It was never protected before, but now it is."

"How long have you had the computer?"

"Three years."

"And when did you first notice the password change?"

"About six months ago."

"I assume his erratic behavior started around the same time?"

Beverly nodded, feeling ashamed.

"Mrs. Cooper, remember this isn't your fault."

"I just feel like such a damn fool."

"What about phone records? Is he calling a number you don't recognize?"

"None that I've seen. Which has me confused because if I'd seen one, and believe me, I've checked, then I'd have called it myself. There isn't one at all."

The Cleansing: A Thriller

The waitress returned with their order. Jack took a sip of beer and a bite of his burger while Beverly squirted the lemon in her drink and stirred the ice around, finally taking a sip.

"Have you tried to talk to him?"

"Yes."

"So right now he is just trying to explain away his behavior, but you're not buying it?'

"Right."

"So why have you decided now to have him followed and not sooner?"

Beverly reached down beside her and lifted up a single plastic grocery bag. She set it on the table with its contents making a plastic clunk. Jack peered into the bag's opening to see approximately twenty DVD-Rs sitting inside. None of the DVD-Rs had any labels and some of them were without a slipcase. Jack wondered what were on the discs.

"What are these discs of?"

"I found them the other day rummaging through Stefan's things. They were in these bags in the back of his closet."

"What are they of? Did you watch any of them?"

"Only one. That's all I could do."

"What was on it?"

"The most violent disgusting sex acts I've ever seen."

35

Jack was still sitting in the booth going over his notes from the meeting with Beverly Cooper when a stranger sat down in his booth across from him.

"Mr. Angel," the stranger said emotionless.

Jack looked up the moment the man sat in the booth. His first impression was disbelief. He was surprised the sickly gaunt looking man didn't have an oxygen tank to help him breathe or walker to aid him around. Jack thought for sure the man was not only at Death's Door, but had turned the knob and was entering Death's House. As the man stared at Jack, he tapped out a non-filtered Camel and lit it.

"What can I do for you?"

The Gray Man chuckled. "You're already doing it."

Jack squinted in confusion trying to process the man's comment. "What do you mean I'm already doing it?"

"Mr. Angel- "

"Call me Jack," Jack interrupted.

"Very well...Jack. I have an interest in what you seek."

"I'm sorry, but who the hell are you?"

The Gray Man held up his hand as if to say, *I will be getting to that.* "As I was saying," the Gray Man continued. "I have an interest in what you seek."

Jack leaned back, crossing his arms, and laughed. "And what is it I seek?"

The Gray Man eased forward. "Answers."

"Answers to what?"

"Jack we can volley back and forth like this all day. Quite frankly, I don't give one care whatsoever. You know damn good and well what you currently seek in hopes that it provides the answers to the questions you've harbored inside for too long." The Gray Man took a drag of his cigarette. "I'm a messenger of sorts and I'm here to help you...to help you...*see*."

Jack knew deep down this man was referring to Ainslie's abduction and murder. A flash of anger shot through his nerves. He hated the fact that this stranger was dangling the information in front of him. As if taunting him. Jack leaned across the table, letting the man know he was treading through dangerous territory. "What do you know about my daughter?" he demanded.

The Gray Man rolled his cigarette between his crusty thumb and index finger and stared through Jack's eyes and into his heart. "I want you to pay attention to what I have to say to you."

Never before had one person made Jack feel as uncomfortable as the person sitting before him did. The man was in control. Jack knew this and so he relented.

"I'm listening."

"There are three types of people in this world. The first are Pleasure Killers. Pleasure Killers kill for either enjoyment, out of anger, or to fulfill some insatiable desire. The reason they kill doesn't matter because it pleases them to kill and watch their victim die..

"The second type is also a killer. I call them, Hunter Killers. This group of killers has the ability to take lives and don't give it a second thought if the killing is warranted. Understand this, they *are* different than Pleasure Killers. Hunter Killers don't prey upon the innocent. Instead, they use their Hunter Killer instincts to catch the first group of killers to prevent further death or they might use their given abilities to find those who brought them harm and seek retribution. You need to recognize that Hunter Killers *are* killers. Only distinction is what drives them to kill.

"The last are Observers. They may or may not have the killer instinct, but it doesn't matter because they do nothing. They just watch. Just like driving by a fatal accident. They slow down, strain to get a view, and then go on. To me, this is the worst kind of person. They make me want to vomit. At least the other two types are doing something. But the Observers do nothing. They don't even try. They just waste the air you and I breathe. To me, it would've been better if they had never been born."

"So what does this have to do with me?"

"You fall into the second group Jack. Your entire adult life, you've been a Hunter Killer. You used your killing instincts to stop people from the first group." The Gray Man paused a beat to let what he was saying begin to take effect. "But recently you've become an Observer. You're a waste of life and you're wasting the air I breathe. Unless you become the killer you were born to be, you'll just be a waste of flesh. You might as well sit in that shithole you live in and rot away. If you don't figure this out – what it is you seek - more blood will flow from the innocent."

Jack sat in numbed silence. He wanted to jump across the booth and show this guy just what kind of killer he truly is. *But wasn't that what the stranger wanted? Wasn't that his point?*

"Make up your mind what you're going to be Mr. Angel. A Killer or an Observer. Observers go to their graves with unanswered questions. Killers get results. Quit wasting everyone's precious time." The Gray Man slid out of the booth and stood up, staring into Jack's eyes. "I hope I've made myself clear."

Jack nodded.

Before the Gray Man walked away, he slid a folded napkin towards Jack. "Don't forget, in life, the road you are on to seek what you find often intersects with others in their journey as well. It will be up to you to open your eyes to clearly see when those roads intersect and become one. We'll be seeing each other again soon. Have a nice day."

Jack watched the man exit the restaurant before he opened the napkin given to him. He hoped the napkin would give him a clue about Ainslie. Instead the message was mysterious, having nothing to do with his daughter: *Through Hellfire Eternal, Infernal Obedience Neverending.*

Jack looked up, hoping to see the man standing outside and looking in on him making sure he had read the napkin. To his disappointment, the stranger was nowhere in sight. He looked back down at the cryptic message recalling what the man had said, *"Observers go to their graves with unanswered questions. Killers get results."*

The man's words made sense. It's what Jack had known all along and the reason why he struggled recently in the current investigation. He knew, to solve this case or his daughter's case for that matter, the type of person he had to become...*again.*

A killer...a *Hunter Killer.*

36

For this first time since Susan Cleavenger had been abducted and brought to the house, she laid in darkness unbound by straps. Her captor, the man who wore the burlap mask, hadn't returned for another "intimate time" as he liked to put it. The pitch-blackness of the room hung like a fog. It was thick and reminded her of how alone she was. She spent these alone times plotting how she was going to get away and wondering how successful she would be if she tried.

She finally resolved in her mind, if her captor's intention was to ultimately kill her and dispose of her body, then she should at least try something to get away.

Anything.

But what?

While in the darkness, Susan scoured the floor blindly as if reading the contents in Braille, hoping to find something.

Anything.

Preferably something sharp for stabbing.

While on her hands and knees, she moved slowly, becoming familiar with every piece of detritus in her prison.

She inched herself around the darkened room while on her hands and knees and remembered the time she toured the Alcatraz prison with her mom on their trip to San Francisco. She was taking the audio tape tour and went into the solitary confinement cell. The inmate on the audio tape described how he passed time while in the darkness of solitary. He would take a paperclip, throw it in the dark cell, and then spend the next few hours on his hands and knees looking for the item. Once he located it, he would do it again.

Over and over.

Just to pass time.

What a horrible way to spend your days, Susan thought to herself while standing in the Alcatraz cell. But now she was the inmate, not passing the time, instead, here she was, running out of it. She swallowed the panic that was trying to suffocate her and continued her quest. She was looking for anything she could use to get away from the evil man in the burlap mask.

As she moved around the darkness, her hand bumped against something. It scooted across the floor with that familiar metal-against-concrete sound. Her breathing quickened as she felt the first seeds of hope spring to life in her heart.

She moved towards the sound and spent the next few moments lightly moving her hands on the concrete trying to find it again.

Success.

Her hand touched it.

She picked it up and let her hands become her eyes as she rolled the item around in her palm. Then she passed it to her other hand and repeated the same action. Then she let her fingers hold one end of the item as she used her other hand to press firmly against the opposite end.

A nail.

She found a nail. *And it was an enormous one.*

Not one of those skinny nails someone would use to put up paneling. No, this was a thick nail and it was long. Almost the entire length of her hand. The tip of it wasn't as sharp as she hoped it would be, but Susan knew it would have to do. With enough force, she knew the nail would do damage and hopefully give her the time she would need to get away.

She made her way back to her mattress and lay there in the darkness and practiced thrusting and slicing with the nail and plotted how she was going to use it.

She knew her only time for escape was coming.

He would return soon for another "intimate time" with her and her actions had to be quick and precise.

She imagined him trying to lay on top of her how. She planned how she would stab him and where she would sink the rusty nail into his flesh.

Despite the grin of hope on her face, tears filled her eyes as she feared what he might do to her if she failed. She quickly put the thought out of her mind. She couldn't think about failing. Instead, she concentrated on what she needed to do if she was to survive.

Her only chance to escape was upon her.

She could hear the latch on her prison door come undone.

He was coming in.

And now she had to be ready. Ready for anything. No matter what.

"Come and get it," she whispered and prepared her heart for what was to come.

37

Jack had been following Stefan Cooper for the last hour. He followed Stefan doing his errands and Jack was convinced the man was dull. He dropped off a book at the library in the nightly deposit box, got some gas, went through a *Burger King* and picked up a bite to eat, and then parked in front of a bar and went inside.

Jack exited his car and followed Stefan inside. He took up his surveillance from across the bar while Stefan sat at the counter and nursed a light beer.

Jack brought the melted videotape he picked up from William Brookings car earlier and began to study it while looking up often to see what Stefan Cooper was doing.

Stefan continued nursing his beer and Jack looked back at the videotape. While studying the tape, he dialed his voicemail again to listen to William's frantic message. His words were quick, panicky, and desperate. Jack was certain that William, finding and watching this videotape, signed his own death certificate. He possessed new information from Pastor Tom Sullivan that was on the tape, tried to call Jack, and someone found out about it.

Jack sighed and thought for a bit and concluded because of what William found out, he paid for it with his life.

Four pastors connected in all.

Two killed themselves.

One was at the hospital.

One, yet to be identified, was still on the loose.

They were all connected. Whether they knew each other or not, they connected to each other in some way.

"Who is this fourth pastor?" Jack spoke while scribbling notes on a napkin. "Why didn't he take his life?"

Jack drew four circles and placed them far enough from each other as if he was about to connect each circle with single lines to make a square. In the first circle, he wrote down pastor #1, in the other, pastor #2, in the third, pastor #3, and in the final, pastor #4. He placed an "X" on the first two circles indicating the two pastors who died. On the third, he wrote the word *saved* indicating that was Reverend Ray. On the fourth circle, he placed a question mark. This was the one who was still unaccounted for. In the middle Jack drew one more circle. All together now the circles looked like the dots one would see representing the number 5 on a single dice. It was then that Jack drew a line from the corner circles and connected each of them to the one circle in the middle.

"One person connects them all," Jack said while staring at his drawing. Then a new thought, "Or, perhaps, that one person is controlling them all."

Jack spun the day's activities. The one event he had trouble getting past was his meeting with the strange man at *Crisper's*. The man knew things that weren't secret to anyone who watched the news and knew who Jack Angel was, but the conversation was still unsettling.

The *man* was unsettling.

His words.

His demeanor.

How cold and uncomfortable he made Jack's heart feel.

Jack remembered William's words from the voicemail he left. His words were panicked, but precise, "*He also talked about a gray man. He didn't know if this man was a messenger of light or darkness. I have no idea who this person is, but this man has a connection somehow.*"

A messenger of light or darkness.

A messenger.

At that moment, Jack remembered his conversation with the strange man from earlier. His words sent a shock of coldness through his heart. "I'm a messenger of sorts and I'm here to help you...to help you...*see*."

A messenger.

"Unbelievable," he said under his breath. "The strange guy who came and talked to me earlier. It was him. It was the Gray Man."

Jack hit the number 2 on his cell phone and held it down as it speed dialed Frank. While it rang, Jack wrote, *Gray Man*, in the center circle of his drawing. On the second ring, Frank answered.

"Jack I'm glad it's you. I was getting ready to call ya."

"Frank, I've may have gotten us somewhere."

"Really? Whatcha got?"

"I think I talked to the Gray Man William told me about in his message."

Jack could hear Frank shut the door to his office, followed soon after with Frank sitting down. "You've got to be shitting me."

"Not at all."

"When was this?"

Jack told him about his meeting with Beverly Cooper and the stranger who came to him after she left.

Frank was in disbelief. "So this guy comes from out of nowhere and says he has an interest in what you seek, tells you about three types of people in this world, calls you a Hunter Killer and you think this is him?"

"Shit Frank, you should've seen this guy. He looked like he just walked out of a morgue after assuming room temperature days ago. I was surprised this walking corpse just didn't die right in front of me. I can see why he's called the Gray Man. It's no wonder Pastor Sullivan feared this guy. Trust me on this one Frank. I know my instincts are right. It just didn't hit me until now."

"Okay, okay. So how do we get in touch with him?"

"That's the problem. I don't know. He passed me some note on a napkin. I read it and when I looked up he was gone. He wasn't there anymore. It was as if he vanished."

R. G. Huxley

"What?!?!"

"I know. I thought the same thing."

"Are you drunk?"

"Frank I'm being serious here.

"So am I," he responded with a slight snicker.

"No, I'm fine."

"Okay, so what did the note say?"

Jack reached into his pocket and pulled out the napkin, unfolded it, and read it to Frank. "Through Hellfire Eternal, Infernal Obedience Neverending."

"What in Sam Hell does that mean?"

"I have no idea. Right now we have two pastors who decided to burn themselves alive. Maybe a reference to that."

"It's circumstantial. We can't hold anyone on what some old buzzard gives you on a napkin."

"But we find him. We interrogate his ass until he opens up with what he knows."

"Think we'll find him soon?"

Jack lit a cigarette and inhaled deeply, "I have a feeling he'll be finding me soon enough."

"Okay, well detain him if he does."

"Absolutely." Jack then remembered Frank's initial comment when he answered. "Hey, what were you going to call me about?"

"Oh yeah! Almost forgot. I got a call from the Medical Examiner. They finished the autopsy on that prostitute from the other day."

"And?"

"The M.E. said he wants to see us tonight. Can you make it?"

"Yeah, nothing is going on here," Jack responded while staring at the back of Stefan Cooper.

"Meet me there in an hour."

"Absolutely."

Jack closed his phone and stared at his notes. *So, you're the Gray Man?* Jack thought to himself. "Infernal obedience huh?

138

The Cleansing: A Thriller

Like you said, I'm a Hunter Killer. Come around me again and you'll find out just what kind of killer I really am."

38

Jack arrived at the Medical Examiner's office forty-five minutes after he hung up with Frank. He followed Stefan Cooper home, completing his surveillance for the evening, and drove across town to meet up with Frank. All the while, he kept thinking about what the Gray Man had said to him earlier about being a killer and having those killer instincts.

The Gray Man was right.

He needed to start relying on those again if he was to get anywhere in the investigation. Up until now, he felt as if he was spinning his wheels and making no progress whatsoever.

That needed to change.

He knew he would have to use those same Hunter Killer instincts in following Stefan Cooper as well. He didn't think his following Stefan would take much longer. He could tell the guy would slip up soon enough and then Jack could be done with him.

He made a mental note to start watching the DVDs Beverly had given him to surmise what was going through her husband's head. Jack just hoped he didn't have to spend the next week watching Stefan drink light beer from across a smoky bar.

Jack didn't care for light beer and other than women drinking it to continue to look sexy, he never understood men who drank it continuously. *If you want to save on calories, eat a rice cake*, he'd think to himself. *Don't drink a light beer.*

He always compared the light beer drinkers to the people who called into those late night syndicated radio shows to request a song because his wife left him for another man.

Maybe it was because you kept drinking light beer. She needed a real man who knew what beer was and how wonderful it tasted.

Jack finally pulled into the M.E.'s parking lot and then walked in the front door and saw Frank waiting in the lobby for him. The M.E., Neil Hamsik, soon greeted both.

"Hey Frank how are ya? As always, it's nice to see you too Jack," Neil Hamsik said smiling, holding out his hand. Jack and Frank returned the gesture. "Why don't you both come back with me?"

Neil passed through the double doors with Jack and Frank following close behind. They entered the autopsy room and saw Sonja Ericson's savaged, naked body lying open on the metal table. Bloody tools used to open her up were in the steel bowl beside her with the overhead lamp shining on her chest. The knife cuts of Rev 21:8 were still visible on her stomach.

"Well, let's get started. She died of blunt force trauma to the head as you can see here, here, and here." Jack and Frank followed where Neil was pointing. "She had massive amounts of bleeding inside her head. Looks like she had a brain hemorrhage and then the perp cut on her stomach. Other than crack cocaine, no other foreign chemicals were found in her body."

Jack couldn't help but stare of the prostitute's lifeless face. As he studied her, his eyes began to burn. His heart rate picked up and then his breathing became increasingly irregular. He closed his eyes.

An image pierced the darkness, trying to come to focus.

It was happening.

A flash of light and quick movements.

A face. At first featureless, but then clear. It was Sonja's face.

Then another flash showered with screams and violent movements.

The image seared into him.

Something else.

A man. Screaming.

Another bright flash and more screams.

A woman.

This woman.

Shielding her face and head from the rage.

Shielding her body.

From him.

Death came to her in a rage. His rage. Blow after blow. She felt her life seep out of her.

In the end, she begged God to save her and stop brutality.

Then just as quick as it started, it stopped. Jack opened his eyes, steadied his breathing, and stared at the body.

"Jack? You okay?" Frank asked.

Jack, in numbed disbelief, still wondering if he had truly regained his ability again, looked at Frank and Neil and walked closer to the corpse. He laid his ear over her lips as if she was whispering something to him from beyond the grave. He then took his hand and laid it on her stomach where the REV 21:8 was scrawled into her abdomen.

Neil Hamsik spoke first. "I think he was trying to tell us what she was by that verse. She's a whore. He's calling her a whore."

"No. I don't think so," Jack said quickly trumping the Medical Examiner. "Our killer is justifying himself to God. He wanted God to know exactly *why* he did what he did to her. He wanted her purged from existence. In his eyes, she's an abomination. And that's what makes him the worst kind of killer."

"Why's that?" Neil Hamsik asked.

"Because he isn't going to stop."

39

Susan lay in the darkness with the rusty nail palmed in her hand when the door to her prison opened. The man in the burlap mask walked in, not saying a word to her. He began striking wooden matches to light candles he brought and then set them up around the room. He lit four in all and spaced them apart to allow enough illumination in the room. Susan sat on the dirty mattress trying to steady her breathing, waiting for an opportunity to stab him with her weapon. She watched her captor light and setup the candles ceremoniously.

Her hands were shaking.

When he finished, he sat down at the foot of her mattress.

"You're shaking Susan. Are you okay?"

She nodded, trying to regulate her breathing and heart rate. "I'm fine."

The Burlap Man looked around at the candles as they flickered, causing shadows to dance on the walls. "What do you know about fire? Tell me Susan."

Why is he asking me about fire? She felt confused. Where was it coming from? In the past, he never came in to be with her to ask her questions. He always would come to her, force himself inside, and then leave.

This time it was different.

He was different. She could sense it. Almost *smell* it.

He seemed disconnected.

Susan continued to wait for the right time to pounce on him. She didn't know exactly when she would, but deep down, she believed her conscience would scream at her. *"Do it now! Stab him! Get it over with! Now run!"*

143

"I asked you a question Susan. What do you know about fire?"

Drawn from her thoughts, she quickly answered him, not wanting to make him upset. "It keeps you warm when you're cold."

"Ah, yes it does. What else? Tell me more."

Susan hated talking to her captor like this. His voice caused bile to rise and burn the back of her throat. He talked to her as if she were a student. Someone he looked down upon and needed to teach.

Yes! That was it exactly! A student!

A student in debauchery.

Debauchery AP class.

Biding her time, Susan answered, "It can be used for cooking food."

"Anything else?"

Struggling with his questions, Susan stammered, "I uh…well…remember in ceramics class…umm…our teacher used a kiln to cook our pottery."

"Now we're getting somewhere." The man moved closer to Susan sliding his hand up her leg. "Tell me about the ceramic making process."

Susan began to tremble a little more. *What are you trying to do to me?* She thought to herself.

She took a few deep breaths, felt her rate slow just a bit and continued to play along. Freedom was near, she just needed to bide her time.

"Well, we took our clay, shaped it into the cup or vase we wanted to make and then let it dry out. Our teacher, Mrs. Hammond, called it *"bone dry"*. After that, we brushed our glaze on it."

"Wait a minute! You're missing a step."

The outburst caught her off guard. Susan trembled.

"W-what do you mean? What step?"

"Before you put on the glaze, you had to do something. What did you have to do?"

Susan paused and tried to run through the steps in her memory. Then it came to her and it was this recollection that caused her to fight back tears. "We had to fire it in the kiln."

Her captor nodded. "Exactly!" he yelled, moving his hand to the top of her dirty, blood-smeared thigh. The conversation aroused him. She was finally getting it. "You had to fire it in the kiln. Do you know what would've happened to your piece of shit pottery if you tried to fire it in the kiln before it was...what did Mrs. Hammond call it?"

More bile rose in her throat. Susan swallowed hard to keep it down. "B-B-Bone dry."

"Yes! Do you know what would've happened to your pottery if you fired it in the kiln before it became bone dry?"

Susan shook her head.

"Well, it could crack or even explode," she answered.

"Exactly right. So it is very important that the pottery must be bone dry."

Susan stared at the Burlap Man wondering if she was the pottery he was referring to.

"So Susan, do you think Mrs. Hammond, if she could see you now, would say you've become *bone dry*?"

Susan sat in silence. She didn't want to play this game anymore.

He placed both his hands on Susan's legs, spreading them apart. "I do. I think you've become *bone dry* and it's about time I start putting on your glaze before I fire you in the kiln."

40

Frank stared in disbelief at his former partner. He'd seen Jack do this before, but it had been awhile since Jack was able to get his mind and heart inside the crime scene. He'd forgotten how eerie and amazing it was all at the same time to watch what Jack did best.

Use his ability.

As far back as he could remember, Jack had never been wrong, and that's why he didn't even bother to question him in front of Neil Hamsik.

He'd asked Jack in the past if he was psychic and Jack just laughed. "No, I'm not psychic. Never claimed to be. I don't know what it is, but I just get feelings, sometimes visions, and it burns inside me."

"Can you feel what the victim feels?"

"Not yet and I hope I never do. I just see quick flashes and I can get inside the head of the victim and the killer."

"That sounds psychic to me."

"Well, call it what you want. I'm telling you I don't consider myself psychic. Psycho maybe, but not psychic."

Frank laughed at his friend's joke. He never asked him again and ever since would just watch Jack in stunned astonishment.

Since Ainslie's murder two years ago, Jack questioned whether or not he would be able to use his ability again. *Ever.* But now, here they both stood, and once again, the Jack Angel Frank remembered, was starting to come back.

The Cleansing: A Thriller

Neil walked away from the body that was once Sonja Ericson, along with Jack and Frank following both across the room.

"I want to show you two something. This is one of the reasons I called you Frank."

Neil grabbed a clear plastic bag and held it underneath a light. Inside the bag was a thin flat disk about the size of a quarter. The item had a purple tinge to it, but it was obvious to everyone present the original color had been white.

"What is it?" Frank finally asked.

"I pulled this from the victim's throat. Her killer forced it down postmortem. Look at the design on it."

Neil laid the bag deliberately under the light so the object's design could be more visible.

"Right there," he said pointing to the disk. "What does that look like to you?"

Frank and Jack both leaned and strained to see the design.

"A lamb," Frank finally spoke.

Jack nodded. "Yeah it looks like a lamb."

"That's precisely what it is. A lamb engraved on a wafer."

"A *wafer*? Like the ones given in communion at church?"

"Yes," replied Neil. "This explains the purple tinge to it."

Frank connected the dots. "The killer soaked it in wine and forced it down her throat."

Neil nodded at Frank.

"But why?" Frank asked. "What does that mean?"

Jack looked up and stared at them both. "He had communion with her after she died. He wanted her to drink the blood and eat the flesh of Christ. He may view himself as Christ's equal."

"Shit."

"Frank, we need to find out which churches in the area use a wafer with a lamb on it at their communion. If we find the church, we're that much closer to finding the killer, and hopefully our fourth pastor."

"Neil? Do you have anything else for us?"

147

"Yes. One last thought before you go. After what we've seen and talked about here, I'd have to agree with Jack. This killer isn't done. Not even close."

"Why's that?" Frank asked.

"To this killer, it's all about power and control. Who would want to relinquish that?"

Jack nodded in agreement and walked once again to the body and held the hand of Sonja Ericson. "He's planning something big. I can't escape the feeling that our killer, this fourth pastor, is planning something on a grand scale and possibly soon."

"Like what?"

"What else is left if thinks of himself as Christ's equal?" Jack stared at Frank and Neil, pausing a beat. "His ascension to Heaven."

41

Susan shook with fear. *What did he mean by wanting to put the glaze on me and fire me in the kiln? Is that what the candles were for?*

The Burlap Man moved closer to her. He studied her countenance. Her body language. Her eyes.

The eyes were the mirror to the soul.

"Do you know the three types of color for a flame?"

"No," she lied. Susan knew what they were, but was hoping her lying could buy her some time. She knew he would have to give her a lesson in physical science because of her assumed ignorance.

"There are three colors, red, orange, and white. Do you know which one burns the hottest?"

"I guess red?" she lied again.

"No. Not red, but white. White burns the hottest. Have you ever heard of dicyanoacetylene?"

"No." She wasn't lying this time.

"Dicyanoacetylene, also referred to as carbon subnitride, burns in oxygen with a blue-white flame at nine thousand and ten degrees Fahrenheit. Carbon subnitride is the hottest flame of any chemical. To give it some scale, each of those candles burning, burns at about one thousand degrees Fahrenheit. So, let me ask you. Do you know what makes fire amazing?"

Susan shook her head.

"It purifies," the Burlap Man said, looking away in thought as if to picture what he was saying. "Some believe when the soul leaves the body it goes to the nearest fire and from there to the heavens. Before it can go to the heavens, the soul must first endure purification by fire. One must descend into darkness to find the source of light. To put it another way, one must die in order to be reborn. The fire burns away the transient, the imperfect; therefore the soul can finally be free and immortalized, to live forever in peace. It's as if the fire purified, or rather *cleansed*, the dark soul." The Burlap Man paused, looking deep and concerning in Susan's eyes, like a father scolding a child. "Do you believe in the cleansing Susan?"

Susan sat motionless. She feared no matter how she answered, her judgment would be the same. She began gripping the nail harder, maneuvering it in her palm so the point was between her thumb and index finger. She thought about bringing it down on top of his flesh with the point at the meat of her hand, but she was afraid he would quickly stop her. She reorganized in her mind.

Susan swiftly moved the nail around to its new position. She was ready to strike him. If he should turn away, even for a second to reference the burning candles again, she would stab him. She hoped to land the nail in his neck, but right now she would take anything just to give her time to run away.

She answered, trying to buy some time. "I do think fire can cleanse. Yes."

"Good. I hoped you would say that. You see, sometimes life can be a trial by fire. To test one's ability. To see how they perform under pressure. Kind of like your pottery. You formed it, dried it, and then fired it in the kiln to purify it before you put on the glaze. I faced the kiln this past Sunday. I stood in front of it. I stared at it, but you see I wasn't ready yet. I would've exploded because I wasn't completely ready, but now the day is drawing closer where it may be time for me to go to the kiln. Finally, to the fire."

The Burlap Man lashed out his hand and grabbed Susan by her jaw and squeezed it hard between his fingers. Susan sreamed in pain. His eyes burned with intensity and anger, no longer the care and love he said he had for her. He'd become different. Susan knew something had changed in him and now, instead of seeing her as a lover, he saw her as an object.

The Cleansing: A Thriller

"I think you're ready for the fire too Susan," he growled. "We must burn for our transgressions. Our souls will join the flames and we shall ascend to the heavens. From there we may spend an eternity in the lake which burneth with fire and brimstone, but I have tried to pave the path to reckon all I've done. Go with me Susan. Join me in my cleansing of fire."

The Burlap Man turned for a moment towards the candles and Susan lunged towards him. "NEVER!" she screamed, thrusting the nail in his chest and piercing his flesh. "You sick - son of a bitch!"

The Burlap Man fell back on the mattress grabbing at the protruding object now in his chest. Susan quickly leapt towards the open door, running up the stairs, out the front door, and into the dark night before her.

42

Jack and Frank walked out of the Medical Examiner's building and into the darkened parking lot. They stood by their cars underneath the only lamppost which hummed with the light energy it provided. Swarms of insects flew chaotically around the light bumping into the bulb and into each other.

An occasional bat flew from out of the darkness to devour an insect and then moments later, either the same bat or a different one would come back for more. No matter how many times the bats came, the population of insects seemed to stay the same.

Jack leaned up against the driver's side door, tapped out a cigarette, and lit it. He took an unusually long drag and exhaled the smoke up towards the swarming insects.

"What happened in there?" Frank finally asked.

Jack spit on the ground and took another drag. "What are you talking about?"

"You know damn well what I'm talking about. Out of nowhere, the Jack I remembered reappeared. You said you've been having a hard time lately with getting into the mind of our victims and killer. Now, you didn't seem to miss a beat. What happened?"

"I think it was my talk with that Gray Man guy."

"Really? Why's that?"

"I don't know. Just something he said I guess."

"About you having the instincts of a killer?"

Jack nodded and took another drag. "He's right. That's why I can do what I do. I know how to get into the killer's

152

mind. For some reason, it's as if I can see through his eyes. I can see the victim. Shit, I can even see from the victim's viewpoint as well. For this to work, I need to stay focused. I need to breathe like him. See like him. Touch like him. Most of all, I need to think like him. And I know how to do that."

"And you don't call that a psychic ability?"

"I don't call it anything. It is what it is. I don't question it."

"So what happened. Why do you think you lost the ability?"

"Because I stopped relying on it. I couldn't focus since Ainslie's death and I thought for sure I could use my instincts to catch her killer. Well, I didn't catch him. I felt like a failure to my daughter. I let her down Frank! Dani left soon after because I failed her. My ability let *me* down. When I needed it the most, it wasn't there. It…failed…me! So I said, 'Fine! Forget it!' Since I didn't have anyone, I didn't need anyone."

"Well you've always had *me* Jack to talk to. You just never reached out. Instead you ran to alcohol and began shutting everyone out of your life. Including me. I was the one who reached out to you to bring you back in. I was worried about you man."

Jack nodded. He knew Frank was right. He'd never come to terms with Ainslie's death and wondered if he ever would.

"Ainslie's killer is still out there Frank."

"I know and we'll get him. Together. But don't shut down on me again. I am here for you Jack. I'll listen to whatever you have to say. I'm your friend. I care about you and your welfare. That's why I was able to get the lieutenant to get you on this case."

Jack took a deep breath. "I know and appreciate what you're doing for me. I'm feeling alive again and I owe that to you."

"By the way, I want you to know, for what it's worth, Dani still cares about you too."

"I know she does."

Jack and Frank stood silent letting their words hang in the air a little longer. This was the beginning for Jack on his way to

153

recovery and Frank wanted his friend to know people cared. After a few minutes, Frank held out his hand and curled his fingers back and forth. "Give me one of those."

"A cigarette?"

Frank nodded.

Jack laughed. "You don't smoke. You're mom would kill us both if she knew I gave you one."

"Well I won't say anything if you don't. Now give me one."

Shaking his head in disbelief, Jack pulled out his pack and handed Frank a cigarette. Frank leaned into the flame of Jack's lighter and lit the cigarette. Jack's eyes squinted watching his friend hacking and coughing while trying to smoke.

"You look stupid Frank."

"And *you* don't when *you* smoke?"

"I at least know how to hold the damn cigarette in between my lips. You look like you're trying to kiss the butt end of that thing. Not to mention, it's not a joint. Please hold the damn thing right if you're going to smoke near me."

"Hey Mr. Hunter Killer Instinct, can you get inside my head and figure out what I am thinking about you right now?"

Jack laughed at his friend's comment. He missed being around Frank and knew that he would always be grateful for what he had done for him.

"So what do you want to do tonight Jack?"

"I'm going home to watch some of the DVDs Beverly Cooper gave me from her husband's stash. Tomorrow, I say we meet for breakfast and start visiting some churches to see what they use for communion. Start eliminating some people."

"Sounds like a plan. Where ya wanna eat?"

"You pick," Jack said getting into his car.

"Waffle House?"

"Sounds good. How's six AM sound?" Jack asked while closing his car door. He started the engine and cracked his window.

"I'll be there. By the way, you're buying."

The Cleansing: A Thriller

"Then take it off the hundred I owe you," Jack responded while pulling out of the parking space.

"No way! You owe me a lot- *remember*!?"

Jack started to drive out of the parking lot acting like he couldn't hear Frank yelling at him. He looked in his rearview mirror and saw Frank continuing to stand in the same place, still holding his cigarette. Jack picked up his cell phone and dialed Frank's number.

"What now Jack?" Frank asked answering his phone with a hint of laughter in his question.

"Please for shit's sake, put that cigarette out. You'll never get away with being a smoker."

Frank laughed while hanging up on Jack and then waved to him while his friend pulled into traffic to head home. He couldn't help but smile watching him leave and knowing deep down Jack was going to be okay.

"Welcome back friend. Welcome back."

43

The darkness of the night devoured Susan Cleavenger. She was blind to where she was running. The snaps and cracks of twigs and leaves underneath her bare feet was a reminder she was free.

Finally. Free.

To quickly escape the Burlap Man's clutches, she decided to leave with only what she was wearing.

Her t-shirt and panties.

Nothing else.

She kept looking back to see if the Burlap Man was following behind her, allowing herself an occasional stop to catch her breath and to conduct a status check and listen if he was close behind. So far she heard nothing.

What scared her most, outside of the Burlap Man catching her again, was she didn't know where she was running to. She had no idea where *exactly* she was. Questions bombarded her as if an invisible entity interrogated her as if she had committed some crime by not thinking her escape plan to its fullest.

Now what?

Where will you go?

Where's the closest town?

How do you get there from here?

How do you tell your mom where you are if you don't know yourself?

As soon as the questions came, Susan had to shut them down. *I can't think like this. Need to focus. Need to keep running.*

But as she kept running, it became harder with each step not to feel discouraged. The blackness of the night and density of the woods around her offered no guidance to any nearby road she could follow or any visible city lights she could run to. All she had was her instinct.

The instinct to survive.

The instinct to run.

And the instinct to kill him if she must.

That's all I need, she reminded herself. *Instinct.*

Susan paused for a moment to catch her breath again and felt around on the ground for a rock or a piece of wood she could use to defend herself if needed. She found a thick piece of wood, picked it up, and squeezed her palm around its base to get a good grip. She shook the wood to get an idea of its dense heaviness and felt comfortable she could use it against her former captor to get away. She also picked up a few rocks she would toss in the distance to make it sound like she was elsewhere to throw him off her whereabouts if he started closing in.

After a final deep inhale, she started to run again. She hoped to find an area she could hunker down in and hide for the night. She resolved in her mind if she needed to sleep to get her strength, she would only do so in short catnap bursts.

Her eyes finally adjusted to the night and she was able to start making out shapes of trees, logs, and branches. This was good because she didn't want to injure herself by running into a tree, knocking herself out, or hurting herself so much that she couldn't move.

Surely he'd catch me if I twisted my ankle or broke my leg.

She dismissed the thought as quick as it came. She needed to focus. She needed to run and not stop.

And run she did until she heard a snap of a twig about fifteen yards in front of her.

Susan abruptly stopped.

It's him, she thought to herself.

She knelt down, gripped her weapon, and tried to fight back tears.

Her heart was pounding out of her chest with thundering beats in her ears. Her breathing was fast, chaotic, and she began taking deep breaths to bring it under control.

The steps came closer.

Susan flung a rock beyond where the steps were coming from to throw off the intruder. From what she could tell, the rock landed and rolled, making it sound as if she was running through the woods in a different direction.

The approaching steps stopped.

Whatever or whoever it was didn't take the bait and run towards the noise the rock made.

The sound of the steps just stopped.

Susan said a quick prayer, but still remained quiet and still. She waited.

The steps resumed and came closer towards her.

Susan readied another rock. She had to try again. If this one failed to lure him away, she would have to stand and fight.

Closer, the steps came.

Fifteen feet away.

She threw her rock.

This time it hit the trunk of tree with a loud thump and then rolled through the black night.

Once again, the sound of nearing steps stopped.

He knows where I am. He's coming for me. Dear God, please don't let me die this way. Please make him go away.

The steps resumed.

Ten feet away.

Her breathing became irregular once more. Her grip tightened. Susan felt she could snap her weapon she was holding it so hard.

Eight feet away.

Still approaching.

I'll let him pass me by. Maybe he doesn't know exactly where I am. I will hit him from behind and won't stop until I know he's dead.

Five feet away.

Let's do this you shit! Come and get me.

She pressed her back against the tree.

Three feet away.

God be with me.

Two feet.

She held her weapon above her head ready to swing it down like an axe.

One foot.

The intruders head appeared from the other side of the tree. At that moment her arms swung down, barely missing the approaching doe. The deer flinched and darted away from Susan the moment it saw her swinging at its head. The sudden jolt of the deer caused Susan to scream. She turned in the opposite direction of the deer and began running once more. The rush of adrenaline gave her enough fuel and second wind to run on and on and not look back.

Meanwhile, the burlap man stumbled onto the porch clutching his bloodied chest. He looked around wondering where Susan ran to and when he heard her screams off in the distance he knew exactly where she was and he began going after the one who would soon join him in the afterlife.

44

Jack walked into his front door and tossed his keys onto the counter. Decker greeted Jack by nuzzling his head into Jack's leg. Jack tried to ignore him, but instead quickly rubbed Decker's head.

"How ya doing Deck? Did you have a lazy day?"

Decker sneezed as if to answer his owner and then rushed to the patio door to let Jack know he needed to go outside and relieve himself. Time was of the essence or Decker would just have to do it right there on the carpet. He didn't want to disappoint Jack so he whined and ran in circles as if he were holding himself.

"Okay. Okay. I'm coming," Jack replied walking over to let out his friend.

After he let Decker out the sliding glass door, Jack opened the plastic bag that had the DVD discs. He pulled out each one and started stacking them and studying them by manufacturer. Of the twenty DVD-Rs, ten were Sony, two Memorex, two TDK, five Maxell, and one JVC. Jack decided to stack by manufacturer.

Jack knew when it came to video recording, people could be sticklers in which brand they liked. In most cases, not all, the person rarely deviated to another brand and were very loyal to what disc they used.

About six years ago Jack and Frank were investigating the murder of a quiet suburban family. What plagued them both was who would've wanted them killed and why? Nothing made sense.

The Cleansing: A Thriller

That was until one day, while going through the house, Jack found a hidden camera in the master bedroom. He pulled it down and ejected the videotape. The tape was a Kodak Gold VHS, the same one used by the family's insurance company to get a record of all items. The investigation team was able to lift the prints off the camera. The prints matched the killer's exactly.

They went to the State Farm Insurance Company and arrested Stephen Lavell in connection to the murders and booked him on five counts of first degree murder. During the interrogation Stephen broke down and confessed it was he who murdered the family. He said he fantasized nightly about the wife, Tracey Linder, and realized he would never be good enough to have her. So when the family took his suggestion about having their household items inventoried for insurance purposes, he decided to set up a hidden camera that would record Tracey.

He would often break into the house, change out the tapes, go home, and watch the woman he had fallen in love with. Deep in his heart, he knew she would never love him in return.

One day it became too much for him to bear. He waited for them to return from a family outing. When they were all in bed, Stephen Lavell came up from the basement and shot them all execution style.

Tracey was the last to die, but not before Stephen had his way with her. He washed his condom down the toilet and then laid her body in the shower to wash away any hair or fibers he may have left behind.

Stephen's attention to detail in cleaning the crime scene worked because the investigation was going nowhere. That was until Jack found the hidden camera. When it came to the murders, the camera recorded nothing because the tape ran out. Jack did find their insurance-taped recordings and was able to piece it together by matching the brand of the insurance tapes with the brand of videotape in the recorder.

The jury found Stephen Lavell guilty of the brutal crimes.

Instead of getting the death penalty, he copped a plea with his full confession and was given a term of five life sentences. One year into his incarceration, the prison guard found Stephen bludgeoned to death in his cell. His cellmate confessed to the murder and said it was his way of cleaning up the mess the justice system left behind.

Jack knew if he hadn't found the two videotapes, it was going to be hard to find the Linder Family's killer. Stephen was used to buying the same VHS tapes because he liked their quality.

He was loyal to the brand.

Now Jack stared at five different stacks of discs wondering if he was looking at five different loyal DVD customers or twenty different ones instead.

He knew the only way to find out was to start watching them one by one. Jack wasn't looking forward to having to sit and start watching twenty discs worth of some sick sexual deviant's addiction.

He grabbed the top disc from the Sony stack, grabbed his remote control, turned on the TV. and inserted the disc into his DVD player. Jack sat on the couch, lit a cigarette, and hit play.

What appeared next on the TV's screen caused Jack's stomach to turn with nausea and anger.

45

Jack watched the video intently. At first the only image which appeared on the screen was an empty apartment. Except for a few dirty dishes on the counter, the apartment appeared clean. He figured right away the owner of the apartment lived in North Carolina because of the telephone book sitting on the counter near the dishes. In big letters across the front it said Raleigh/Durham and Vicinity. Jack knew anyone could have moved from the Tarheel State and brought their phone book with them, but for the moment, Jack assumed this was a video taken from North Carolina.

Within a few moments a man appeared on the screen. He knew the camera was recording because when he appeared on screen he adjusted the angle to make sure he was getting the best shot possible. The man smiled at the camera and then pulled out a knife.

He held the silver blade close to his cheek and began running it from his cheekbone towards his bottom lip. He did this a couple times, all the while smiling.

"This is what you get bitch for ignoring me in the office! You could've been happy. You could've had all the happiness life had to offer, but through your vulgarity, you ignored me. I'd watch you in the break room getting a Diet Coke and talking to your friends. When I came in, you would all suddenly get quiet. You think I didn't notice? You think I was too thick and stupid to know you weren't talking about me? You were! I knew you were! When Adrian asked you out you told him you would love to go out. Problem is, I asked you out two weeks ago and you said that you were still getting over your recent break up from Gary. You're a lying bitch and lying bitches get what they deserve!"

After the man was done talking, he walked into the kitchen, opened what looked to be the door to the pantry and hid inside.

Jack's stomach turned as he feared what would happen to the woman the man was speaking to when she opened the pantry.

Jack hit the fast forward button and watched the video race to the point the woman walked into view of the camera. After a few minutes of forwarding the disc, she finally appeared.

She was a tan, slender blonde woman, about thirty years of age. Her shoulder length hair pulled back into a ponytail. She placed her purse onto the counter and walked over to the phone to listen to the messages.

There were two.

The first message was her mom calling about the weekend family reunion.

The other was from Adrian thanking her for the nice date they had and couldn't wait to go out again sometime soon.

Jack felt himself wanting to scream at the TV warning her to run. Leave the apartment now! Call 911!

But he knew she wouldn't be able to hear his warning. He would have to watch it all play out on the video. Jack didn't know if he could do it.

The woman turned and walked towards the pantry. She paused for a moment to pick up her cat who was now snaking itself in between her legs and wanting attention. She bent down, picked up the cat, and rubbed its chin and head.

"It's okay Binky. Mommy is going to get you something to eat."

She placed the cat down and returned to the pantry door. She turned the knob, opened the door, and within seconds the man hiding tackled her to the kitchen floor.

The woman let out a scream, but the man's hand covered her mouth and silenced her.

The Cleansing: A Thriller

He showed her the knife he brought with him, bent towards her ear, and warned her if she shouted again he'd gut her and then her cat.

She nodded in quick agreement.

Then the man started to take her pants down along with unzipping himself and started to force himself inside his co-worker.

Jack had seen enough. He reached up to turn off the video, but before he could, the woman started begging for more.

"Yes!" She screamed. "Like that! That's what I've always wanted!"

Confused, Jack sat back on the couch. "What the hell?"

In a fury of movement, clothes came off and both the man and the woman were having sex together on the kitchen floor. Both the man and the woman were smiling and enjoying the moment.

"This is staged," Jack said disgustedly under his breath. "This is a damn staged video!"

Jack turned and looked at the remaining discs wondering if he had the stomach to watch the rest.

He stopped the disc, ejected it, and placed it on the counter. He grabbed a second disc along with his bourbon and returned to the couch.

"Why the hell did I agree to follow this man?"

He popped in the next disc and soon realized his decision to follow him was the right one.

46

The next disc Jack popped into the DVD player was from the Sony stack. He returned to the couch after inserting the disc and downed a shot of bourbon. The TV's screen flipped around a bit from the video and then the picture came on.

There seemed to be some grain on the video and Jack wondered if it was a fault of the disc being scratched or if done purposely.

He didn't know and didn't care.

He heard the camera operator speak. "Here, I want you to try this."

A hand from the side of the camera came into view and handed an emaciated looking male a small Ziploc baggie. The male, who looked to be in his early twenties, took the bag. The camera panned over to the couch. When it did, Jack's blood began to run cold. Numbness overtook his hands as his mouth turned dry.

He couldn't believe who was sitting on the couch.

It all seemed surreal to him.

"You've got to be shitting me," he said as his full attention took over.

Sitting on the couch was a man wearing a burlap mask.

"Why don't you shoot it in his veins this time?" the cameraman asked the guy sitting on the couch with the burlap mask. The man nodded and got up and after heating what appeared to be heroin in a spoon, he shot the liquid into the addict's arm.

Just like Reverend Ray said he did before the kid went into convulsions.

166

The Cleansing: A Thriller

Within moments, the cameraman moved forward to record the eyes rolling back into the head of the addict and the blood pouring from his mouth and nose. The addict shook violently. The man in the burlap mask started to scream for help.

His pleas went ignored.

He began doing CPR, but the addict was already dead from the injection.

"I KILLED HIM!" the man screamed. "Oh my God! I killed him!"

The man turned towards the camera and kept screaming for the cameraman to help him.

The camera continued to film the incident.

Then Reverend Ray pulled off his mask and screamed some more at the camera. The body of the addict lay lifeless on the floor. Blood continued to pour from his blue face. The last portion of the video recorded the screams for help and a dead body on the floor.

The exact incident Reverend Ray described to Jack and Frank yesterday from his hospital. Ray was beginning to describe the man who visited him. Jack was now convinced it was the Gray man. But before Reverend Ray could go into his entire meeting with the Gray Man, he had a seizure.

Now Jack just watched for himself the incident that caused the Gray Man to come to Ray Stevens.

An event recorded and obviously sold for profit.

Jack was following a man who could be a bridge to this investigation.

He picked up his cell and dialed Frank's number. Frank answered on the second ring. "Frank! You remember our talk with Ray Stevens yesterday?"

"Jack we've got a problem."

"I know we do," Jack continued. "The guy I've been-"

"Jack!" Frank shouted cutting him off. "Listen to me. Reverend Ray is gone."

"What?"

"He's gone. I just got the call a few minutes ago."

"From who?"

"The charge nurse at the hospital. He came up missing an hour ago."

"Son of a bitch! How?"

Frank didn't answer.

"Tell me Frank! How did this happen? I thought someone monitored the patients. Especially someone we consider of interest. How did he just disappear?"

"No one knows, but they would like us to come down and review the security cameras with them to see if we recognize anyone or anything."

"When?"

"Now."

Jack looked at the time on the microwave. "It's almost midnight."

"I know, but something's not right. Ray isn't in any condition to just up and leave. Something happened. We need to know what exactly."

"I think I already do."

"What is it then Jack?"

"The Gray Man."

THURSDAY

47

Jack arrived at the hospital shortly after 12:30 AM. He couldn't believe that just two days ago he and his partner had been talking to Ray Stevens. Now he's missing.

This couldn't have come at a more inopportune time. Especially since he just got a hold of the video of the incident Ray confessed about to him and Frank.

Jack surmised that not only were the pastors who killed themselves involved in some disturbing fantasies, but these events were being recorded, distributed, and sold for others to view.

It made sense to Jack why the people on the disc were wearing burlap masks.

To hide their identity.

The cameraman knew that what he was giving the young man to inject in his arms was going to kill him. If he hadn't, he would've turned off the camera to help. Instead he kept the video rolling and recorded the shock and horror of the man's tragic death.

Jack concluded that along with the fourth pastor, they also needed to find this cameraman, whoever he was. While driving to the hospital, Jack knew the only connection he had now to the event Ray Stevens described was Stefan Cooper, the husband of his newest client, who he'd been hired to follow.

He would confront him later today, after he got some much needed rest, and do what he did best.

Interrogate Stefan.

He would make Stefan understand he had only two choices. The first one would be the easiest: talk and tell everything he knew. The second choice, and Jack's personal favorite depending on his mood, physical punishment. The punishment lasted long enough before Jack reminded the person of the first choice.

Jack yearned for Stefan Cooper to choose option two, physical punishment. It had been a long while since Jack truly punished someone and he was ready to introduce that son of a bitch to the person known best around the police station:

The Death Angel.

Watching those discs caused an acute anger to burn inside his heart and he couldn't help but think of the helpless innocents on the other discs who may have been hurt. On top of that, this sick pervert, Stefan Cooper, watched these DVDs for entertainment.

Jack didn't care about the staged rape or sex scenes. He still considered it sick, but he knew there was a market for that type of fake gratuitous violence.

It was the discs of real people being hurt for the amusement of another.

That's what he hated.

That's the anger that had flared inside.

A seething anger he traced back to the death of Ainslie.

Jack refused to let another innocent person be a victim of some sick depraved man.

Not this time.

Not ever again.

It was his desire to find out how Stefan acquired these discs and then follow that lead to the person either supplying or recording them. Either way he knew that Stefan's knowledge could be significant to the investigation.

But first, Jack just wanted to punish him for awhile. Make him rethink his behavior.

He wanted to open Stefan's eyes to see what had become of his dark and perverted heart.

Looking forward to meeting you Stefan, Jack thought to himself as he pulled into the hospital's parking lot. *I hope you allow me the*

The Cleansing: A Thriller

opportunity to break you. To make you suffer a bit before you come clean with what you know.

Jack smiled and for the first time since Ainslie's death, he felt like he was truly himself again.

48

"This is where he was when I last saw him," Lynn Hollister said. "When I came on shift, I started doing my rounds and checking vitals. That was the last time I saw him. When I came on shift. A few hours later, about nine-thirty or so, I went into his room to change his IV drip and he was gone."

Frank and Jack were staring at the now empty bed of Ray Stevens. The same place he'd been a couple days ago when they both came to visit him.

The same day he started to open up and tell them about his sexual encounter and the drug use that ultimately lead to the death of a young man. Ray had started to tell them about the strange visitor that came to him. The man who looked like death. The pale gray man with tattoos.

The same man who came to visit Jack.

You're a Hunter Killer, the man had said.

It was the Gray Man.

It was during Ray's explanation of his encounter with the Gray Man that he started to seize. That was the last time Jack and Frank talked to him.

"He was our only connection to the unknown fourth pastor," Frank said to Jack.

"I know he was, but like I was telling you, we're not out of options here."

"Because of the video you watched."

"Exactly!"

The Cleansing: A Thriller

"How do you know the guy you're following isn't the one making these recordings? Maybe *he's* the cameraman Ray was telling us about?"

"I wondered that too, but I don't get that feeling about him. I think he's just some sick guy who gets off watching this kind of shit."

Frank sat down and crossed his legs. "I wish we could have seen that tape William Brookings had found, but we can't," he paused a beat and sighed. "Because he's dead too."

"Gotta love it. Two pastors who torch themselves, a third who is now missing from here, and a fourth who has yet to show his face."

"And a cameraman who hopes to make a name for himself in Hollywood one day."

"And," Jack emphasized. "The pale rider who likes to show up to scare the shit out of people."

Frank chuckled at Jack's comment.

"Can we see the security tape?" Jack finally asked the nurse.

"Absolutely. Let me take you down to the security desk."

After taking the elevator down eight floors, Lynn Hollister escorted Jack and Frank to the security office. After a brief introduction, the security guard took them to the monitors to play the tape back. Lynn Hollister decided to stay in case the two detectives had any more questions for her.

"I understand one of our patients is M.I.A.?" the security guard sarcastically asked.

"Yeah, we need to see the activity from the eighth floor for the last seven hours," Jack said to the guard. "And by the way. I'm curious. Why didn't any of you see Ray Stevens leaving?"

"Mr. Angel, ever since it was reported he was missing, we checked the cameras, all the floors, and the hospital grounds, and no one saw him leave. It was just like he vanished."

"Did your cameras pick up on anything at all? Any visitors?"

175

"Just one," the guard said rewinding the tape to the point he was referring to. "This guy right here."

Jack and Frank leaned into the monitor to look at the black and white video.

"That's him," Jack said with cold certainty as if he was picking out someone from a lineup.

The guard looked up at Jack. "Who?"

Frank knew immediately who Jack was talking about. "Is that the guy who came and talked to you Jack?"

"Yes. That's our Gray Man."

The security guard spun back around to the monitor and rewound the tape some more. "Well that was the last time he visited. He came earlier in the day as well."

The guard rewound the tape to the point where the Gray Man came the first time to visit Ray Stevens. Frank noticed the time on the video.

"That was an hour after we left."

"I see that," Jack responded taking a seat and now facing Lynn. "Did anyone mention anything to you about Ray when you came on your floor shift this evening?"

"All they said was that he'd been unresponsive for most of the day," Lynn replied.

"Unresponsive how?"

"Sleeping mostly. Later on when he was awake, he wouldn't answer anyone. He'd just nod or shake his head, but refused to talk. I found it odd because he was a talker the first time I met him."

"Did anyone tell you when he started acting like this?"

"It was in the shift change report. Records showed it was late morning."

"After his visit with that man right there?"

"I guess one could assume that, but I don't know what could've happened to cause Mr. Stevens not to talk."

"Okay," Jack said standing up and heading towards the door. "That's all we need to know."

Jack opened the door and walked out. Frank couldn't believe that Jack was leaving suddenly. The guard and the nurse shared his confused look. When he walked out the security office, he saw Jack was halfway down the hall. He jogged up to his friend.

"What's going on Jack? I have some questions I need to ask those two."

"You're not going to get any answers. We're wasting our time."

"How do you know I won't get any answers?"

"Because. The Gray Man silenced Ray Stevens. He didn't want him to talk to us or anyone else."

"How the hell do you know that?"

"That's why he came. He came to see Ray to see if he'd talked to us and Ray had."

"So you think Ray was "silenced" by him?" Frank asked, quoting his friend.

Jack nodded.

"How the hell could somebody cause someone not to speak? That makes no sense at all."

Jack stopped and spun towards Frank. "That's the point! None of this makes sense and we need to start thinking outside the box. This guy, this Gray Man, is trying to force my hand. To control my way of thinking. To make me become what I am."

"You referring to that Hunter Killer thing?"

Jack nodded. "I am and for whatever reason he wants me to find the answers on my own."

"Such as?"

"It goes back to when I interviewed Ray the first time. It was something he said to me."

"You mean about why you need to be involved with this investigation?"

"Yes! To understand Ainslie's death, why Dani left me and the reactions that took place. Ray said, 'Seek, and ye shall find. Knock and it will be opened unto you'."

"Okay, so aren't you doing that already? I thought that's what you've been doing here."

"Not by talking to Ray I wasn't. I need to seek on my own and knock on my own doors."

"You think this Gray Man is somehow guiding you then? Maybe pushing you?"

Jack nodded. "I really do."

"C'mon, don't you think that's a little farfetched? Why does he care Jack? Why you?"

Jack swallowed hard. He'd had similar thoughts as well. "I don't know. Maybe he thinks I'm the only one capable. There's something he doesn't want me to miss."

"Does that bother you a little?"

"I can't let it. Not if this investigation leads me to Ainslie's killer."

"Fair enough. Well, if we find Ray, I'm sure we'll find this guy as well. We *need* to do just that. We need them both in custody to break this case open."

"Don't worry about it Frank. I have a feeling they're gone and we will see them only on *his* time and not any sooner. In fact, I'm sure of it, but it will only be on *his* time."

"You referring to the Gray Man?"

"Yes. And like I said, we shouldn't think he will let us see Reverend Ray any sooner than when he wants us to. I have a feeling this is the order of things to come. *Control*. It's always been about control."

"And when do you suppose we will get it back? The control?"

Jack snickered at Frank. "You're assuming we had it. We never did. But I do know how to acquire it and it starts with us doing things differently: thinking differently. *Acting* differently."

Frank knew what Jack was referring to.

Being a Killer.

But not just any killer - a *Hunter Killer.*

"Okay then." Frank said giving in. "We'll do this your way. Outside the box. Unconventional."

"It's the only option we have left."

49

The Burlap Man seethed at feeling rejected since Susan had left him. He thought she loved him like he loved her. He'd been wrong.

She lied to him.

Liars need to be punished!

He planned their cleansing ceremony down to the detail and was excited Susan would join him in the afterlife. But now she was gone and he would have to spend the evening looking for her. He would find her. He was certain of that. It would just be a matter of time. And when he did...

She would have to repent for her sins.

He was fine with repentance. The Burlap Man knew all about asking God for forgiveness. He'd done it many times himself, but recently knew that words were not enough. Action was required.

You say you have faith, but I will show you my faith by what I do.

To become effective faith needed action. To be a true believer in God, one had to demonstrate their faith through action. The Burlap Man knew what the Bible said about the whores, the gays, and the idolaters. He knew where their place in the Lake of Fire would be, so why not send them there now? Why not bestow judgment on them now? Isn't that what God called him to do as a pastor? To lead? To shepherd? Guide the flock?

His actions were an extension of his faith in God and he knew God would be pleased with him. He knew God would forgive Him. He had to. He was acting in accordance to God's word. He even gave that whore prostitute communion when she died so God could see he wanted her to eat the flesh and drink the blood of His Son.

No one would ever understand it though.

But my ways are not your ways. For my ways are the ways of God.

That's what the Bible said.

The Burlap Man started to lose hope in humanity and was ready to cleanse himself like he was told to do. He had been delivering his sermon, just like the other pastors had been instructed to do. He was pounding his fist on the podium, driving home the point about the Lake of Fire and what was in store for those who followed the path of wickedness. He was about to pull out his jug of gasoline that was given to him by the Gray Man. He was going to bathe himself in the fuel and then set his body ablaze in front of his flock. He was eyeing the jug. He reached down to pick it up from the podium's shelf along with the lighter sitting beside it.

But then a glimmer of hope appeared.

It was as if God wanted him to wait.

Sitting in his congregation was a young girl.

Letting him know his work was not yet complete.

A girl who reminded him of all the purity and innocence of life.

There is but one task left.

She was stunningly beautiful.

You're time will come.

He couldn't go through with his cleansing. Not yet anyway. He had to have her all to himself. He didn't want her tainted by a wicked boy who wouldn't love her the way *he* would love or treat her.

She was a virgin.

He could feel it in his heart.

A virgin like Mary, the mother of Jesus.

And it was through this virgin that God's plan for humanity was born. And now the Burlap Man had found *his* virgin that his ultimate plan could be born in.

So he sent for her.

He sent for her to come to him.

The Cleansing: A Thriller

She belonged to him. Her heart belonged to him. Her love belonged to him. Her virginity belonged to him.

He resolved when he found her, he would offer her forgiveness, but forgiveness does not excuse the consequences. Surely she would still love him after he punished her.

And why wouldn't she? The children of Israel still loved God after receiving *their* punishment. Yes, she would love him still. But first things first, Susan must be punished for her sins. And so the Burlap Man looked forward to punishing the love of his life.

Just like God.

50

Susan Cleavenger nestled down in the leaves and thatch on the ground. Fatigue was setting in. She wanted to keep running because she knew if she stopped she would want to take a short nap. Another problem she faced was what direction she was heading. She couldn't tell if she was getting closer to a road she could follow and maybe hitch a ride or if she was heading deeper into the woods.

The sounds of the night did nothing to comfort Susan, but instead acted as if to remind her she was alone and lost. She decided to stop for a moment and listen for his approaching footsteps. Susan decided to cup her hands around her ears and push them forward a little bit. It was a trick she learned in Girl Scouts to get a feel how an animal's ears work. Cupping her ears was effective enough to pick up additional sounds as she lay quiet.

To wait.

To listen.

And to think.

What if I never see my mom again? I don't want to die out here not saying I love her one last time. I don't want her memories of me to be replaced with thoughts of how I must've suffered at the hands of this monster. I just want to live. I want to laugh again. I want to be home.

I want to see my mom.

And then she heard it.

The sound she had hoped for ever since she started running. The sound was far off, maybe a hundred yards away, but it was close enough and it gave her the hope she needed.

The sound of a passing car on the road.

She was near a road.

She could make it and then follow it and hope another car passes by and she could get to safety. Maybe they would have a cell phone she could use so she could try and call her mom to tell her where she was. Tell her she was okay and coming home. But she had to get to the road first. She had to get there without him catching her. Without him finding her first.

She *had* to get there.

To the road.

She eased up trying to stay silent and began running towards the direction of the passing car. She willed herself to push through the fatigue and said a prayer for the strength she would need to get through the night.

51

Susan slid down the small hill leading to the road. Her bare legs scraped against the rocks, dirt, and debris causing small lacerations along the back of her thighs and calves. She used her feet to slow her down while reaching the bottom of the hill. She ignored the pain of the sharp-edged rocks and jagged sticks her feet stepped against. All Susan could focus on was reaching the bottom and trying to get to freedom.

Freedom.

Just the mere thought of never having to endure his sexual assaults on her body ever again gave her the determination to keep running.

When Susan reached the road, she paused and looked quickly to her right and then left to see if any cars were coming. She willed for any set of headlights to break the darkness in front of her. Seeing none, the darkness sucked her hopes and Susan kept running and moving forward along the road. She knew he was behind her somewhere in the night. He knew these woods better than she did and would probably be making his way towards this road as well.

Panic creeping in, she kept moving. She couldn't stop. She didn't want to think what he would do to her if he caught her again.

She turned to her left and started jogging along the shoulder of the road, staying close the woods. She wanted to be able to slip back into the trees if she spotted him ahead or heard him from behind.

As she jogged, her head kept scanning the scenery ahead. *Road signs,* she thought to herself. *There has to be road signs along here somewhere.*

She continued to scan the area.

Quick left. Pan right. Keep running.

Then she heard it.

An approaching car in the distance.

When the headlights crested the hill and cut into her path she jumped in front of the oncoming truck and frantically waved it down. She didn't want to scream for the truck to stop just in case the vehicle passed her and fearing her voice would give her whereabouts away to the Burlap Man.

The truck came to a screeching stop, swerving and barley missing Susan. Dust and gravel sputtered around Susan as she ran towards the driver's side of the vehicle.

"Dear God," she cried with relief. "Please help me."

The driver, a man in his seventies, got out of the vehicle and rushed to Susan's side.

"Oh my God!" the man boomed staring at the half-naked soiled girl. "Are you okay?"

"No!" Susan cried pushing the old man back towards the truck. The driver grabbed her by her shoulders, trying to calm her down.

"Miss! What's going on?"

Susan looked over her shoulder in the direction she came. She continued to tremble. "Please! We need to get out of here! He's coming for me!"

The driver couldn't help but look in the same direction as her. He couldn't see anyone coming. He squinted as if that would grant him some superior vision.

He still saw nothing.

"Sweetie! Who's coming?"

Susan was sobbing uncontrollably. Her heavy panicked breathing was soon matched by her start-and-stop stares of the dark surroundings.

"Mister! Please listen. He's going to kill me *and* you. We need to leave. Now!"

Taking her tone as a final warning that he better trust her, he nodded, placed his arm around her, and then quickly guided her into the truck. When the driver put the truck in gear and started pulling away from the shoulder, Susan's head collapsed in her hands and she sobbed.

"It's going to be okay sweetie," the man said. "I'll take you to the police station. You're going to be okay."

"Where are we?"

"Route 235. Twenty minutes east of town. You want to call your mom and dad?"

Susan nodded, taking the man's cell phone. She flipped it open and punched in her home phone number."

Her mom answered on the second ring.

"Hell-"

"MOM!" Susan screamed, cutting her off. "It's me!"

"SUSAN?" Linda asked already brought to tears. "Is that you?"

"Mom, I need help! Oh my God he was going to kill me. He wanted to burn me. Kill me!"

"Who sweetie? Where are you?"

"I don't know. East. On 235. Somewhere."

"Who has you?"

"I got away. A man picked me up. He has me now."

She was looking out the rear window, trying to see if the Burlap Man was behind her.

He wasn't.

But the shots fired, the ones that shattered Susan's hope of escaping, came from in front of the truck.

The glass cracked and splintered with a single hole entering the driver's side. The bullet from the Burlap Man's gun slammed into the driver's head. Blood peppered Susan's face as she screamed into the phone.

Then the phone went dead.

"Susan? *SUSAN!!!*" her mom screamed. But her cries fell into the abyss of silence.

52

"And when He had taken some bread and given thanks, He broke it and gave it to them, saying, 'This is My body which is given for you; do this in remembrance of Me.'"

Susan's body felt groggy. Her heavy eye lids struggled to open to see through her mind's thick fog. *Where am I?,* she thought to herself.

But she knew.

The same stench of mildew and damp coldness blanketed her skin like before. The thin mattress lay underneath her.

Susan choked back the tears.

Once again, she was in the basement.

Two sets of plastic zip-strips were used. One set to bind her hands and the other set for her feet. She tried to move her wrists together, but the plastic strips were pulled tight enough not to allow any give. Her captor wouldn't make the same mistake as before.

As her mind cleared she was able to make out two shapes in the room. The first was her rescuer, the man who picked her up in the truck. The second, standing in front of her behind a pulpit and staring at her, waiting for her to wake up, was the Burlap Man.

Her eyes continued blinking rapidly trying to bring the room into focus. When she was finally able to focus, she saw what had become of her rescuer.

His body was up against the cement wall with arms stretched apart to the side and hands nailed into the mortar with his feet dangling a foot from the floor, bound by the same plastic zip strips as her.

Her rescuer, to her disgust, was displayed in a grotesque crucifixion. She shuddered inside wondering what was to come of her. Was she next?

"You sinned against me Susan," the Burlap Man said to her. "When you tried to hurt me and then run away, you sinned. But it's okay because just as God provided a way for Israel to rectify her sins and come back to Him. I too have provided a way for you to redeem yourself, become pure once more, and come back into my presence. But remember, sin is so hated by God that He requires death. Since you sinned against *me* - this man - had to die for *you*. That's right, he died for your sins."

The Burlap Man walked over to the dead trucker and cut a piece of flesh from his naked body. To Susan, it looked like a butcher preparing meat for sale at market. When he finished cutting, he walked towards Susan with the bloody skin flap in his hands and knelt beside her.

"This is his body which he gave to you. Do this in remembrance of him."

The Burlap Man held the flesh in front of Susan. Her stomach churned. She knew if she followed through and ate it, she would spew vomit all over herself.

"Take...eat...he did this for you Susan."

Susan struggled. She stared at the piece of meat presented to her. Tears of defeat filled her eyes as she closed her lids to try and black out the reality of what was happening and being asked of her.

This is it, she thought to herself. *I experienced freedom. Even if it was for a moment. I was free. The strength I had to run, now gone. The will to survive, it died. It died with the man who picked me up in the truck. I am going to die here. In this basement. My prison. I am going to die. Just like the man who rescued me. No more boyfriends. I won't know what it's like to go to prom. There'll be no college. No career. I will never know the happiness of finally walking down the aisle in a beautiful dress and getting married one day. I will not know the joy of having a husband or experience the miracle of having a baby. The life I always dreamed I would have was nothing more than that...a dream. This is where it will end for me. Alone. Away from my mom. Why me God? Why am I here? Why did it have to be me?*

"Susan," he said in a calm, yet controlled voice. "I don't want to have to tell you again. You must atone and become pure for what you have done. I require it and so does God."

Fearing what he would do to her if she didn't eat, Susan closed her eyes and barely opened her mouth. The Burlap Man placed the piece of meat on her lips, forcing it into her mouth. Susan squirmed, gagging and crying at the same time. Frustrated that Susan wasn't chewing the flesh fast enough, the Burlap Man grabbed her jaw, shoved the bloody piece into her mouth, and then clamped her mandible shut. Feeling defeated, Susan relented and finally chewed fast and swallowed hard. Just as she feared, she vomited as soon as she swallowed.

"Oh God!" she cried in between retches. "Please stop! No more! I'm begging you. Don't do this. PLEASE!"

The Burlap Man ignored her pleas for an end and returned to his crucifixion. He held a cup to the man's stomach, took a knife, and began slicing once again into his flesh.

"And in the same way He took the cup after they had eaten, saying, 'This cup which is poured out for you is the new covenant in My blood.'"

He returned to Susan, kneeling once again, and held the cup to her lips. She shook her head, refusing to follow through.

"Drink this Susan," he said calmly. "You must purify and atone for your sins. You can only do so by eating the flesh and drinking the blood of the sacrificial lamb."

"I can't," she cried in defeat. "I can't do this anymore."

"You must Susan or you will be punished for your unconfessed sins. Don't make me punish you."

Susan understood what she must do and closed her eyes. He took the cup, brought it towards her mouth, and placed it purposefully to her lips. Her mouth remained tight.

"Open Susan. It's the only way."

Reluctantly, fighting her inner self, and remembering how he forced the flesh inside her mouth, she parted her lips and accepted the offering. The cup then tilted closer and the warm liquid spilled inside her mouth and down her chin. Its iron taste slid back across her tongue and down her throat. Fighting the wave of nausea, Susan turned her head and continued weeping and begging for an end.

The Burlap Man stood, placed the cup on the ground, and walked over to the hanging man. His back was to Susan, but she could see that he was making her dead rescuer take communion as well. Instead of feeding the man his own flesh as he did her, her captor was giving him a wafer.

"Now Susan, we must go, for you and I need to be cleansed of all unrighteousness and purged of the sins we committed here today."

53

Thursday morning.

Jack took a sip of his coffee and fiddled around with his plate of waffles. Frank flipped through the newspaper and skimmed the day's headlines. He couldn't help but notice Jack staring across the restaurant, but not looking at anything in particular. He was looking beyond the walls and into something else.

"Your food's gonna get cold Jack."

"That's fine. Not really hungry anyway."

"Are you thinking about Reverend Ray?"

Jack took another sip of his coffee and nodded. "That and the video."

"Well don't worry. We got units looking for him. He'll show up."

For the first time since Jack started looking across the Waffle House, he finally turned to Frank. "No he won't. You and I both know that. Ray will only be found when *he* deems it so."

"You mean the Gray Man."

"Yes, the Gray Man."

Frank took a bite of his breakfast. He chewed the bite of his waffles slowly as if chewing on what he was going to say next. He knew where Jack's mind was going. He'd seen this look before and it was not good.

"I know what you're thinking Jack."

"Really? Why don't you tell me? Maybe *you're* the one who's psychic."

Frank took a sip of coffee. "You're going to go after Stefan Cooper...aren't you?"

Jack smirked. "And what if I do? There's no harm in that. We need to think outside the box. Unorthodox methods. Do this my way. Remember?"

"Unorthodox is one thing. Doing what I know you're going to do is another."

"And what's that? What am I going to do?"

"Two words Jack. Terrance Reid."

"Listen Frank. I had to do what I did to get the information from him. His wife and daughter were bound and placed inside a casket. They were buried alive for Christ's sake! What did you expect me to do? He wasn't talking."

"I understand your motivation, but putting a single bullet in your revolver, spinning the barrel, and then pulling the trigger to get him to talk, well, may have been out of line."

"Playing Russian Roulette wasn't out of line. You all trying to play good cop to get him to talk was *out of line*. We were running out of time and you know it! He thought he had all the cards, so I needed to play an ace. I did. He talked. And we saved them."

"And what would you've done if the gun landed on the bullet and you shot him?"

"The gun *did* land on the bullet."

"How do you know."

"I saw it in his eyes. Don't you worry though. The bullet was a fake."

Frank leaned back and crossed his arms. This was the first he'd heard it was a dummy round. Jack licked the inside of his bottom lip and took another sip of coffee. He knew Frank didn't always agree with his methods, but he Jack didn't care. People called him Death Angel for a reason. What he did to Terrance Reid was just another example of his nickname.

"Well, Stefan Cooper isn't a suspect. Don't treat him like one."

Frank's comment stung Jack. "Let me ask you something Frank. You know how I handle investigations. As extreme as my methods may be at times, you and others know I get answers."

Frank nodded. "And?"

"Knowing what I do, why'd you bring me on?"

"You know why. To get you out of that prison you made for yourself."

"Bullshit! That's complete bullshit and you know it. You brought me on because you know no one dares to push the limits like I will. I do it better. I do it faster. I get results."

"Jack, let me remind you, you're the one who asked to come on in this investigation. I didn't ask you."

"You're right. You didn't ask me. But Reverend Ray did. He said if I want the answers to the questions I have about Ainslie's murder I needed to be a part of this investigation. You knew that, went ahead, and obliged him. I don't care how I got here, but I'm here. I will do what it takes to get to the bottom of this and we both know it."

Frank folded his hands, leaned in, and looked directly into Jack's eyes. "Listen to me Jack. No matter how any investigation turns out, you are not going to bring Ainslie back."

Jack mirrored Frank's actions and leaned into him as well. "I know that Frank. I've known that from the beginning. You're right, this isn't about bringing Ainslie back. No investigation is or should be. But I will be damned if I was going to sit back on this one and not get the answers I need for her."

Frank leaned back in the booth. He knew he crossed the line. "Fair enough."

"And let me add this. My vision is clear. I can separate my past from the present, but make no mistake. I will find the son of a bitch who killed my daughter. It may not be today. It may not be a month from now. Maybe not even a year from now. But I will find him. When I do, that abortion of a person will wish they'd never touched her. Until that day, I know how to focus. But my anger at what happened to her is the fuel I need to help solve cases like this and my conscience is clear with whatever methods I choose. I know you risked your reputation by getting the Lou to agree to have me assist in this case. I won't do anything to make you regret that decision. Are we clear?"

"We're clear Jack."

"Good. You're my dearest friend and I don't want to lose that."

Jack grabbed their breakfast bill and walked away from the table. "I'm gonna take care of this. Deduct your food from the hundred I owe you."

Frank smiled, nodded and looked out the window at the patrons coming and going. He questioned whether he should've said what he did. He finally decided he was in the right. Jack needed to hear Frank's concerns. He needed to know where Jack's temperature was and no one else dared ask those questions. Because of their relationship, Frank knew he could.

Watching Jack leave through the front door, Frank stood, took a final swig of coffee, and reached into his pocket to grab a few bills to throw on the table for the tip when his cell phone chimed.

"This is Frank."

"Frank? It's Sergeant Rand," he said hurriedly.

"What's up?"

"Got a phone call from Mrs. Cleavenger. The one who came to see you about her daughter missing?"

"Yeah?"

"You need to get down here fast. She heard from her daughter Susan. This is not good Frank. Not good at all."

54

Jack and Frank joined the rest of the squad cars on State Route 235 within twenty minutes of receiving Sergeant Rand's call. Red and blue lights swarmed the road with K-9 units following a possible trail to find Susan Cleavenger. Radios were squawking as the trail became hotter and officers walking abreast of one another through the woods to cover as much ground as possible. Shattered glass was on the ground, but the vehicle Susan called from was nowhere to be found.

"It looks as if the person who abducted Susan shot the driver and took his car. Mrs. Cleavenger said she heard the gunshots and then the phone went dead," Sergeant Rand said approaching Jack and Frank.

"Any news on Susan?" Frank asked.

Rand shook his head. "We assume she's still alive and her captor took the vehicle along with the driver's body. We are working on the assumption the driver's dead, most likely killed in the altercation. We're scouring the area. We think the house he's been using is nearby. We'll find it soon enough."

Jack walked where the shattered glass littered the pavement. He kneeled down and touched the blood with his forefinger. With the little bit of blood he had on his finger, he rubbed it between his index finger and thumb.

"He won't be there when you find it. You do realize that don't you? He's vacated the area with Susan."

"That's our assumption as well," Sergeant Rand agreed. "Hopefully we'll find some evidence that leads us to his whereabouts. Excuse me for a moment. I'm getting waved at."

Jack and Frank nodded as Sergeant Rand walked away.

"Jack," Frank said turning to face him. "I'm sorry I got called away for this. Two cases going on here. I promise we'll go and find Stefan Cooper later if you want or you can take my car now and I'll meet up with you when I'm done here."

"It's okay. I'd like to stand by and see if I can offer any assistance if that's okay with you."

"It's fine with me, but I want you to be prepared just in case."

"Just in case *what*?"

"What if you're wrong about the girl being taken with her abductor and we find this house and inside is Susan Cleavenger's beaten and bloodied body? Are you prepared to see that?"

Jack paused a beat. "I am. I'll be okay."

Rand held up his hand waving for Frank to join him. Frank walked over to Sergeant Rand leaving Jack behind. Frank and Rand shared a few words, nodded, and talked to a few other officers.

Finally alone, Jack continued to take in his surroundings by breathing in the air deep into his lungs. He closed his eyes and tried to reenact in his mind the shooting of the driver and abduction of Susan. Opening his eyes, Jack scanned the wooded area and the road the girl ran to towards freedom. Not too far from where the other squad cars were parked, Jack saw the road split.

Flash.

Pop.

Jack slammed his eyes shut - his pulse raced.

The Gray Man's words thundered in his head from their meeting at *Crisper's, "Don't forget, in life, the road you are on to seek what you find often intersects with others in their journey as well. It will be up to you to open your eyes to clearly see when those roads intersect and become one."*

"Son of a bitch," Jack said opening his eyes. "Are these two cases the intersecting roads you referred to?"

"They found the house," Rand said rejoining Jack with Frank beside him, interrupting Jack's thoughts. "And just like

The Cleansing: A Thriller

you figured, neither Susan or her captor are there, but her would-be rescuer's body was found. Doesn't look good at all."

"I *need* to see it. Now!" Jack demanded while turning and running towards the group of officers, leaving Sergeant Rand and Frank behind.

Sergeant Rand turned to Frank with a puzzled stare and held up his hands as if to say, "*What's with him?*" Frank, confused by Jack's sudden determination to see the house, sprinted to Jack along with Sergeant Rand. After catching up with him, Rand moved in front of Jack and led him through the woods to the house that held Susan Cleavenger as a prisoner for the past week.

55

Jack and Frank entered the abandoned house. The empty hollowness created an atmosphere reminding all who entered that the place was a house of evil. Footsteps echoed on the dirty wooden floors. Jack surveyed the main living room. Dirty furniture blanketed by dust and stained blood was seen by everyone in the room. As Jack stepped into the kitchen, he saw dinner plates with half-eaten food covered with roaches and feasting rats. The kitchen smelled of rotten meat and spoiled milk.

Jack turned and stood in the entryway that separated the living room from the kitchen. The house was familiar to him.

He'd seen it before.

He walked over to the couch and stood in front of it as if he was going to sit. He stared at Frank and Sergeant Rand and continued to scan the room with his eyes and taking in the revolting environment.

He knew if the walls could testify to what they had witnessed, they would tell him of the blood spilt, the screams shouted, and the excessive violence forced on the innocent.

Jack closed his eyes while breathing in deeply to blank out the officers walking through the house.

He knew what had taken place here.

He'd felt it the moment he walked in.

Crime scenes like this told a story. The walls were eyewitnesses to the viciousness directed on the victims brought before it. The blood coated furniture and floor held the remnants of those no longer here. The wood in the house was a sponge, absorbing the blood curdling screams of the innocent.

The smell of death blended with the smell of rotting meat and food.

The crime scene told a story.

The house was the book.

The perpetrators were the authors of murder and violence.

The investigators have now become the readers to the horror story that took place within the walls.

Jack walked away from the couch, stood in the middle of the room, and continued to look around. He took his right hand and made the letter "O". Closing his left eye, he held up his hand and looked through the "O" shape at the couch. He continued to scan the room through his hand with Frank and Sergeant Rand looking at him confused by his actions.

"What are you doing Jack?" Frank asked.

Jack held up his hand and waved Frank's question off. Jack walked around the room, still looking through his hand. He walked from the front door towards the couch and then to the kitchen. Once inside the kitchen, he turned and walked back into the living room, still looking through his "O" shaped hand.

"This is where it took place," Jack finally said.

"We know that Jack."

"No, I'm not just referring to Susan Cleavenger. I'm talking about Reverend Ray and all the others. We're looking for the same guy Frank!"

Frank felt a cold chill shoot through his veins as Jack's comment drove its way in.

"Are you sure?"

"Yes! This is the same room on the disc I saw with Reverend Ray. This is where their crimes took place. This is where the pastors committed their heinous acts. In this house. This is the room I saw."

"You've got to be shitting me Jack! Are you certain?"

Jack put his hand to his side and stared at Frank and Sergeant Rand. "Susan's abductor is the fourth pastor we've been looking for. He took her to this place. *This* house. The one Reverend Ray told us about. This is where the pastors came. This was their sanctuary of evil."

56

Jack opened the door to the basement and started his descent down the rickety stairs with Frank and Sergeant Rand following close behind. The dry rotted wooden steps creaked underneath their weight informing them they could soon give, eventually crack, and ultimately break.

As they reached the bottom, they saw the door that led into Susan's prison. Jack was the first to open the door and enter, soon followed by Frank and Rand. All three men entered and stood in the room where her captor visited and sexually assaulted her in.

In the middle of the room was the dirty mattress Susan laid on and received her daily abuse. Jack couldn't take his eyes off the bed. He saw the stains of blood and semen. The smell of urine, feces, blood, and bodily fluids permeated the air. Candles adorned the walls. An erected mock pulpit sat on the far side of the room. Strung up on the wall, behind the pulpit, was the man who tried to rescue Susan. His arms stretched wide as if hanging on a cross.

"Oh my God," Frank said looking at the horrific display.

Everyone who entered the room saw the man's flesh had been cut into by a knife with a portion of his skin sliced and taken away. Written on the wall in the man's blood was the word, *THEION*.

Off to each side of the pulpit stood a half-melted candle. Sitting in front, on a table, were a cup and a plate. Jack walked over to the pulpit and looked inside the cup. A small amount of a dark red liquid lay at the bottom. Jack picked it up, swished it around as if it were a fine wine, and finally smelled it.

The Cleansing: A Thriller

"It's blood."

He then looked at the plate and saw something he hadn't expected. Laying on the plate, the size of a restaurant steak, was a piece of flesh which appeared to have been cut away from the driver. Next to the flap of skin, assembled next to each other, were three wafers; the type given at communion. Jack picked up one of the wafers and turned it over. And then it all started to come together.

"Look at this Frank."

Frank walked over to the plate and looked at what Jack was pointing to. "It's the same lamb engraving on the wafer found in Sonja Ericson's throat."

"Exactly."

"It's the same guy who killed our prostitute, Sonja Ericson." Frank said still staring at the wafer.

"Absolutely."

"My God Jack. What happened in this house?"

No sooner than Frank asked the question did Jack's eyes slam shut. Flashes appeared again. Rapid flashes. One on top of the other. Coming quick.

A man.
Wearing a mask.
Looks like a sack.
A sack made of burlap.
The same man.
Forcing himself on someone.
A girl.
A teenage girl. Frightened.
She hurts the man.
She runs up the stairs.
She's crying.
Screaming.
Running.
He chases her.
She runs into the woods.

"Jack?" Frank asked breaking Jack's concentration. "Are you okay?"

"After she ran away," Jack began, oblivious to Frank's question or any conversation taking place in the basement. "He caught her. He brought her back here."

"Why would he risk bringing her back here and *then* leave? Why not just leave after he caught her?"

"I think he wanted her to be pure. He *needs* her to be pure. She needed to atone for her sins."

"All because she ran away?"

"Yeah, that's what I'm getting."

"What about the driver?" Frank asked. "Why would someone crucify him after he's already dead?"

Jack looked at the cruel display of the crucified man on the wall and closed his eyes again.

A flash.

Bright.

Quick.

Two images.

A man. The driver.

A girl. Must be Susan.

Crying. Not wanting to drink from the cup.

"Because," Jack answered emotionless. "Just like Christ died for the sins of humanity, the driver died for the sins of Susan. I think that's what he's saying by doing this to him and he wants Susan to know she can be forgiven by taking this pastor's communion."

"Unbelievable Jack. Just when I think I've seen it all."

"There's more."

"What?"

Jack walked over to the wall where the word *THEION* was written in blood. He studied the word, concentrating on each letter, letting his right hand hover over the word. "I think I know what that word means."

"You do? What?"

"I think it's an acronym. Only I've seen its meaning written out before, but never like this."

"Well hell! When was *that*?"

"Yesterday. When I was visited by the Gray Man."

57

Jack remembered when he was sitting in the booth at *Crisper's* after talking with Beverly Cooper and then how we was visited by the strange individual known as the Gray Man.

They had mused about what kind of killer Jack needed to realize he was. Soon after their visit, the Gray Man stood and passed Jack a handwritten cryptic message on a napkin that read, *Through Hellfire Eternal, Infernal Obedience Neverending.*

At the time Jack thought it was more musings by the Gray Man, but now it made a little more sense. Jack reached into his back pocket and pulled out his wallet. He grabbed the napkin he kept tucked away and produced it for Frank and Sergeant Rand to read.

Frank reached for the napkin, read the message, and then looked back at the wall where the single bloody word *Theion,* stared back at them.

"You think these two are connected?"

"I do. Look at the first letter of each word. It spells *THEION.* The message on the napkin made no sense to me. I put it in my wallet and didn't think of it again. Then later on, when I was watching the video of Pastor Sullivan, he kept screaming a single word when he was on fire. He kept shouting it before he fell down and died. I couldn't make it out. I thought he was saying Leon, Neon, or Theon. It didn't make any sense at the time. Now it does. He was shouting that word! He was shouting Theion."

"What the hell does 'Through Hellfire Eternal, Infernal Obedience Neverending' even mean?"

Jack shook his head and shrugged his shoulders

"I think I do," Rand finally spoke up.

Jack's attention was on Rand. "What? What does it all mean?"

"Before I decided to become a police officer I went to a Christian college. In my first year I had to take a Bible class. Since the Bible is broken up between the Old and New Testament, I had to learn Hebrew and Greek. Well, the New Testament is written in Greek. And that's where I saw this word before. I remember it so well because I had to write a paper on it."

"What does it mean?" Jack asked.

"There is a verse in Revelation, chapter fourteen I think. I can't remember the verse, but I do remember it dealt with being tormented with burning sulfur. In the Greek, in that instance, the word *Theion* doubles for the word sulfur or even brimstone. The root word for *Theion* is *Theos* which means God in the Greek. Like in other passages the same word, *Theion*, is translated as *Divine*."

"You've lost me," Frank said.

Sergeant Rand held up his hand. "The lake of fire is considered divine because it comes from God. It is divine fire, but what's more is that it purifies. It purifies all who come in contact with it."

Jack digested Sergeant Rand's words. He knew what Rand was implying. He now understood the message sent by the fourth pastor.

"So our missing pastor and those who killed themselves were looking for purification by fire?"

Sergeant Rand nodded. "You said that this Gray Man gave you the acronym written out?"

"Yeah. Yesterday."

"He gives you *his* interpretation of the word *Theion*, but Theion is not an acronym for anything. It is what I told you it was. It's just a word with a dual meaning - sulfur and divine. It's not an acronym for anything whatsoever."

Jack walked over to the wall and looked at the bloody word: *THEION*. "I think there is more behind this word.

You're on to something Sarge. I think you're right about what you said. It makes sense as to why these pastors shouted what they did when they died, but I have a sick feeling there may be something more. I just can't figure out why each of them shouted this word. Why not just shout out for God's forgiveness? Instead, something inside each of them forced them to shout *this* specific word."

Jack turned and walked past Frank and Sergeant Rand, leaving them behind staring at one another.

"Where you going Jack?" Frank asked.

Jack stopped at the entrance and turned back. "To get to the bottom of this. Someone knows something and he's not being forthcoming at all! It's time to turn the heat up on a certain associate pastor. I'm tired of playing these mindless games. Toss me your car keys Frank."

Without questioning, Frank tossed Jack his keys. Jack snatched them out of the air, turned, and ran up the steps leading out of the basement skipping every other one. When he was gone Sergeant Rand turned to Frank, "That's the Death Angel I remember. God help that pastor."

58

"Sir you just can't go in there!" the church secretary shouted while chasing after Jack.

"Watch me dammit!"

Jack burst into Associate Pastor Barry Spencer's office without knocking. Barry jerked up from his Bible and looked at the door to see Jack barging in followed by the church secretary.

Barry stood up and held a hand to his secretary. "It's okay Barbara. Come in Jack"

Jack slammed the door and bypassed the office couch typically used by church members when talking to the pastor. Jack stood at the front of Barry's desk, staring unflinchingly at him.

"You better start talking to me asshole! I don't have a lot of time. I now have a missing girl who I need to find. Time is crucial and I know you've been jerking my ass around. Start talking Barry or I'll beat your ass here in your office. I don't give a shit who sees."

"Sit down Jack," Barry said not raising his voice, trying to defuse the situation.

"It's okay. I'll stand."

"Very well. Suit yourself. I'm getting ready for a candle light service tomorrow night to remember this week's fallen Christian brothers." Barry sat down at his desk and closed his Bible. He leaned back in his leather high-back with the chair creaking trying to support his weight. "What has you so upset that you had to come and barge in like a crazed lunatic?" Barry asked while folding his hands, waiting for Jack to explain.

206

The Cleansing: A Thriller

"I need some answers and I'm not leaving here until I get them. Are we understood?"

Barry nodded dispassionately.

"Four days ago two pastors set themselves on fire. One of them was your very own David Stout,"

"I'm very well aware of that. I just finished his funeral yesterday. I recall you thought it was some orchestrated event. Do you still believe that theory?"

Jack nodded. "I do. You know why?"

Barry shook his head, still sitting in the same nonchalant position. Jack started to walk around the office, picking up various religious knick-knacks that sat on the shelves, studying each of the items as if he was going to purchase them. When he was done with each piece, he placed it back on the shelf as if undisturbed.

"I went home and watched the DVD you burned for me and something peculiar stuck out to me. It was right in front of my face, but maybe blind to you."

"And what was that?"

"First, you and I both agreed when it comes to a group of pastors preparing to deliver a sermon, and assuming those pastors were from different denominations, it wouldn't be unusual for them to preach on the same subject on the same day. You still believe that right?"

Barry scratched his chin and thought while chewing on Jack's question. "Yes. I'd agree with that. We are all out there trying to relay God's message to the world, so it's not too out of the ordinary for different pastors to possibly preach from the same passage. It's bound to happen. Like on Easter Sunday or at Christmas time."

"So let me go one level deeper. Would you consider it strange then if two, possibly even three pastors, in different locations, at the same time, didn't just preach on the same message, but instead, said the exact same lines from a sermon message verbatim?"

For the first time since Jack stormed in, Barry leaned forward. "Yes, I would consider that strange. I would need more details, but going with what you're saying, I would have to agree. But it could be just a coincidence."

Jack placed his arms on Barry's desk and leaned into his face. "Then would you consider it still a coincidence if these pastors shouted the same final word when dying while on fire?"

"Not unless.." Barry's voice trailed off.

"Not unless...*what?*"

Barry's eyes changed. He finally understood what Jack was implying. His voice, no longer defensive, "Not unless their messages were coordinated between them and rehearsed."

"Exactly," Jack said smiling, knowing he'd finally gotten through to Barry Spencer.

"So what do you want from me?"

"I want to know what the hell David Stout was involved in. This is no coincidence and I think you know more than what you've led me to believe. You've got about five seconds to start talking or I'm going to beat it out of you. Are we clear?"

59

"Do you mind driving?" Sergeant Rand asked, tossing his keys to Frank. Not waiting for a response, Rand got in the passenger side of his car and shut the door. Frank checked his cell phone's voice mail, quickly returned a few calls, and then wrote in his planner some notes from the voice mails.

He pulled the car onto State Route 235 and started driving back to town. Sergeant Rand looked out the passenger side window at the trees as they zipped by. The further they went down the road, the more he directed his head and looked back at the still parked squad cars. When the cars were out of his visual sight, he looked forward again.

"What's on your mind Marcus?"

Sergeant Rand turned to Frank. "Just trying to fathom what must be going through that poor girl's mind right now. How she thought she was safe, only to be taken again, and then having to witness the brutal scene in the basement. I can't even begin to imagine what she felt."

Frank nodded. "This guy's a real monster. Jack wants him caught more than anyone else I think."

Marcus Rand nodded and turned to look ahead at the oncoming road as it curved and bend towards them. To Marcus, each curve was an example of the unknowing.

A mystery.

Ultimately, the bends and curves acted like the unknown that lay ahead. Was something waiting to reveal itself? What unexpected tragedy could possibly be there for the on comer coming around the curve?

"Do you think Jack is motivated by more than just his burning will to find this girl?" Rand asked coming out of the monotony of watching the road's bends and curves.

"Meaning what?"

"His daughter."

"Sure. I think it may have something to do with this. Some people think it has a lot to do with this. But I've talked to him extensively about his motivations and I'm convinced his head's on straight. His focus and drive are where they need to be."

There was a moment of silence between the two men. Marcus digested what Frank said.

"And what happens if this doesn't turn out the way Jack hopes?"

"As in, what happens to Jack? Does it send him over the edge for good?"

Marcus nodded.

"Honestly, I don't know what would happen to him."

"Then maybe his head isn't on as straight as you think."

"I don't know. Maybe you're right. Anything is possible, but I'm just not thinking about that right now. We focus on today. We deal with tomorrow when it comes."

Frank continued to drive as he and Marcus sat, not saying a word, but just looking at the road. As Frank rounded another curve he heard Marcus starting to sniff. It wasn't the type of sniff from someone with a cold, but rather someone starting to cry. Frank turned and saw a single tear start to fall down his face.

"You okay Sarge?"

Marcus shook his head.

"What's wrong?"

"I just want to see this come to an end. I want to see all of this come to an end. We've seen so much of the human side of evil and I wonder how much one person can handle."

"You still talking about Jack?"

"Yeah, and the rest of us. We all have a breaking point. We may think in our head we know exactly where that point is, but we never know. None of us do. Something, somewhere, down the road, finally comes at us and it tests us. I think we are all being tested here, but I just wonder when our breaking point will remove the veil and finally reveal itself to us."

"I've thought the same thing from time to time. I don't know when it will be more than I can handle. I don't know if I will ever see it coming."

"And if you don't? If none of us do?"

"The way I see it, I hope we can each make it through that valley of the shadow of death, but some of us never really do. We can ultimately exist in the valley with no hope whatsoever of coming out of it."

Marcus nodded. "And I wonder if Jack will exist in that valley for the rest of his life."

Frank didn't respond. He knew what Marcus was saying was right. As police officers, each of them knew at one point the job would test them emotionally and mentally. It came with the territory. It was part of their life now. It was only a matter of time when the job would consume their emotions so much that there could no longer be a separation from job and life at home. When that time came, when there could no longer be the separation, it was time to move on. Maybe retire. Maybe move in another line of work. Until that day, the sadness and pain would continue to consume their hearts and minds.

The rest of the drive back to the city was in silence as both Frank and Marcus thought about Jack and wondered if the sadness and evil he witnessed over the years, especially what happened to Ainslie, had consumed him enough to leave him in the valley of the shadow of death permanently.

60

Jack clenched his fists, supporting his weight on the desk while he leaned into Barry's face. "I want to know what connection your pastor had with these others. Your five seconds are up."

Barry slowly stood up from his chair and walked over to the window. He kept his back to Jack as he looked outside at the passing cars and people walking by. Each person that passed by appeared to be in their own world. Their oblivious facial features were a giveaway to the unknown around them. Barry found himself often standing by this very window daily praying for those who walked by. He never knew if he'd ever see them again and so he always took the time to pray for their souls, their hearts, and their families.

"They're lost you know," Barry said still looking out the window.

Jack quickly shook his head as if being bothered by a fly. He couldn't understand what Barry's comment had to do with his question. "Who? Who's lost?"

Barry pressed his index finger on the glass. "Them. The city." Barry finally turned and looked at Jack. "And the senior pastors."

Jack walked to the window and stood by Barry, occasionally looking out the window. To Jack, the people walking by seemed to have direction in their walk, except for the occasional passerby who would realize he was going the wrong way and just turn around and head in the right direction. Jack turned and looked at Barry who was still looking out the window. "What was David involved in?"

Barry stepped away from the window and walked over to one of the large cherry wood bookshelves. He thumbed down the different shelves of books and came upon what he was looking for. He grabbed the book, leafed through it, and then locating the page he wanted, he walked back to Jack.

"I want to show you something."

Jack walked over to Barry's desk and looked over his shoulder at the black and white yearbook picture Barry had turned to and left open for Jack to see. The picture was of a group of men standing around at what seemed to be a party. The men had their arms around each other, holding up plastic cups of punch, smiling, and acting silly for the camera. It was obvious from the picture that it was taken late into the party since the decorations seemed to be coming down, jackets were off, and sleeves were rolled up. Every one of the men in the picture were holding up their hands and flashing some hand signs. Their left hand made the letter "O" and the right hand was making the lowercase letter "d" sign.

"What's that all about?" Jack asked Barry.

"They are the Order of Divinity. Their left hand is showing the sign for the letter "O" in sign language. Their left hand is the letter "D"."

"What were they?"

"A group of seminary students who felt their calling from God, in this life, was of a *divine* nature and nothing more."

"Like in religious divinity?"

Barry shook his head. "You would think so, but nothing could be further from the truth. There are multiple meanings for the word *divinity*. Many think of the word when it comes to a supreme being. Like a deity. Another use comes with a divine force or power. You see, divinities have a relationship to the transcendent force or power typically credited to them. So much so, that in some cases the powers or forces may invoke themselves independently. This is the use of divinity the Order believed in and felt called to do. In this case, which is a less common use of the word, it refers to the operation of transcendent power in the world."

"I don't understand."

"Simply put, it means divine intervention."

"Divine intervention of what?"

"By bringing evil and evil-doers to justice through the conventional workings of the world. What is commonly referred to as, *divine retribution*, like in Sodom and Gomorrah or the Great Flood."

"And this group felt they were to bring divine retribution?"

"In a way."

"You lost me."

"The Order of Divinity felt divinity was bestowed upon them. In the Greek, it was called apotheosis, or, *to deify*. In the Latin, *gióvino*, it means *made divine*. The Greek word, *apotheosis*, refers to the idea that an individual or group has been raised to godlike stature. The Order of Divinity felt they are a chosen Order by God."

"To bring divine retribution?"

"Yes, to anyone and anything they felt was evil or could become evil."

61

Jack was losing his patience. Time was running out. "What does this have to do with these pastors?"

Barry pointed to man in the middle. He looked to be in his early twenties and based off the date of the yearbook, that would make him now in his early fifties.

"He's the founder of this chapter."

"This chapter? There were more?"

"Precisely, but he was the most radical out of all chapter presidents."

"What happened to them?"

"Some of the members didn't care for his methods and eventually quit the chapter."

"So this chapter of the Order became no more then, right? They just disbanded?"

"No. Once a member, you are always a member. You could never leave the Order. The ones that left always went and joined other chapters, but it was up to the chapter president who lost its members to recruit more. And that is what this one did," Barry said pointing to the man in the middle of the picture. "But this time he recruited more men who were like minded as he."

"So why did the others leave this chapter?"

"Well, the Order of Divinity was known for their righteous anger. It was common knowledge of what they did."

"Which was?"

"Going into the community to confront what they felt were the dregs of society. Drug dealers, sex addicts, prostitutes, and rapists. Sometimes they would get arrested, but not in all

215

circumstances. After awhile the police and judges ignored them. They knew they didn't have the manpower to control all the dregs and so they allowed the Order to act like vigilantes, so as long as they remained under control."

"And did they?"

"For the most part."

Jack processed Barry's words. He felt as if the fog of confusion was starting to lift and it was starting to make sense. "Murder? Did they commit murder?"

"It could never be proven. Speculated, but never proven."

"Were there any investigations?"

"Let me say this, you don't have to be in the Mafia to buy a few judges and police officers. Okay?"

Jack nodded. "So what about him?" he asked pointing to the chapter president.

"Rumor had it he felt as if it was okay to assault not only prostitutes, but women who dressed like whores. He felt they were on the road to sexual immorality and therefore he would take care of them before they went any further."

"And that's why the others left? They didn't agree with his methods?"

"Exactly."

"And what happened to him? Who is he?"

"He moved on after graduation. No one really knew what became of him. That was until recently."

Jack's realization caused his eyes to widen. He now knew who the man was in the picture. He knew whom he was staring at. It finally made sense.

The body of the prostitute found in the river.

Young Susan Cleavenger.

He now had a face to go with who he was looking for.

"That's the fourth pastor isn't it? That's the one I'm looking for!"

Barry nodded. "His name is Julian Watts. He was the chapter president for the Order of Divinity and is the current pastor for New Beginnings Christian Church. He's the one who has the girl you are searching for."

62

"Why didn't you tell me about this before?"

Barry began pacing the floor. He looked down at the burgundy crush carpet as if hoping to see the field of answers Jack Angel was wanting, willing them to crop up. If they had appeared, he would kneel down, pluck them, and hand them over to Jack. Barry knew the reality though. It wouldn't be that simple.

It never was.

"I need to show you something." Barry crossed the room and opened the credenza to pull out a pamphlet. He closed the credenza drawer, reviewed the pamphlet, and handed it over to Jack. After receiving the pamphlet from Barry, Jack read the inside, flipped over to the back, and finished.

"What's this?"

"Earlier this year there was a men's conference that David was going to attend. The pamphlet you're holding is that conference."

"The Builders of Men Conference?"

"Yes. David Stout was invited to go by Julian Watts along with Tom Sullivan and Ray Stevens."

"Tom Sullivan and Ray Stevens were the other two pastors involved in Sunday's incident. Tom and David both succeeded in killing themselves, but not Ray."

"That's right. If Pastor Stevens hadn't been stopped by his congregation, there would've been three suicides total."

Jack scratched his head and began rearranging the pieces of evidence from the last few days in his mind.

"So what's the significance of this conference? What happened there?"

Barry exhaled the weight of all he'd been carrying since this began. He finally sat down and gathered his thoughts.

"I don't think anything happened at the conference. I think things were happening before then and that's why they went together."

Jack thought back to his conversation with Ray Stevens. The story Ray shared when he met with David Stout and told him about his struggles with homosexual porn. *Was that what all of these pastors had in connection with each other?* He wondered. *Were each of them somehow involved in these video recordings?*

"Each of these pastors struggled with something didn't they?"

"Yes."

"Such as?"

Barry fidgeted uncomfortably in his chair. "What the church and society deem as sexually immoral acts. Prostitutes. Child porn. Underage sex. Sexual immorality or impurity."

"So why would they want to go together? What's the point in that?"

"To come together finally as one. As a unit. Commit to each other what they knew they were and what they wanted to do."

"And what was that?"

Barry looked at Jack. His eyes spoke before his mouth uttered the words. Jack knew what he was going to say by watching his body language.

"To deal with their struggles and be led by one man to become a new Order of Divinity."

63

Julian Watts, known as the Burlap Man, stood in front of the bound and gagged Susan Cleavenger. His back was to her as he placed on the floor a gallon jug of gasoline, a lighter, and his Bible. Susan's heart thumped inside her chest as she willed it to stop beating, bringing her death, before her captor resumed his distorted ramblings about cleansing the sexually immoral whores of the world.

Julian walked ceremoniously to the other side of the room and grabbed a wooden podium and placed it in front of Susan. His eyes didn't look upon her. At least not the way they used to, with care and love for her. Instead, his focus was on a different task at hand.

His new mission.

Julian picked up his Bible and placed it on the podium. He opened it, flipping the thin pages to the passage he wanted to read to Susan from the Old Testament.

"I know you can't turn with me in your Bible Susan, but you *will* listen with your heart as if you could. You will hear the words I must read to you. You will understand with your mind what I have to do. You will watch as your eyes act as a mirror to your soul."

Susan did not acknowledge him. Not by word or by nodding her head.

She sat silent and motionless.

Julian continued to turn in his Bible until he eventually found the passage he wanted to read. "I will be reading from the first book, Genesis, chapter nineteen. I will read only the verses you need to hear. Again, you *will* understand. Let's begin

219

with verse six of Genesis nineteen." Julian cleared his throat and began reading. "Lot went outside to meet them and shut the door behind him and said, 'No, my friends. Don't do this wicked thing. Look, I have two daughters who have never slept with a man. Let me bring them out to you, and you can do what you like with them. But don't do anything to these men, for they have come under the protection of my roof.'"

Julian stopped reading and looked up at Susan who was staring at him as if she was a member of his congregation. Her body language told him she was listening to every word he had to say. Julian was pleased. He smiled at her and looked back down at his Bible and continued reading.

"'Get out of our way,' they replied. And they said, 'This fellow came here as an alien, and now he wants to play the judge! We'll treat you worse than them.' They kept bringing pressure on Lot and moved forward to break down the door."

Again, Julian stopped. He looked to Susan to see if she understood the message behind his reading. He walked over and knelt down in front of her. "To this day Susan, we are all in some way characters in this story. Some of us are the character Lot, trying to protect those he loves. Some of us are the two daughters who must endure sexual sacrifice to protect the house of guests. Some are the mob outside the house, feeling as is if the judge is an unknown person. A stranger, an alien, if you will. Do you agree with that?"

Fearing what Julian might do if she didn't participate, Susan nodded.

"What character are you Susan? Are you Lot the judger? The two daughters? Or are you the mob?"

Susan's mouth had become dry. She moved her tongue along the roof of her mouth to wet the inside. Her voice trembled when she began to answer, "I'm the two daughters."

Julian smiled. "Yes you are Susan. You're the daughters who never slept with a man. You are being offered up sexually to let men do whatever they please. I'm sure you've thought ill of me for what we've shared intimately, but as you can see, even Lot knew it was okay. If God allowed Lot to give his daughters up to these men, surely it's okay for you too. Wouldn't you agree?"

Susan didn't respond to his question. Anger coursed through her blood, turning her face fiery with rage.

Julian's hand snapped to her face, grabbing her chin. "Answer me Susan! *Wouldn't!? You!? Agree!?*"

Fearfully, she nodded.

"Good. I thought so." Julian released her chin. "And which character am I?"

"Y-y-you're the mob outside the door."

"Very good. I *am* the mob outside the door and why am I angry Susan?"

Susan thought about this one. She didn't want to anger Julian any more than he already was. She knew the answer, but she needed to say it delicately. She didn't want to invite more harm on her than what had already been done.

"You are being judged by outsiders," she replied answering his question.

"And what have the outsiders, these Lots, done?"

"They came here and don't understand you."

"Again, you're correct. I'm proud of you. You *were* listening. And what did the mob want to do to Lot?"

"They wanted to hurt him."

"Not only that. They wanted to do worse to him than what they wanted to do to the strangers. They wanted to make him suffer. I assure you, these judgers of me will suffer. The Lord allows for it Susan."

Julian stood up and returned to the podium and flipped the pages in his Bible. "I will now read to you from the book of Ezekiel, the twenty-third chapter and forty-ninth verse, 'You will suffer the penalty for your lewdness and bear the consequences of your sins of idolatry. Then you will know that I am the Sovereign Lord.'"

Julian closed his Bible and stared at Susan. Even though his heart seethed anger for her trying to leave him, he understood that her maturity was not where it should be. In time, he might forgive her, but for now, he felt compelled to teach her.

"You are the daughter in this story Susan. You were so right about that. As for me, I am the mob and for a moment now, you will be given to me and I will have my way."

64

"I'm confused. I thought the Order of Divinity was against sexual impurity. Weren't these pastors struggling with this? How can they be part of the Order if they were guilty?"

"Because in the new Order of Divinity, I think Julian felt he was the only one who could purify them. He would control the acts and help flush the filth from their hearts."

"And then what?"

"They would no longer be blinded of course. Then they could be used and work together as a group. Only then could they purge the world together."

"So what happened Barry? I feel as if you're stalling. Why did they kill themselves? Why didn't Julian do the same? Why did he take Susan Cleavenger? What does he want with her? Time is running out and I need to find her."

Barry knew the question was coming. It was only natural. Even *he* asked himself many times why Julian didn't go through with it like the others. He was convinced when it finally came down to it; Julian abandoned the courage to set himself on fire.

But *why?*

The others had followed through.

Why them and not Julian?

Barry spent hours since Sunday wondering what would prompt somebody to do a horrific act such as what they did. He knew what the Order of Divinity had done in the past and assumed Julian was starting it up again. A new sect. A different sect.

A violent sect.

Barry had theories, but nothing concrete as to Julian's motives and actions. Even when Julian started talking to David and they would meet for lunch or breakfast under the guise of pastoral leadership counseling, Barry started getting suspicious.

What did Julian want with David?

After a period of a few months, since David started associating with Julian, Barry noticed a change in his pastor. He'd become short tempered, distant, and withdrawn. Even more so after the Builders of Men conference. Barry knew there was more. He was convinced the three pastors that joined Julian, including David, were in the first stages of bringing the Order of Divinity together. If this were the case, David had been involved in sinful acts that were probably illegal.

Was this the reason behind the change in his personality?

Barry believed so. He set up a meeting with Julian Watts and it was at that meeting that Barry made a decision. A decision that changed Barry Spencer from that moment on. Julian needed assistance in a partner he could trust and asked to use Barry's services. After contemplating what Julian wanted, and the money being offered, he agreed to help him at any capacity. All seemed adequate.

Until the suicides.

Suicide was never a personal act of the Order of Divinity. No one ever showed their loyalty to the group by killing themselves. What happened on Sunday was not an act of loyalty to the Order. Barry was confident in that assessment. He knew what it was.

An act of regret.

A righteous kill, a *righteous* suicide, for what they did.

Barry was certain someone had found out about the Order and what acts they'd committed. Now that person was threatening each of them with exposure.

Did the pastors get together and decide to take their lives in this manner? Were they the whoremongers and sexually immoral they preached about? Had they become so guilty in their hearts they knew what judgment awaited them.

A judgment of fire.

The Cleansing: A Thriller

But who knew?

Someone came to the pastors. Spoke with them.

Taunted them perhaps?

Threatened them?

Someone wanted retribution. Barry figured the pastors needed to act quickly. *They must've decided this together*, he thought. *They would take their lives at the same time on the altar where they preached every Sunday. All of them must have agreed to do this.*

All of them but one.

Julian Watts. The leader of the Order of Divinity.

And it wasn't until now, while sitting in his office with Jack Angel, did Barry fully realize why Julian didn't kill himself like the others. He had his theories since Sunday, but it wasn't until Jack asked him did he finally comprehend.

Julian wasn't ready.

His calling wasn't complete.

This was the reason Julian called Barry after Sunday and made one final request. There was one last act he needed to fulfill and it required Barry's help.

"I asked you a question Barry," Jack finally said feeling annoyed. "Why didn't Julian Watts kill himself?"

Barry stared down at his hand, shrugging his shoulders, and lied. "I don't know what to tell you detective Angel. I've been racking my brain about this and I just don't know why he didn't. I'm sorry. I know I am not much help, but I just don't know."

65

Jack fumed. Barry was holding back information and still stalling. Jack was certain. Time was running out and he'd had enough of Barry Spencer's stall tactics.

Jack walked over to Barry who was still sitting and looking at the floor. Jack thrust out his left hand, grabbed Barry by the shirt and slammed him on the floor.

"WHAT ARE YOU DOING?!?!" Barry yelled.

"Shut up! I'm tired of doing this your way. Now we're going to do it *my* way. I'm going to make you suffer! You'll hurt in the end, but you'll be better for it you shit!"

Barry, now laying on his front, struggled against Jack. The sudden sting of Jack slapping Barry's face caused him to stop. Jack slid his left hand up to Barry's throat and squeezed it. Barry screamed and then gagged, almost vomiting on the floor. Hearing Barry's raised voice, the secretary that tried to stop Jack from coming in was once again coming into Barry's office.

"Pastor Barry!" she screamed.

"Get out!" Jack yelled with his knee in Barry's back who was still on the floor.

"Call the police Barbara!"

"Don't bother Barbara. I *am* the police and I'm going to arrest your pathetic pastor for obstruction of justice. And if you don't get your worthless face out of here I'm going to arrest you for public intoxication. Do you hear me?"

"What?" she asked offended at Jack's comment. "I'm not drunk."

The Cleansing: A Thriller

"Please! You don't think I didn't smell your boozed breath when I came in here? You smell like my apartment and trust me, *that's* not a compliment. Now leave us!"

Barbara backed out of Barry's office shutting the door quietly, her body saying, 'You're on your own Barry', not wanting to upset Jack anymore than he already was.

Jack planted Barry's face in the carpet with his knee still in his back. He grabbed Barry's hair, turned his head so his right cheek lay against the carpet, and leaned into Barry's ear. "Start talking Barry. You know too much back-story on Julian and these others. I know you have an idea why Julian didn't kill himself. You're smarter than you appear to be. I promise you, I'll beat it out of you. You have no idea who you're dealing with."

"Yes I do," Barry replied through a string of coughs. "I know more than you think."

"Talk you piece of shit," Jack growled pulling out his gun and cocking back the hammer. "You're living on borrowed time now."

Jack forced the end of the barrel to Barry's head.

"I'll have you arrested."

Jack laughed. "Good, but before I'm taken away, I assure you, I'll get what I need and pass it along. But know this, I will beat your sorry face so hard, your mouth will be wired shut for the next year. You'll be sipping burgers and fries from a straw. And for what? All because you didn't want to talk? Ask yourself something, is *he* worth it?"

"I'm afraid to. You have no idea what you're involved in detective."

"Don't worry, you'll be protected, but right now, no one is going to protect *you* from *me*."

Barry closed his eyes and wept. He was done. He'd had enough. "My pastor, and friend, David Stout used say he felt our society had become the second coming of Sodom and Gomorrah. He told me once that Julian agreed, but it went further."

"What does that mean?"

"Julian felt judged. He encouraged David to see how the eyes of others were the eyes of condemnation."

"Go on."

"I didn't understand what David was talking about until I took his Bible and saw his notes. There were dozens of notes and scribblings. All referring to the passage in Genesis about Sodom and Gomorrah, the visitors who came to Lot, and how the mob felt Lot was judging them for not giving them what they wanted."

"So what! That has nothing to do with Julian."

"Yes it does. He sees himself as the mob of Sodom and Gomorrah and he wants to punish those who pass judgment on him."

"And who are *they*? Who does he want to punish?"

Barry looked up at Jack. "His congregation."

Jack's blood ran ice cold.

Of course.

Barry continued, "But unlike the mob who wanted the visitors who came to see Lot, he's decided to take one of the daughters first. A virgin. When he's done, he'll cleanse himself like the other pastors, but not before he punishes his judgers. His congregation."

66

When Barry said those haunting words, Jack saw a flash in his head. It went off like a bulb. His eyes slammed shut, his heart rate quickened. Then he saw them.

The congregation.

Each of them, male and female, sat motionless. Everyone staring straight ahead. Their eyes were transfixed on nothing. No one moved. No one breathed. It seemed their wooden posture resulted by an unseen force. Keeping them in the pews. Forcing them not to move. As if they were under a spell.

They looked hypnotized.

Their eyes seemed to be black coals. Jack knew why this was. It was a result of their eye sockets being empty. To Jack this made sense. The human eyes were always compared to the energy of life. The empty eye sockets meant one thing: the congregation was void of life.

Every member in the congregation looked aged decades past a hundred years old. Long stringy gray hair extended beyond their shoulders with receding hairlines exposing age spots on their scalps. Their sunken faces and cheeks were accented with dry-cracked moisture-less lips.

There were children.

Children of all heights, some as tall as adults while others were the size of toddlers. But all were still children none the less.

They had aged just like the adults. The children were old. Emaciated. Hungry. Forlorn. Pasty mouths. All of them wearing soiled diapers.

A baby was shrieking in pain. Jack couldn't see where the baby was at and not one member moved to the baby to console its discomfort. *Where was its mother?* he thought to himself.

The congregation continued to sit.

Dry mouths. Occasionally smacking their lips hoping to spring forth any amount of moisture to cure the lack of wetness. As expected, these acts were done in futility. Still, not one member uttered a sound.

This was death. This is what it looks like. If Jack had ever been asked to paint the picture of death, this would've been it. Not a painting of the Grim Reaper holding a scythe, but instead it would've been a painting of this vision. These people. The mood elicited in his heart would've transferred to the painting from what this vision gave him.

This is what was waiting for New Beginnings Christian Church.

Julian's flock.

This was the congregation that was going to judge him. And these were the people he was going to punish: to deal with.

Each and every one of them.

Julian's eyes opened.

Barry laid beneath him, looking up in confusion. *What just happened?*

"You're going to go with me."

"What?" Barry asked astonished at Jack's demand. "Where to?"

"You're going to take me to Julian's church. He's preparing his heart and Susan Cleavenger as well. You're right about that. I've seen it and he's going to make them suffer."

"How?"

"I don't know how just yet, but he's going to make them all taste death the way he sees it. He wants them to experience pain. I saw it. I saw *them.*"

"But why me? Don't you need to call for backup?"

"I will. I'm calling my partner. Then we're heading over to the church. Get up and get moving."

The Cleansing: A Thriller

"He may not even be there you know."

"Barry, something tells me he's hiding Susan Cleavenger inside the church somewhere. He's holding her. Making plans for Sunday."

Barry paused. He remembered something. He rushed to his desk and opened the drawer. He reached in, pulled out a church bulletin and handed it to Jack.

"You may not have until Sunday."

"Why's that."

"Look on the inside. There's a multi-church event at New Beginnings Christian Church tomorrow night. Julian is supposed to deliver the message. Their expecting close to a thousand in attendance."

Jack cursed under his breath. "Grab your stuff. Let's go."

"What about my appointments this afternoon?"

"Have your boozing secretary call to cancel them. She'll be glad so she can sleep off her hangover."

Barry did as Jack demanded. While Barry was talking to Barbara, Jack pushed through the church doors dialing Frank's number.

It went to voicemail.

"Frank? Jack. Listen when you get this. Call me. I know who we're looking for. He's going to commit some Jonesboro massacre tomorrow night. Call me. I'm on my way to New Beginnings Christian Church. Get there! Now!"

67

Frank was still driving back to the station when his cell phone rang. He looked down to see the caller id. "It's Jack," he said to Marcus.

"Don't answer it."

Frank turned his head bewildered as to why Marcus would say not to answer the phone. When he turned, he saw that Marcus had his weapon drawn and pointing the barrel at Frank.

"Marcus? What are you doing?" Frank asked, trying to watch the road and keep his attention on the gun that was now pointed at his face. In his entire career as an officer never had he been this close to the end of a gun's barrel, knowing his life could be over with a quick pull of the trigger, or if he made a mistake and hit a pothole and caused Marcus to accidentally pull the trigger. Frank's heart raced with trepidation.

"I'm doing what I should've done a long time ago. I just didn't have the audacity. But I do now."

Frank's cell rang again. He reached for it, wanting to answer it and alert Jack.

Rand pushed the gun's barrel against Frank's temple. "Answer it and I'll blow you away. I'm not bluffing Frank."

Frank remained calm, "Okay. What do you want me to do? What's this about?"

"I want you to drive to Byron Cemetery."

"Why Marcus? We need to get to the station. We can talk out whatever is on your mind. This will stay between us." Frank said trying to defuse the situation.

"You know why I'm doing this. You know exactly why. You just thought I was too ignorant to know."

"Know what?"

"What you did."

What I did? Frank thought to himself. Marcus' words baffled Frank. *What was he talking about? What did going to the cemetery have to do with anything?*

"Marcus," Frank pleaded. "Can we talk about this without the gun please? You're scaring me. *Please.*"

"You know something? I wouldn't mind seeing your brains splatter against the window. Killers like you deserve such a death."

Frank kept his eyes on the road, trying to make sense of what Marcus was talking about. He'd heard about this happening to other cops. The lifestyle becomes too much. There was no more black and white. Everything simply becomes gray. No more good versus bad. Everything and everyone seemed the same. He'd heard of cops who were partners for years and then one day their partner just shoots and kills the other for no reason. All because the one partner couldn't take it anymore. They no longer saw themselves as the "good guys". Instead, they became the ones perpetuating the situation. Keeping the environment just right. Letting the perps get away. Never doing anything about it. Letting the world corrupt them as well. Then one day when the stress comes in like a roaring flood, they snap. That's why cops had psyche evaluations. To try and foresee such conditions. Not all evaluations caught the signs. Sometimes the person slips through until one day they snap. They either off themselves, their loved ones, or even their partner. The end may be different for each one, but the emotional trauma leading one to commit such an act seemed to follow the same destructive path.

"Marcus, why am I a killer? What have I done?"

"And you even call yourself a friend of Jack's. You're a liar. He'll hate you when he finds out what you've done."

Frank's face grimaced with confusion.

"What *have* I done?"

Marcus cocked the hammer of his gun and pressed the barrel harder against Frank's temple.

"You know exactly what you've done. You didn't think I knew. You thought you'd get away with it."

"With what Marcus?"

"You're a murderer! A child killer! And the reason why Ainslie Angel isn't here anymore."

68

The Gray Man sat across the dark room from Ray Stevens who lay bound to a bed in an unknown location. Cigarette butts littered the ground around the Gray Man's feet. He was halfway through another cigarette when he heard Ray stir awake.

Ray's eyes blinked a few times as he tried to get his bearings and realize where he was. His surroundings reminded him he was no longer at the hospital and the reality of what was happening.

The Gray Man stood up and walked over to Ray. He stood over him, grabbed Ray's wrist, and checked his pulse.

"You're doing fine Ray. You still can't speak, so don't even try."

Ray nodded.

"Everything is working according to plan. Mr. Angel has pieced together what he needs to go and find Julian Watts and young Susan Cleavenger. Sergeant Rand is now taking matters into his own hands. Something I didn't foresee, but it works nonetheless. If he can maintain his sanity then the outcome will bring Mr. Angel even closer to the answers he seeks."

Ray looked around the room trying to see if he recognized where he was. The Gray Man took another drag on his cigarette.

"It's interesting, when you think about it, how all of us are connected in this ocean of life. Did you know that even the smallest creek empties into the oceans?"

Ray nodded.

"It's okay. If you didn't, don't try and act like you did. I hate liars."

235

The Gray Man stared at Ray's eyes trying to read his thoughts.

"You didn't know that did you? Or maybe you did, but just never really thought about it before today."

Ray shook his head.

"That's what I thought. You had no idea. Probably didn't even care."

The Gray Man pulled a knife from the inside of his pant pocket. He flipped the blade out and grabbed Ray's right hand.

"Sure, maybe the smallest creek won't have the greatest impact if it were dammed up, but there could still be an effect. Possibly on the nearest scenic river it empties into. But when you have multiple creeks and streams pouring into one main river and if you cut them all off from their intended destination, then the river will surely feel that result."

While holding Ray's hand, he folded down all of Ray's fingers, except his index, and held the blade next to the knuckle.

"For example, I could slice this finger off. It would hurt. You'd feel it. You'd mourn the loss, but in the end you'd be able to manage. Wouldn't you agree?"

Again, Ray nodded not wanting to upset his captor. The Gray Man then folded down Ray's index finger and held up his thumb. Again, he placed the blade up against Ray's knuckle.

"Now the thumb. That's something different. I bet you didn't know how important the thumb is did you?"

Ray agreed.

The Gray Man laughed.

"Again, I'm not surprised. Did you know the thumb helped the human species develop motor skills? It did. Trust me on this. Try and write without it. Pick up an aspirin off the counter without one. Better yet, try and button your shirt without one."

The Gray Man started to gently slice the blade slowly against Ray's thumb. Ray tried to pull away, but the Gray Man held on tighter.

"Yes, the thumb is very important. You could lose one of your other fingers and be okay, but to lose your thumb would almost make you incapacitated."

The Gray Man sliced harder into Ray's flesh causing him to scream in agony. Ray's scream was the only audible ability he had at the moment.

"That's right Ray. You may have thought you were a valuable person in this life, but you weren't. You had the opportunity to be a thumb. But you failed. You were nothing but a finger. You could vanish and life would still go on. That's too bad. Sorry to say, but you won't be missed when you're gone."

The Gray Man continued to cut through Ray's flesh and bone with his knife. Blood poured from Ray's hand as he writhed in excruciating anguish while the Gray Man removed his thumb.

"But when it comes to me, well, let's just say I'm the thumb that makes you and everyone else need me."

The Gray Man laughed as he removed Ray's thumb and left him to bleed and scream on the bed.

69

Jack parked a block down from New Beginnings Christian Church. Both men exited the car and jogged towards the church. The moment they stepped foot on the church property, Jack pulled his gun. He checked to make sure it was fully loaded and then chambered a round.

Barry scanned the parking lot and saw no vehicles in sight. He started to wonder if this was all in vain, coming here to search for Julian, but didn't want to upset Jack's already volatile state of mind.

"No one's here Jack."

"Just because you don't see any cars, doesn't mean no one's here. He's here. I know he is."

"What if he's not?"

"Then we'll wait!" Jack growled. "He won't miss tomorrow night. It's part of his plan. Remember? Now stay close. If you don't, I promise I'll shoot you."

Barry nodded and followed Jack as he jogged behind the church. They first came to the office administration doors and checked them to see if they were unlocked. Jack wasn't surprised to see they weren't.

"Now what?" Barry asked as if the administration doors were their first and last hope. Jack scanned the area, studying the property, and hoping to find the next vulnerable entrance.

"We'll try all the doors. I don't expect to find any unlocked, but it's worth a shot."

"Why do you think he's in there? Don't you think someone would've seen him come in with a girl who's been as assaulted as you described?"

Jack stopped, turned, and got nose to nose with Barry. "Let me ask you something reverend. How do *you* know Jesus is the way to eternal life?"

"What's that have to do with anything?"

"Just answer my question. How do you know?"

"Well, after many years of reading the scripture, praying, and feeling Him talk to me, I have faith in who He is and what He's going to do."

Jack smiled. Barry didn't know it, but he just made Jack's point.

"Exactly! So when you ask me, 'Why do you think he's here?' I can tell you, after many years of chasing sick minds like this perp, I can honestly say, he's here. I have faith in that. And without faith, you have nothing. Am I right?"

Barry nodded.

"And," Jack continued. "As you feel that Jesus talks to you, those who commit evil talk to *me*."

Confusion flooded Barry's eyes.

"I didn't think you'd understand that point. But don't question me and I promise not to question you and why you believe what you do. Deal?"

Barry nodded and for the first time since Jack walked into Barry's office, he smiled.

"Okay, let's check the doors. You lead. I'll follow."

Jack went to the next set of doors. The plastic sign drilled into the metallic door stated, Children's Wing. He tried them and once again had no luck in opening the doors. Not out of options, the two made their way around the church grounds going from door entry to door entry. Each time they found locked doors. After fifteen minutes, they arrived back at the same administration doors they had first attempted when they arrived.

"Now what?" Barry asked.

Jack took a few steps backwards into the church parking lot and looked at the building, studying the walls, the roof, and the windows as if he planned to scale the church.

"I'm willing to bet not everyone closes or locks a window in this place. It's been hot the last few days. I say we try a window."

Before Barry could object, Jack was already walking towards the first set of windows he saw. He went from window to window, pushing on the pane hoping to find one that was open.

The tenth window on the Children's Wing side of the church was what he was looking for. They found the window closed, but not locked. Jack pushed on the pane and the window folded inward and up. He looked back at Barry who smiled and gave him a thumbs up. Jack motioned to Barry to go first.

"I'm too big. I won't fit."

"Yes you will. I may have to force your ass a bit, but you can get through. So get moving."

Barry, not wanting to have a debate with Jack on whether or not he could manage to squeeze through the open window, decided to attempt the entry. He hoped his effort and result of unsuccess would be enough to show Jack that he was right when he said he couldn't fit. Barry got about half way when his large ass started to get hung up. "You see. I can't fit."

"Yes you can." Jack stood behind Barry and started pushing him through the window. After a few moments of struggling, the window finally gave way and Barry fell onto the floor. "Told you you'd fit."

Jack was next. He placed his left leg first through the opening, followed by his head and upper body. After a brief struggle of getting his right leg to follow through, both Jack and Barry were inside the New Beginnings Christian Church.

70

The gravel popped underneath the tires of the car as Frank pulled into the rocky driveway of Byron Cemetery. He drove past the multitude of headstones all the way to the end of the drive.

The sun was starting to set.

Soon, he feared, he would join the darkness of night through the darkness of death.

"You can stop right here," Marcus Rand said, still pointing the gun at Frank. He reached over and grabbed Frank's gun and removed it from the holster. "Go ahead and get out. When you do, well, you know the drill. Put your hands on your head and start walking slowly."

"Where to?"

"You know damn well where to Frank. Don't play stupid on me now."

Ainslie's grave. Marcus wanted him to walk to Jack Angel's little girl's grave.

"And when I get there?"

"I want you to kneel down. We'll go from there."

Frank exited the vehicle and did as Marcus asked. He walked to Ainslie's grave site and knelt down on the ground with both knees. He kept his hands on his head and faced Marcus who was still aiming the gun at Frank's head.

"Turn and face her gravestone. Don't look at me! You don't deserve my pity. Face her grave. *FACE IT!*"

Before he turned, Frank quickly glanced around to see if any cars were pulling into the cemetery. He saw nothing, just the passing headlights on the cross streets and the street lamps beginning their slow burning process of flickering on for the night.

He finally faced Ainslie's gravestone.

Marcus was directly behind him. Frank could hear the crunch of grass as Marcus slowly walked closer. Each step seemed forced with determined calculation. Frank closed his eyes. He sensed if he closed harder he could almost see the sands of his life's hourglass run out with each step Marcus took.

"You're a murderer Detective Frank Madiolie," Marcus said nearing Frank. "Did you hear me? A murderer."

"Marcus," Frank's said, his voice trembling slightly. "I don't know what you're talking about. Whatever you're thinking about doing, please don't."

"You don't know what I'm talking about because you, and people like you, have become blind. But I haven't. I see clearly. I know what you did. Soon, Jack and Dani will know too."

Marcus, standing directly behind Frank, held the nose of the gun up against the back of Frank's skull. He pressed it hard enough to move Frank's head forward slightly.

"Now, bow your head and close your eyes. It's time to make peace for your transgressions. I want you to repeat after me Frank. Do you understand?"

"Marcus," Frank pled. "Please listen to me."

"Dear Jesus," Marcus said ignoring Frank. "Say it."

"Marc-"

"*SAY IT!*"

Frank closed his eyes and began, "Dear Jesus," he repeated, barely audible.

"Louder! I can't hear you!"

"Dear Jesus…"

"Louder!"

"*DEAR!* JE-SUS!"

"Much better. Let's continue…Hear my words."

"Hear my words," Frank repeated.

"I bow before you."

"I bow before you."

The Cleansing: A Thriller

"You bow before Him in humility Frank! Say it!"

"I bow before you in humility."

"Beg Him for forgiveness Frank. I want to hear you beg. He'll give it to you, but you will need to beg Him."

Frank shuddered in fear. Death was close. He could feel it. The closer he drew to the end of his prayer, the closer the reality of death became. "I beg you Lord...I beg of you...please forgive me for my sins. Even the ones I'm not aware I've committed."

"You know the sins I'm talking about Frank. They're the sins of being an accomplice to murder. You need to say that. The Lord needs to hear you confess it."

"But-"

"Do it!"

Frank trembled in fear. With each second that ticked by, with each word he uttered, he anticipated a bullet slamming into his head.

"F-f-for being an accomplice to m-m-murder."

71

The sun was setting when Jack and Barry entered the dark church through the window. Except for the limited sunlight through the windows, darkness abound. They both exited the room they entered and then crept into the hallway.

"Which way do you want to go?" Barry asked.

Jack looked from his left to his right. Examining the hallway. Taking in the darkness. Trying to *feel* where Julian might be.

"The place feels empty."

"That's what I've been trying to tell you since we got here. We're wasting our time. No one is here."

Jack shook his head. "That's not what I'm talking about."

"Then what?"

"Like there's no spirit here," Jack scanned the room they occupied, inhaling deeply to get a sense of the environment. "It's as if God himself left. It doesn't feel like a church. It just feels like any other building you would see on the street."

Barry closed his eyes, trying to get the same sense Jack was talking about.

"I don't know. It feels like a church to me."

"Not any church I've been to before."

Not allowing Barry a chance to respond, Jack turned and slipped quietly into the hallway. He grasped his gun with both hands, holding it next to his shoulder, ready for whatever unexpected event should play out.

Jack, followed by Barry, made his way to the end of the hall with only the red-lit *Exit* sign lighting their way. When he arrived at the end he paused, listening for any sounds.

Nothing.

Jack closed his eyes, *"Where are you Susan?"* he asked in a whisper.

Not feeling an answer in return, he turned and went up the steps leading to the next floor.

"You been here before?" he asked Barry as he stepped up to the next floor.

"Yeah. A few times."

"Okay, so where does this hallway lead?"

"Don't know for sure. Youth wing I think."

Jack looked at the walls. He could barely make out Crayola drawings on the wall through the darkness.

"Okay then. Let's head towards the worship center."

"Why there?"

"I don't know what it is, but I just feel we need to be there."

Not giving Barry a chance to object, Jack saw on the wall the directions leading to the worship center. He followed the sign and made his way to the worship center doors. Sitting by the sanctuary on a table was a bouquet of flowers with a sign underneath reading, *To our beloved pastor, Julian Watts. Thank you for your loving kindness. May God bless you as our pastor for many years to come.*

"Yeah, if you only knew," Jack said disgustedly. He looked back to see if Barry was still with him.

"I'm right behind you."

Jack pulled on the door and let out a sigh of relief finding them unlocked.

"Let's go," he said to Barry.

"He's not going to be in there Jack."

"I know, but he has been since last Sunday. I guarantee it. I want to read him. I *need* to read him. To *feel* him."

Barry nodded and followed Jack into the dark sanctuary letting the big wooden door slowly creak shut behind them.

The worship center was a blanket of darkness and Jack finally knew why it didn't feel like a church when they first entered through the window.

R. G. Huxley

"It cold in here," Barry said just above a whisper.

"That's not the cold you feel." Jack turned to Barry in the darkness. "That, my reverend friend, is the actual presence of evil itself."

<u>72</u>

When the black and white world for a police officer becomes gray, the environment which was once familiar, soon becomes indistinguishable. It happens when agents go undercover to bring down an outlaw motorcycle gang. They create a criminal record to seem legit. They see the drugs. They go out to bang with other members. They may even run guns, sell women in prostitution, or even deal meth.

Sometimes, someone within the organization begins to smell a rat. *A snitch.* They want to see some sort of action on the part of the undercover agent to prove their allegiance to the gang.

They will ask them to commit murder.

For the deeply involved agent, who becomes afraid of being caught, he begins to make choices. The black and white world can begin to turn gray. They start to justify their actions. They may begin to shoot meth or sell it on the streets. Once the barrier is crossed, committing crimes becomes easier.

What used to be black and white, now becomes gray.

The only way to survive is to create a new black and white within the world of gray.

Frank knew he now existed within a gray world of Sergeant Rand and feared what the police sergeant now viewed as the new *black* and the new *white*.

"I've prayed to God and asked for forgiveness. Is there anything I can do to spare my life?" Frank asked.

Marcus pressed the gun harder against Frank's skull. "I don't know if there is anything you can do now. Not anymore. Ainslie's dead. She's not coming back."

"But how am I an accomplice? I tried to help solve the case before it ran cold."

Marcus became agitated. He didn't want to have *this* conversation.

"Because! You saw the evidence. You created the profile of the killer and you ignored doing anything about it. You let him walk the streets."

Frank was confused. "I'm lost. How am I an accomplice? I didn't kill Ainslie. I tried to *catch* her killer."

"You had thoughts to who it might be," Marcus said whispering in Frank's ear. "Deep down you wondered. You suspected, but you put the thought out of your mind. You didn't want to believe."

"Believe what?"

"You hoped you were wrong. But you knew."

Frank tried to regain his composure. "Who was it Marcus? You know who killed Ainslie don't you?"

"I know who had a part, but I wanted you to see it for yourself. Jack couldn't do it. His pain and hurt was too much."

"Who Marcus?"

"Think hard. Remember the evidence you read over and over. Think about the killer's profile. Admit what we both already know."

Frank closed his eyes. He tried to remember all the evidence gathered on Ainslie's killer. From the time of day when she was abducted. Where she was playing. The actual murder. The location of her body.

He couldn't help but draw a blank.

"There was a single piece of evidence that you and everyone else overlooked. It's nothing you would have found at the scene, but should have questioned anyways. What *was* it?"

Then it finally hit Frank like a freight train. Marcus was right. It was the *one* piece that could've caught Ainslie's killer, but he ignored it. Nausea came over Frank as his stomach twisted with disgust at the handling of the case. He not only let himself down, but he let his friend and partner Jack down as well.

Frank realized the crucial and most important connection to Ainslie's killer was standing behind him and was soon going to be his own killer as well.

His name was Marcus Rand.

73

Jack walked up onto the stage and stood behind the podium where Julian Watts preached from on Sundays. Jack's eyes barely adjusted to the dark sanctuary as he struggled to look at the empty pews. He tried to picture how the congregation looked to Julian through his eyes, but the darkness acted as a shroud and shielded the view.

Standing behind the podium, Jack sensed the sanctuary was set up like every other church.

Piano to his right.

Organ to his left.

Choir loft and baptismal behind him.

Congregation sitting in pews in front of him.

Jack placed his hands on the podium and closed his eyes. It didn't matter to him at this moment the sanctuary was already dark, but Jack needed to close his eyes. He needed to get inside Julian's mind.

"What are you? Psychic?" Barry asked while watching Jack.

"No," Jack responded quickly, trying to put Barry out of his mind. "It's just what I do to get inside the person, to see what he sees. To feel what emotions are running through their heart and mind."

Barry didn't respond. Instead he just stepped back and away, leaving Jack alone and to himself.

Pain seeping inside.

Jack felt it pierce his body as if administered by a needle. It was the same pain which infested Julian Watts. But something was different about this particular type. It wasn't the sort of pain one would feel from falling down stairs. Nor was it the kind of pain one would feel from the loss of someone close to them.

No. This was different.

It was intentional pain. The kind one would want to inflict on someone else.

It was the pain Julian Watts wanted to cause.

The pain was cold in its delivery.

The type that was fueled by malice and delivered through hatred.

This type of pain had a different name.

Evil.

Julian Watts wanted to inflict evil on others.

Jack felt it as it came to him in a single inebriated wave of dizziness. He grabbed onto the podium to stable himself as visions of living dead church members filled his mind. Bodies, strewn across the sanctuary. Vomit and blood poured from their mouths. Children sat crying next to their dead parents, shaking their dead parents, struggling to wake them up.

As the children raised their heads to the ceiling above, looking to heaven for an answer, their eye sockets were empty. Only black holes where eyes of innocence used to be.

This was the picture of pain.

The pain of evil.

The kind of evil Julian wanted his congregation to experience.

The evil they would soon feel.

"We need to find him Barry," Jack said opening his eyes, still staring at the empty pews. "We need to find Julian tonight."

Barry didn't answer.

Jack turned hoping to hear a response of agreement. Still, he heard nothing. For the first time since he and Barry entered the church, Jack felt the icy presence of loneliness. The darkness that surrounded him was the only company he had.

"Barry?" he asked, still hoping Barry would respond. "Where are you?"

Silence.

Jack walked across the stage in the same direction he had originally come from. He walked toward the same front doors he entered when he came into the darkened sanctuary.

Maybe he left while I was trying to get a fix on Julian, he thought to himself.

"Barry?" he asked one more time, not expecting, but hoping, to hear a response. As he neared the doors he heard the subtle sounds of footsteps behind him. Jack turned towards the noise. He strained his eyes in the darkness, barely making out the figure that now stood before him.

"Barry? Is that you?"

The blow that came to Jack's head wasn't from the dark figure now standing in front of him, but rather from the unknown figure that suddenly came from behind.

Jack hit the floor, his eyes closing, and became one with the darkness. The darkness came swift, similarly as it had when he first entered the sanctuary. The darkness...

It wasn't comforting.

It was cold.

It was the presence of evil.

74

"You were the one who found Ainslie's body," Frank said. "You called it in. Because of the intensity of the crime scene, no one even questioned you."

For the first time since they exited Frank's car, he heard Marcus breaking down. Frank knew he needed to seize the opportunity to try and spare his life from being ended unjustifiably by Marcus Rand.

"It's okay Marcus." Frank said with his hands still on top of his head. "We can work through this."

"I don't think we can. I know where Jack is heading. He's going to find out the truth and then nothing will stop him. He'll come at me with a blind rage." Marcus tried to regain his composure. "I didn't even know it was his daughter."

Frank saw another crack in Marcus' wall. "You can talk to me. You know that don't you? We've always had a good relationship. You've kept this inside too long. I'll listen to you Marcus."

"No one will believe me, not even Jack, but it wasn't even me. I'm not her killer. I can't get that image out of mind, seeing her violated and torn body laying there. I'm not the one who did it, but I might as well have. I was too scared. I did nothing. I'm just as guilty."

Frank turned his head trying to look back at Marcus.

"Don't look at me! Turn around!"

Frank quickly faced forward once again.

"I'm here for you Marcus. Whether you believe me or not, I'm here for you. I'm here to help."

253

"I'm beyond help. I can't face not one more day. I've carried this too long."

"Have there been others that you knew about?"

"No," Marcus answered solemnly. "But I did try and stop this madness from spreading."

"You see! You sought redemption. That's something good, right?"

"It's not what you think."

Frank felt like he was playing Whack-A-Mole with Marcus. Every turn in the conversation was a mole popping up through the hole. Frank would strike it and hope to score a point. He'd miss, but then he'd see another mole, *a possible chance to save his life*, and he'd whack at it, only to miss it too.

Another mole. Then the whack.

"It's okay. Just talk to me. Talking helps."

Followed by the miss.

"But my life is over."

Then another mole followed by another whack.

"It doesn't have to be. I know you'd never do anything to hurt someone on purpose."

"You're right. Not an innocent little girl like Ainslie."

Finally. A hit!

"Do you want to tell me what happened?"

Frank felt Sergeant Rand's intensity subside slightly.

"I'm afraid. I haven't talked about this to anyone since that day."

"It's okay. I'm your friend."

And another hit.

"I'm ashamed of who I became Frank."

"I'm listening."

Tears were streaming down Marcus' face. Each drop was a reminder and a testimony to his emotional pain. What kind of person had he become? How could he have let his urges corrupt his heart so much that he was no longer a reflection of the man he'd hoped to become. Marcus Rand wanted the weight lifted - to be free. He knew, freedom started with confession.

"I was addicted to child porn Frank. I actually tried to get help. I sought counseling from a pastor named Julian Watts. I can't even remember how I was referred to him, but that doesn't matter now does it.

"It's okay. I'm not going to judge you. Friends stand by one another."

Another hit.

Marcus continued. "He said he could help me. He said it was best if I confronted my addiction and not to run away from it. So he arranged for me to meet him at a coffee shop. I did. He then took me to a house. The *same* house we just came from. When we got there, he let me watch videos he had. Some seemed homemade. Others weren't. I couldn't believe I was watching that filth. I felt guilty and sickened by what I was doing. I actually vomited. I told him I wanted to leave. I was done. Before he would let me go, he asked me to do something."

Frank was stunned by what he heard. He felt the bile rise in his throat. He hated sexual predators. He talked to them before and they all made him feel the same way.

This time, it was different.

For the first time in his twenty-plus-year career, he felt compassion. The Marcus he knew was not the one who was confessing this story. They seemed to be two different people. The Marcus he knew was someone he genuinely admired and cared for. *This* Marcus was the type of person he spent a career trying to lock behind bars. His heart did break for his friend and he was sincere in wanting to help him.

"What did he want you to do?"

"Before he would let me go, he asked me to help dispose of a body someone had left behind."

"A body?" Frank was horrified.

"Yes, I couldn't believe it either. He assured me he wasn't the one responsible and I wouldn't have to see it because it was in a garbage bag. But if I didn't help him, he was going to expose me and make sure I was investigated for child pornography. I didn't know what to do. If I'd been arrested and charged it would've destroyed my family. He justified it by saying the body was a seventeen-year-old runaway drug addict so I shouldn't feel guilty."

"So you agreed?"

"Yes, but he lied to me. When I disposed of it, I knew it was the body of a child. I refused to open it. I couldn't look. I didn't want to look at the lifeless body of a child. So I just dumped it and afterward I drove home as fast as I could and spent hours in the shower scrubbing my skin till it bled. I wanted the filth off me. I didn't want to think about it. I kept denying what I did and kept telling myself it *was* a runaway. It wasn't a child. No way in hell could it have been a child. I didn't say a word to anyone. Then when the search started for Ainslie Angel, my horror turned to terror and disgust. I had this sick feeling it was *her* body I dumped. I prayed I was wrong, but I had to know. I had to know if it was Ainslie. So, I went back to see and found out I was right. It *was* her. I never killed her, but I played a part. A horrific part."

"Marcus, you're not a monster. This is not your fault. We can get through this."

"I should've killed that monster when I had the chance!" Marcus cried out. "If I did, none of us would be here now. Susan Cleavenger would be at home with her mom. And Julian Watts would be dead."

If he wanted to get out of this alive, he needed to play along with Marcus to continue gaining his trust.

"But you helped us end the investigation. We found her *because* of you. I assume you got help for your addiction."

"I did, but that wasn't all."

Frank wondered what else Marcus could've done. *Please dear God, don't let him say he hurt another child.*

"Tell me Marcus. We've come *this* far. You can trust me."

"I didn't hurt Ainslie. But I *have* killed Frank. I had to. I had to stop the disease before it spread. I'm a cold-blooded murderer."

75

Jack stirred awake through the fog of pain. The come-from-behind attack and blow to his head made it throb. His eyelids felt like lead weights, too heavy to keep them open. His wrists, bound behind, as he realized he couldn't move because the chair confined him and prevented any movement. Jack surveyed his dark surroundings, turning his head to the right and then the left.

No longer inside the church.

Someplace new.

Randomly lit candles adorned the room. *I'm not alone,* he thought to himself.

In the corner, by one of the candles, Jack saw a girl sitting alone. Not in a chair, but on the floor. As his eyes adjusted to his new surroundings, he saw her looking at him. It was clear she'd been waiting for him to regain consciousness.

Without having to ask, Jack knew who he was looking at.

"Is your name Susan?" he whispered.

"What?" she whispered back.

"Is your name Susan?"

"Yes! How did you know?"

"My name's Jack Angel. I'm a detective. We've been looking for you."

Susan released her relief through tears. "Oh thank God! Can you take me away from here?"

"I'm going to do everything I can, but I need to know where Julian Watts is. When's he coming back?"

"Is that his name?"

Jack nodded.

"I didn't know. He never said his name to me. He's an evil man Mr. Angel. He's a mean man."

"I know he is," Jack nodded in agreement. He couldn't imagine how Susan felt at the moment. He knew the repeated rape of Susan's body and soul caused her to feel shallow and dead inside. Her innocence, lost over the last week by a monster who wanted only to further his sick religious agenda. Jack hoped there was a special place in Hell for men like him. A special place where the furnace temperature was raised a few thousand degrees and the burning pain felt exponentially more.

"Do you know when he'll return?"

She shook her head in despair.

"It's okay. We'll figure out a way."

"I saw them bring you in. I acted like I wasn't awake, but I was. They tied you up, lit the candles, and left."

They? Jack thought to himself. He was confused. "I thought there was only Julian? Who are *they?*"

"I've only seen him a few times. He records me with the camera."

"Do you know who he is?"

Susan nodded.

"Who?"

"He's the same guy who picked me up in his car. He's the one who took me from my mom and brought me to the mean man who wears a mask."

"Do you know his name?"

Susan nodded. "His name is Barry. Barry Spencer."

76

I had to stop the disease before it spread. I'm a cold-blooded murderer.

Marcus' words slammed into Frank's chest. *What was he talking about?* Marcus admitted having disposed of Ainslie's body after watching child porn videos, but he didn't kill her. Frank saw Marcus as someone involved in the aftermath of her murder, but not involved in her death. If he didn't kill her, then Frank knew Ainslie Angel's killer was still at large.

Why was Marcus talking cryptically? Did he know who her killer was? What was the disease he was trying to stop? Frank was feeling time slip away from him like water through the cracks of his fingers. Jack had called his cell while he was driving with Marcus. Maybe Jack found something out and needed him.

Frank delicately pressed Marcus more.

"This disease you're talking about, what is it? Does it have to do with her killer?"

"Yes," Marcus said nodding, still standing behind Frank. "It has to do with her killer and the countless victims to come."

Frank pressed again, feeling he was beginning to gain Marcus' trust, he slowly turned his body around. "Please Marcus. Please tell me. You and I can put an end to all of this. But I can't do anything if you don't tell me everything."

Marcus continued to hold his guard and kept the gun pointed at Frank. "Let me ask you a question Frank."

"Anything."

"If I were to ask you to take a feather pillow and empty its contents into the wind, what would happen?"

The question confused Frank, but to stay alive he knew he had to play along. "They'd blow away of course."

"Right. And then if I asked you to collect all those feathers and put them back into the pillowcase, could you?"

"Well no. It'd be impossible. You might get half if you were lucky, but not all."

Marcus smiled. Frank made his point. "Exactly! I know we can't stop the disease, but I tried to collect the feathers. I made sure I did my part to try and stop it."

Frank made the connection. The feathers were the people involved.

"Who were they? Who did you kill?"

"Only one so far. I wasn't able to get to the others just yet. But in time I will."

"Who was he? Was he involved in Ainslie's murder?"

"No. He's not Ainslie's killer, but he'd become tainted and he'd soon follow in the steps of those before him. I was certain of it. So I stopped it before it happened."

The two pastors who killed themselves? Was Marcus Rand somehow responsible for their suicides?

"Did you know the pastors who killed themselves this past Sunday?"

"Only one. Tom Sullivan."

"Did you know he was going to kill himself?"

"No," Marcus said shaking his head. "But I wasn't surprised when I heard what was going to happen to him and the other pastors."

Those words cut into Frank. "You *knew* they were going to set themselves on fire?"

Marcus smiled. "Yes. And each of them deserved what they did and more. They went on to face their judgment. They really had no idea what was in store for them."

"How did you know Marcus?"

Marcus knelt in front of Frank, still pointing the gun at him. "I was visited by the same man who talked to all the pastors. The same man who also talked to Jack. The Gray Man came to me and told me what would happen to them."

The Cleansing: A Thriller

Frank's blood turned cold. *Who was this Gray Man? What is his involvement in all of this and why? Was this Gray Man the monster Frank was starting to believe him to be?*

"Why did he come and see *you*?"

"He said I had shown great restraint in my actions, but I still needed to prevent others from doing harm."

"So he was glad you didn't hurt any children."

Marcus nodded.

"So what did he want you to do?"

"To help him collect the feathers that had been ripped from the pillow of course."

"What feathers Marcus? Who are the feathers?"

"The Order of Divinity. But I wanted to gather more. And I did. So far I was only able to collect one."

"Who Marcus?" Frank asked getting frustrated. "Who was the feather you collected?"

"Associate Pastor William Brookings. I made sure he burned and that he cleansed himself just like Pastor Sullivan."

77

Jack heard steps approaching from the other side of the door. Susan, having been through this before, retreated to that one safe area inside her mind. The one private place that no one could ever hurt. The last untouched area in her heart and mind.

Her faith in God.

Jack watched as she cowered back in the corner. He took a deep breath and readied himself for what unseen events he and Susan were about to endure.

The door opened slowly, with an outside light penetrating the room before the two-silhouetted figures walked in. Both men were wearing burlap masks. Jack could tell that one of the burlap men was pastor Barry Spencer, still wearing the same clothes from earlier. He knew the other had to be Julian Watts.

Both men were silent when they came into the room.

They walked past Jack, not saying a word. Barry went and grabbed the video camera and turned it on, just as he had many times before. The other, Julian Watts, walked to Susan. He knelt beside her, gave her a kiss on the cheek, and whispered in her ear. Jack tried to lean towards Susan hoping he could discern what sick comment Julian was saying to her. He could actually envision himself beating the shit out of Julian to a bloody mess. He hoped he would be given the opportunity to do just that: beat Julian to the point he was at Death's door ready to knock and enter its premises.

"It is time," Julian said to Barry while standing up from Susan.

262

Barry knew what Julian meant. He had done this multiple times in the past. He recorded the prostitute Bambi's beating, the heroin addict with Reverend Ray Stevens, Susan Cleavenger after he brought her to the house, and now he was going to record what could be his finest achievement to add to his oeuvre. Like the others, he would distribute the recordings for sale in the underground market. He enjoyed this part the most. Recording raw emotion clothed in anger or fear. Nothing Hollywood distributed to the public could come close to what he was able to capture on camera.

Barry stood behind his camera and pressed the record button. Julian crossed the room and directed his attention to Jack. When he was within an arm's length, he knelt in front of him. Jack watched Julian intently, studying his every move.

Julian opened his Bible, turning the thin pages until he arrived at the New Testament. He scrolled down with his finger and found his verse. He recited a verse in a low whisper, and then looked up at Jack.

"Do you know who I am?"

Jack nodded.

"Who am I?"

Jack smiled as he'd been looking forward to this moment all week. To finally say what he'd wanted to this vile human filth. "You're the shit I see when I flush the toilet after I'm done wiping. That's who you are."

Julian got a chuckle from Jack's comment. He actually admired his audacity. "Fair enough. I'm sure you have many more of those overconfident gems you want to say to me. Don't you?"

"I don't know," Jack replied, shrugging his shoulders. "I guess that all depends."

"On what? Please tell me," Julian asked sarcastically.

Jack smiled while licking his lips. "If you keep asking me absurd questions, then I'll continue giving you these little gems as you call them. I have a quarry full of them."

"I bet you do. I bet *you* do." Julian stood up. "Back to my original question. Let me ask you again. This time I'm looking for a name. Do *you* know who *I* am?"

"You're Julian Watts," Jack responded as if he were a witness testifying in a trial.

"Okay. Good. And I know who you are. Your name is Jack Angel. Sometimes called the Death Angel by those who know you best. Am I right?"

"Yeah. That's right Among other names I'm sure. But that's the one that stuck."

Julian started to walk around the candle lit room with his preaching posture. Bible held in his left hand with his other hand empty, ready at any moment to emphasize a point.

"Let me ask you something Brother Jack. Have you ever wondered if you were called by God to do what it is *you* do?"

Jack thought for a second, and then shook his head. "No not really."

"No? You never thought about it? Or no, you don't think you were called?"

"I guess 'No' to both of those."

"I find it peculiar that you have a name which represents the God I serve. Some people view you as the Angel of Death. As if you were sent to take life. You were given a choice, let the person live or die. Most of the time you chose the latter. Hence, your name. Now here you are telling me you think you haven't been called by a higher power to fulfill a purpose. That's interesting because I believe something fuels your drive. Something greater than you. Let me remind you, the Bible specifically says, 'If you're not for me, you're against me.' So Brother Jack, let me ask you this, are you *for* God or *against* God?"

78

To Jack, Julian Watts was a master of manipulation. This man knew the Bible and how to use its contents to justify his actions and words. It was clear Julian was going to use whatever verse, whether in or out of context, he needed in making his case. Jack had dealt with criminal minds similar to Julian's in the past and knew what he must do to compete against him.

"When you put it like that, I would like to think I am for Him. Maybe I never thought of it in the terms you described. When I think of who I am and what I do, I would have to say I am for Him."

Julian puffed his chest. He relished moments like this. It was one of the reasons he became a pastor. He had the ability to take scripture and hold it up in front of his congregation and make them look at their hearts through the Bible's mirror. It was painful for his congregation, but it was something he had to do as their shepherd. Each of them needed to confront the sins of who they were and their inability on their own to turn from sin. Once they realized, only then, could He protect them from the predators that wanted to devour them.

The wolves of this world.

He opened his Bible to the place he previously saved with his finger. "I want to read you something. It's in the book of Matthew, chapter thirty-nine, verse forty-one and forty-two. 'The Son of man shall send forth his angels, and they shall gather out of his kingdom all things that offend, and them which do iniquity; and shall cast them into a furnace of fire: where there shall be wailing and gnashing of teeth.'"

Julian looked up from his Bible to make sure he still had Jack's attention. When he saw he had, he continued. "In the same chapter, but verse forty-nine and fifty, Matthew continues, 'so shall it be at the end of the world: the angels shall come forth, and sever the wicked from among the just, And shall cast them into the lake of fire: there shall be wailing and gnashing of teeth.'"

Julian closed his Bible and laid it on the ground. He reached into his pocket and pulled out a finger grooved folded Buck knife. It was the same kind of knife with walnut grip and gold plates Jack had seen in hunting stores many times with the locking blade when fully opened.

Julian unfolded the blade. It clicked and locked into place. He was ready. He was the one in control. He was the vessel God had chosen. The rightful angel sent to separate the wicked from the just.

"Jack, the Bible says that the angels will sever the wicked. I love that word. *Sever*. It means to dissolve. To cut up - to *amputate*. Do you believe that?"

Jack steadied his breathing as he tried to anticipate what Julian was going to do. *What will he do if I agree? What will he do if I don't? Is the question directed at me or Susan? Who are the wicked? Who are the just?*

Jack continued to play along. "Well, if the Bible says it's so, who am I to disagree with you and your knowledge?"

"You're right. You shouldn't disagree with me." Julian decided to take a victory walk around the room. His pious shoulders eased back to make himself seem taller than he really was. He took his position next to Barry. "The way I see it, we're both angels, you and me, and it is our job to sever the wicked."

Julian moved quickly. He spun to his right, flicking the blade's sharp edge outward. The movement was fast. He sliced through the air, cutting the darkness.

Jack gasped.

Susan screamed.

Barry felt the cold steely slice across his throat. His hands went to his neck to try to stop the blood that was now gushing from his neck and streaming through his now crimson fingers.

He fell to the ground gurgling unintelligible words through his bloody lips.

"Yes," Julian spoke watching Barry die. "The angels will sever the wicked from the just. I am an angel of God. I am the *one* He called and I too will sever the wicked from among the just."

79

Frank couldn't help but feel confused by Marcus' admission of killing William Brookings. *Does Marcus know something we don't?* Jack thought to himself. *What are you not telling me?*

"Why Marcus? Why did you kill William Brookings?"

"No!" he objected. "Not kill! He was a feather to be collected and *cleansed* from all unrighteousness."

Frank held out his hands as if to say, "*Sorry. I take it back.*"

"He *had* to be cleansed. Don't you see? He'd been tainted and in time, he too would've succumbed just like Tom Sullivan and the others."

Hearing Marcus' confession it made sense to Frank the underlying motive behind his murderous actions.

"You think because William worked with Tom that he would've become like him?"

"Yes."

"And you made sure he never became like that?"

"Absolutely. If I hadn't then I'd be just as responsible for the pain caused on the countless innocents. Just like *you're* responsible for the murder of Ainslie."

And just like that, Marcus reminded Frank why he brought him to Byron Cemetery. To Marcus Rand, Frank was a link. He was part of the cause in not catching her killer. The effect would be others who would now suffer because of their inability to find her *real* killer. Frank realized Marcus was trying to atone for his wrongdoings by dealing out lethal punishment.

"Turn around," Marcus said making circling motion with the barrel of his gun. "I don't have a lot of time and you're done wasting mine."

The mood turned fast on Frank. He hoped he was making progress to get through to Marcus. It hadn't worked. The impenetrable wall that seemed to begin to crack unfortunately had sealed itself once again.

"Wait Marcus!" Frank pleaded again. "Don't do this."

"I'm sorry. What I must do here is for the better. Jack will be pleased with me when I tell him. He may even forgive me for the past."

Marcus cocked back the hammer on his gun. He placed his finger's pad on the trigger and slowly pressed.

"Wait," Frank demanded. He finally saw his one last chance. A final plea. "Then let Jack do this."

"What?" Marcus asked releasing his finger's pressure on the trigger.

"Yes! Don't you see? It should be Jack who does this. Not *you*. Let him get the closure his heart needs. Don't take it from him. That's what he wants. This should be done by him."

Marcus' countenance eased. Frank's words made sense. He could deliver and hand over an extension of the evil that caused Ainslie's death and Jack would *have* to forgive him for what happened to his daughter. "You're right," he said lowering his gun. "We'll go to him. You'll confess. Jack will do to you what I should've done and in the end he will forgive me."

"He will," Frank replied with relief from his stay of execution.

"And if he doesn't execute you, then *I* will. Without hesitation, I will kill you. Now, get up."

Frank did as commanded. He prayed silently that he could find a few more cracks to dismantle the twisted wall in Marcus' heart and mind.

When he got into the car, and with approval from Marcus, he picked up his cell phone, punched in the voicemail password, and for the first time since being taken hostage by Sergeant Marcus Rand, Frank listened to Jack's urgent message.

80

Jack stared at Barry's lifeless body on the floor. The killing of Barry Spencer wasn't expected. With the quick flash of the knife's blade against Barry's neck, death had come quick. He could hear Susan sobbing from fear she might be next. Julian's volatility gave credence to her tears.

But Jack knew there was more.

As knee-jerk Julian seemed, there was a method to his actions. There was a statement he still wanted to make. Jack knew he and Susan would have to endure Julian's ramblings on religion and the rationale behind his intentions.

Julian stood over Barry's body and bowed his head. "Father do unto his soul as You feel is just and necessary. I am your instrument. I am *your* angel. Guide my hand. Guide me to those who judge falsely. Let me strike them down in Your name. Amen."

Julian raised his head and walked over to Susan. Jack pulled against the ties that bound his wrists, trying to free himself. Julian sat beside Susan and placed the bloody knife against her clothed breasts.

"Do you mourn him Susan?"

With a blanket of fear covering her, Susan pulled away.

"It's okay. You don't have to answer. I know you feel sorry for him. It's who you are. It's one of the reasons why I love you. But what if I told you he was going to rape you? He wanted to have you to himself when he first brought you to me. I wouldn't let him. But he still desired you. He wanted to take you here, tonight. What if I told you *that*? Would you mourn him then?"

Susan hung her head in humility and slowly shook it.

"No. I didn't think so." Julian leaned in and gave her a kiss. "What about you Mr. Angel?"

"I don't mourn his loss one bit. Just like I won't mourn yours either."

Julian stood up and walked towards Jack. "You may not mourn *my* death, but others will. Those who know I've been doing the Lord's work. They will mourn my passing. As they should."

"No. You think they will. But I assure you, you couldn't be more wrong."

"*YOU'RE* THE ONE WHO'S WRONG!" Julian screamed, thrusting the knife at Jack. Jack remained composed. He knew *this* is where he wanted to be. *This* is where he would begin to take Julian apart.

"If I'm wrong and you think you will be mourned, why were you going to kill your congregation?"

The words stung Julian. He hit an unseen obstacle. *How did this wretched fool know about his plans for his flock?*

"You know nothing of being a shepherd. I'm here to guide. To lead. And protect. No matter what happens to me, I'm still going to deliver God's message and rid the world of the whores, murderers, judgers, and all that are immoral."

Jack continued to turn the screw tighter.

"Then why did you run in fear on Sunday? Why didn't you follow the others? What, or should I ask, *who* are you afraid of?"

Julian stormed over to Jack and stood nose to nose. "Because the task isn't finished! Others needed to prepare for what is to come. I'm not going to kill myself because some crazy man said I needed to. He doesn't understand. Not like *I* do!"

Jack laughed. "What's to understand? What more do you need to do?"

"Plenty! People must atone!"

"And do you think God will forgive you for what you've done?"

"For the Lord God said, 'If you confess your sins I will forgive you of your sins and cleanse you from all unrighteousness.'"

Jack smiled inside. He was breaking Julian down. "God wants nothing to do with people like you. You'll answer for the death you've caused you bastard."

"I am *His* vessel! You son of a bitch! I answer to only one God. No one else. He'll tell me when I'm done! Until then, you and the mob must die for your sins!"

Jack inched his face closer Julian. "Then what are you waiting for?" he grinded, tempting Julian. "Do it now. Kill her and me both."

Julian stood straight and breathed deeply. "You're right. Your time has come."

81

Susan was confused. She'd been listening to the exchange between Julian Watts and the detective called Jack Angel. She thought the man was here to save her, but that all changed when Julian entered the room with Barry.

Barry.

She had never witnessed an act so cold and heartless as the murder of Barry Spencer. So much blood poured from his neck. It seemed to gush faster with each beat of his heart, sometimes streaming through his fingers, then followed by the gurgling sounds of oncoming death as he gasped for what little life he had left.

For the briefest of moments, she felt sorry for him, but the feeling was quickly extinguished. *"What if I told you he was going to rape you?"*

She questioned whether Julian was lying to her or not, but she couldn't think about that anymore. She had to survive. She had to think of a way to escape one last time or her life may end here next to Barry's. She'd hoped the Angel detective would be the one to take her away, but now she questioned even that scenario. He'd done his best to anger Julian and seemed to be provoking him into rage. *What was this guy doing? I thought he was trying to get us out of here. Now it seemed he wanted us both dead. Why persuade or even challenge this monster? He was enticing him, willing him to kill them both.*

She struggled not to look at the lifeless and bloodied body on the floor. It distracted her from focusing. She knew what her captor was capable of because she'd seen his violent actions before and saw them on display here once again. He didn't

273

need prodding. He would do just as her so called liberator asked.

"Do it now! Kill her and me both." He challenged

Time was running out.

She needed to act.

She looked at her unbound wrists and said a quick "Thank you" to God. She didn't know if Julian had forgotten to tie her wrists or if he didn't think she had the courage or energy to try and run again. None of that mattered now. Her hands weren't tied and finally she could do something.

Susan quickly scanned the room for anything to grab to hit Julian with. Seeing nothing but burning candles, she looked around from where she sat hoping to locate the gallon of gasoline Julian always carried with himself.

Nothing.

Where was it?

It doesn't matter, she thought. *He's going to kill the detective and then me.*

She stood, her knees shaking with fear. *Dear God, don't let him hear me. Give me the strength to leave here alive. Please Lord.*

With those words spoken under her breath, quite possibly her final prayer, Susan crept up behind Julian as he held the bloody knife above his head. He'd readied himself to bring the blade down into Jack Angel's flesh and end the life of one more judger.

As she drew closer, she repeated her prayer again. At the last possible moment, she pounced on the monster Julian Watts.

82

Jack saw Susan pushing herself to get up. This is what he was hoping for. He wanted to distract Julian, hoping Susan would seize the opportunity to get up and strike Julian from behind.

He kept Julian's attention away from Susan and solely on himself. Julian's anger was growing because Jack dared to question him. He felt disrespected. Julian was annoyed by the man's unfathomable ignorance. *How could this non-believer, who has no faith, question my ministry with the God of Israel? Just as God meted out judgment, so shall I.*

Jack was smiling inside as he figured this would be Julian's biggest mistake. People like him *needed* to be in control and became disgusted by people like Jack who wouldn't concede that power.

The window of opportunity to change the dynamic of the situation was small. If Susan didn't snatch this moment, probably the only one they had to survive, Jack would pay for it with his life. She had to act quick.

Julian raised the knife.

He was balanced. His grip tightened on the knife's handle as he steadied himself to slash through the air, sinking the blade deep into Jack's flesh.

Jack saw his rage. Julian's eyes seethed with a fiery anger. His heart was an inferno, consumed with making Jack suffer for his judgmental attitude and contemptuous non-reverence.

Jack knew if Julian thrust the knife into his flesh, the anger Julian felt would ignite multiple stabs of the knife into his body. One on top of the other. Each thrust of the blade would be deeper than the last. Julian would release his fury and wouldn't stop until the anger had purged itself completely.

The steely knife hovered above Jack's head.

Julian was starting its decent.

Within that second, Susan let out a scream as she tackled him from behind.

Jack rocked the chair he was sitting in to the right and away from the knife as Julian fell to the floor.

Susan was on Julian's back pounding her fists into the back of his head. Grabbing his hair. With each blow, she screamed. She was finally releasing all of her fear, anger, and rage towards the man who had repeatedly violated her innocence.

Julian struggled to grab the knife that fell from his hands.

His fingers nicked the sides, just barely out of reach, and causing it to move a little further each time he grabbed for it.

"You whore!" he screamed.

"I HATE YOU! I HATE YOU!" she screamed, coupled with a hammering blow from her fists.

She saw him struggling to grab the knife.

She knew she had to snatch it first or knock it further out of the way.

If Julian got it, her only attempt to escape was over.

They both reached for it at the same time.

Julian's fingers kept nicking it out of his reach.

Feeling desperate, Susan sunk her teeth into his face and bit down hard and ripped upwards.

Julian howled in pain.

Flesh and blood from Julian's face came up in her mouth as she arched her face upwards.

His hands instinctively went to his face, trying to protect it from another bite.

Susan saw the knife.

It was within reach.

Julian held his bloodied face, writhing on the floor.

Susan jumped onto the knife.

In a single swift movement, she palmed the knife, turned, and stabbed. With no intended bodily target in sight, Susan accepted whatever piece of Julian she could stab. She felt the knife make contact and forced the blade deep into the meat of Julian's back thigh.

"*YOU BITCH!*" he howled in pain as his hands instantly left his face and went to his leg.

Susan, still holding the knife, jumped up and ran to Jack, who was lying on his side, still tied to the chair. Susan took the knife and began cutting through his plastic zip strips and looking up intermittently eyeing Julian to see what he was doing. If he decided to come after her, she needed to be ready.

Instead of retaliating, Julian limped quickly away from them toward the only door in the room.

Susan, feeling the pounding rush of adrenaline course through her, struggled to cut the plastic ties.

"Hurry Susan!"

"I'm trying," she cried trying to saw through the thick plastic ties.

Julian continued to limp towards the door.

Finally, she cut through one zip strip and started immediately on the second.

Becoming impatient while seeing Julian trying to get away, Jack grabbed the knife from her and began cutting his final tie, but it was too late.

Julian escaped out the door.

Slammed it.

Locked it.

Imprisoned them once again.

Jack cut through the last zip strip.

Finally free, they both ran towards the door. Jack turned the knob, only to find the door was jammed from the other side.

"DAMMIT!" Jack screamed.

Within a few seconds, they could both smell the pungent stench of gasoline as it seeped into the room from underneath the door.

"He's dousing it with gasoline," Susan cried.

"I know," Jack responded, looking for a way to escape. "Get back, "I'm going to kick it."

Susan stepped away from the door and moved behind Jack, giving him plenty of room to kick the door. Then, in that moment, as Jack feared, he felt heat from the fire Julian Watts had set to the door to burn them in their prison.

Susan's panicked gaze looked to Jack for an answer.

Her fearful eyes were the same as his.

What do we do now?

Within seconds of the fire being set, flames began to lick the cracks of their prison door.

83

After hearing Jack's urgent message of going to New Beginnings Christian Church, Marcus agreed to have Frank drive them both to the church. Marcus wanted to end his years of guilt by confessing what he knew and have Jack deal with Frank accordingly. Killing Frank, right or wrong, was the only solution Marcus envisioned.

It was his only path towards redemption.

When they arrived, pulling into the parking lot of the church, Frank immediately spotted orange flames flicking their searing claws, straining to wrap themselves from underneath and around to the top of the roof of the church's bus garage.

"They're in there!" Frank yelled, speeding into the parking lot towards the burning garage. The car screeched to a stop and Frank jumped from the car ignoring the gun Marcus had pointed at him. "Call 911!"

Heart pounding, hoping he wasn't too late, Frank ran towards the garage not bothering to turn and see if Marcus was behind him or not. He assumed Marcus was making the call.

After a short sprint, he was at the garage and threw the door open scanning right, then left, looking to see where Jack could be. Immediately, a wall of heat hit him in his face. He wrapped his arm around his eyes, shielding them from the blast. The fire was growing and spreading like an uncontrollable monster.

"Jack!" Frank screamed while scanning the garage. Time was running out as the fire quickly grew in intensity. "Jack!"

Then, Frank saw what he was looking for, a metal bar jammed into the frame of a door preventing whoever was on the other side to open it. Covering his face to protect it from the dancing flames, Frank grabbed an oily rag from the floor and tried to dislodge the bar from the door, but the fire was too intense in its ferocity.

Time was running out.

Boom! Boom! Boom!

The pounding of fists on the other side of the door confirmed to Frank what he already knew. "JACK! IT'S ME! FRANK! I'M COMING FOR YOU!"

Frank repeatedly kicked at the door, still protecting his face from the growing flames. The fire was spreading. Sparks popped. Flames stretched. The unbearable heat grew becoming a barrier to freedom.

"Frank!" Jack yelled from the other side of the door. "Hurry! We're in *here*!"

Hearing Jack's voice and ignoring the fire's burns on his leg, Frank kicked harder and the door finally broke way and gave in.

84

Jack was pounding on the door, hoping it would give way. As he was kicking at the door, he heard Frank's voice from the other side.

"JACK! IT'S ME! FRANK! I'M COMING FOR YOU!"

Jack grabbed Susan and backed away as Frank kicked the door in.

Within seconds, the door gave way and Frank shot into the room. Jack and Frank both covered Susan as they dodged the flames and escaped the fire as it consumed the garage.

"Let's get away from the building!" Frank yelled and guided them to the parking lot.

Frank quickly scanned the area, looking for Marcus, but saw no sign of him or his car. *Dammit! Where did you go Marcus?*, Frank thought to himself still eyeing the parking lot.

In the distance, wailing sirens and lights filled the night air, drawing closer to the church.

"Did you see him?" Jack asked.

"Who?" Frank asked still looking for any evidence that Marcus was still in the area.

"Julian Watts! He can't be far. He's been stabbed."

"Jack we didn't see anyone. Just the burning garage."

"We? You mean you and Sergeant Rand? He's still with you?"

"Well, he was! But now he's gone too."

Jack and Frank both searched the area. No car. No Marcus. No Julian Watts.

Fire trucks and squad cars screeched into the parking lot.

"We'll get them later," Jack said turning his attention to Susan who was sitting on the pavement with her legs pulled to her chest and crying. For her, the nightmare that began was finally over.

Jack and Frank sat beside Susan and put their arms around her. They watched as the firefighters started putting out the flames.

"Is anyone still inside?" one of the firemen asked.

Jack nodded. "You'll find a body. Pastor Barry Spencer. He's already dead."

The fireman took note, turned, and left to attend with the other responders.

"Detective Madiolie?" a policeman asked approaching them. "What happened here tonight?"

Jack spoke instead. "Julian Watts, pastor of New Beginnings Christian Church." He went into the details of the investigation, reminding the officer of the suicides, Reverend Ray Stevens, and Susan Cleavenger.

The officer nodded. "We'll get him. Don't worry."

While Jack was talking, Frank was still looking around to see if he could locate Marcus. He was nowhere in sight. He vanished. Along with Julian Watts.

"I don't think *we* will," Frank commented to Jack and the officer about finding Julian Watts. "But I have an idea of who did."

"Who?" the officer asked, but Frank waved him off. Knowing he wasn't going to get anymore answers, the officer walked away.

Lieutenant Richards pulled up and walked over to Frank and Jack. "You two want to tell me what happened here?"

"Absolutely," Jack answered. "But can we first call Mrs. Cleavenger and let her know her daughter is safe?"

Lieutenant Richards nodded and handed his phone to Frank who immediately gave it to Susan. With fingers still shaking, she punched in her home number and waited through a series of rings.

The Cleansing: A Thriller

On the third ring a familiar voice answered on the other end. It was the one voice Susan needed every moment she was gone. The one voice that always seemed to make the hurt and pain go away from the first time she scraped her knee to a break-up from a boy.

"Mom? It's me, Susan."

85

Jack and Frank were sitting in interrogation room 2. The same room Jack had first met Reverend Ray Stevens on Monday. Jack couldn't help but stare at the same seat Ray sat in just a few days earlier. The week was an emotional hurricane for everyone involved in the case, but something told Jack it wasn't over yet.

Julian was still missing.

His whereabouts were unknown. Phone calls were placed to his house. Unmarked vehicles parked outside the residence and surveillance teams watching his church. All of which turned up nothing.

Along with Julian Watts, they needed to find one of their own too, Sergeant Marcus Rand.

The one victory they celebrated was their success in finding Susan and getting to her before it was too late. Jack questioned what could've happened to her he hadn't went back to interrogate Barry Spencer on what he knew about the pastor suicides. His meeting with Barry answered the questions they sought about Julian Watts and his creation of the New Order of Divinity and his connection to the deceased pastors. This was followed by them going to Julian's church and then rescuing Susan Cleavenger. Jack dismissed the two questions that plagued him the most, *What if I didn't go and question Barry Spencer? What would've happened to this sweet girl?*

But Jack knew why he was able to follow the evidence, connect the pieces, and find himself standing in Barry's office.

He'd begun to think like a killer again. A *Hunter Killer*.

The Cleansing: A Thriller

Now once again, here he was, looking at the empty seat that Reverend Ray once sat in: who was still missing as well. Jack remembered Ray's words to him, "*I'm confident that if you personally do the necessary investigating that needs to be done here, you will not only find the answers you've been seeking since your wife left you, but you will also understand the reactions that took place.*"

Ray was wrong.

Jack had more questions than answers and other than finding Susan Cleavenger, he felt his time spent was in vain.

The door to the room opened as Lieutenant Richards entered and tossed a beige folder onto the table.

"You were right Jack," he said sitting down in Ray's empty chair. "They found cyanide in Julian's office. It looks as if he was going to dispense it into the juice that the congregation took during the Lord's Supper. He was going to kill everyone. Maybe even himself. You did good work."

"And the wafers for the Lord's Supper?"

"Same. We should be able to link those to the prostitute and to the man in the basement."

"What about Sergeant Rand?" Frank asked.

"We called his wife. She hasn't heard from him. He's nowhere to be found."

"What about his car?" Frank asked.

"It was found abandoned. Lots of blood on the passenger seat."

"Julian's blood from his leg," Jack concluded with a slight smile.

"That's what we think. We'll run tests, but we're sure it will come back positive for him." Lieutenant Richards looked at Frank. "Did Sergeant Rand give any hint where he was going?"

He shook his head. "No, he was going to kill me, but I was able to stall him so we could find Jack."

"He actually thought I'd kill you because of my daughter's murder investigation?" Jack asked Frank.

"He did. He thinks I'm to blame for not finding her killer and that I should've questioned him more on how he was able to find her body."

285

"Should you have Frank?" Jack asked feeling a quick flash of frustration.

"I don't know. Maybe I should've. I'm sure there's quite a bit we could've done to prevent this case from going cold." Frank reached across the table and put his hand on Jack's arm. "I'm sorry Jack. We will find the guy okay?"

"I know you're sorry. Let's just find Sergeant Rand. Maybe he can tell us more."

"Agreed, but I'm telling you, he's really messed up. On top of that, he's confused to what is wrong or right at the moment."

"So he gave no hint to Ainslie's killer," Jack asked with a hint of hope in his voice.

"I'm sorry Jack. He didn't say anything. Just that it was *him* who handled her body. The scenario of him meeting Julian Watts was eerily similar to Reverend Ray's."

"Do you think it was Julian who hurt my little girl?" Jack asked with tears filling his eyes.

"I don't think so. It didn't sound like his M.O."

"Okay." Jack inhaled deeply to gather his composure. "We'll find him and get the answers."

Lieutenant Richards stood up to exit the room. Jack and Frank stood as the Lieutenant was leaving. "You two go home and get some sleep. Stay near your phones so I can reach you. Thanks again guys. You did good."

"Thanks Lou," they both said.

"Jack?"

"Yeah Lou?"

"I want you to know, it's been great having you on this case. Have you considered the possibility of coming back? You don't have to answer me now. Just go home, let your head clear, and talk it over with Frank and let me know. Alright?"

Jack nodded and watched as the Lieutenant left.

"So now what?" Frank asked turning towards Jack.

"I'm going to call Dani."

"And?"

"There's no *And*. I just want to call her. Hear her voice. Tell her I'm sorry."

Frank put his arm around his friend. "Listen, I want to tell you I'm sorry."

Jack put up his hand to stop him. "Don't. You didn't know. Neither of us did. Mistakes happen in investigations. They're not perfect. At least I know more today than I did two years ago. We'll find him."

"Thanks Jack. I appreciate it."

"And we'll do this together. Fair enough?"

Jack and Frank shook hands and then left the interrogation room with Jack turning off the light.

FRIDAY

86

Jack was sipping on his coffee looking across the table at Dani. Her brown eyes and beautiful smile always had a way of getting through his outer shell. She knew him intimately and probably better than he himself. Her sweet perfume slinked through the air and filled his heart.

She was the most beautiful woman he'd ever met.

"Dani, I'm sorry. I'm sorry for my attitude. You needed me and I wasn't there. I should've been. So much has happened and I want you to know I'm going to finally...what I'm trying to say is... I'm going to do what I should've done a long time ago and finally see a counselor."

Dani smiled. "Really?"

"Yes. Really. Frank handed me a card the other day. Her name's Rebecca McNeil and she specializes in individual, marriage, and grief counseling."

Jack let the words hang in the air. He wanted Dani to know he was serious about working on himself. "Are you telling me this because you would like me to go with you? I can if you need me to."

Jack shook his head. He was comforted by her words, but he knew this was something he had to do on his own. "Not right now. Believe me, I want you to be able to forgive me and see if we can work this out. But right now I need to work on myself."

"Jack, I've already forgiven you. You go and see this counselor and when you're ready for me to come with you, just ask me, and I will. Until then, we just take things one day at a time okay?"

Jack nodded and smiled. "Sounds good."

"I want to ask if you'd do something for me."

"Sure Dani. Anything."

"This Sunday, if you'd be willing, I'd like you to think about coming to church with me."

Jack twitched his head back. It wasn't the question he expected to hear from her. "Church is the last place I want to go right now."

"I know that. I just want you to consider it. I think it would be good for you."

"Why's that?"

"I've been going for awhile now and the sermon messages help me. Not every church and pastor is like what you saw this week."

Jack took another sip of his black coffee and pondered her question.

"Is it a requirement for us?"

Dani reached across the table and touched Jack's hand. "No," she said softly. "It's only a suggestion."

Jack placed his hand on top of hers. "I'll think about it."

Dani smiled. "I think hearing sermons on the positivity in life would be beneficial for you Jack. You see so much of the dark evil side of life, maybe seeing the good in people can really help bring a balance."

Jack returned her smile and let her words massage his heart. She was right, but he needed time. "I'll think about. That's all I can say. Is that okay?"

Smiling, Dani stood and grabbed her purse. "It is. Thanks Jack. Now if you'll excuse me I'm going to the restroom. Why don't you pay the bill and I'll meet you out front."

Jack stood up and kissed Dani on the cheek. She turned and Jack took care of the bill. The smile they both had on their faces was the first they shared in a long time together and Jack hoped it would be the first of many.

87

Jack was walking to his car when he heard a familiar voice come from out of the darkness.

"Mr. Angel," the deep, throaty-smoky voice said. "I'm glad to see you and your wife had dinner together."

Jack turned and saw the Gray Man standing to his right. He approached Jack from between two cars with a half-burned cigarette dangling on his lips. Within a few swift steps, he was inches from Jack's face.

"Where's Ray Stevens?" Jack asked, almost regretting having asked the question.

The Gray Man laughed. "Don't worry about him. As a matter of fact, you don't even have to worry about Sergeant Rand. They're both in good hands."

Jack's face burned. He didn't expect to hear Marcus Rand's name and felt unless Marcus was handed over he would not get the answers he sought when it came to his daughter. Jack's hand snapped to his gun.

"Don't," the Gray Man said. "Trust me. You don't want to make that mistake. Not here. Not when you and your beautiful wife are finally working your problems out."

Jack eased his hand off his gun's handle and placed them in front of him for the Gray Man to see.

"Much better."

"Where's Julian Watts?"

"Now *that* is a great question. I haven't seen him."

"You lie."

The Gray Man smiled. "Well, let me say, he too is not for you to worry about. Don't worry. He'll be dealt with."

"He needs to be brought in. He needs to answer for what he's done."

"He will, but not in your court. He answers to a higher authority."

"Who? You?"

"No. I'm not his judge. Just the executioner that was sent to deliver His judgment."

Jack looked to the front doors to see if Dani was coming outside. He didn't want her to see him talking to the Gray Man.

"You're not authorized to do that."

"Not by you I'm not, but like I said, I don't answer to you."

"Then who? God?"

"Absolutely. I am *Theion*. I am the one God communicates His anger through."

There was that word was again, *Theion*, but now, for the first time, Jack heard it pronounced as if it were two separate words, *"The Ion"* and not as a single word, *"Theion"*. The same word shouted as they burned to death. The Gray Man had defined its meaning by writing out the acronym on a napkin and handed it to Jack. At the time, Jack didn't know what it meant, until he saw the same word written in blood when they found the trucker crucified.

"So you use your name as an acronym for, 'Through hellfire eternal, infernal obedience neverending?"

The Gray Man smirked. The expression caused Jack to feel as if he should've known the answer to the inane question he asked. But the Gray Man's face did something further, it caused him to feel unclean and dirty, as if he were being judged.

"You're right Mr. Angel, it does mean *precisely* that, but there is something particularly divine about it. You have a lot to learn Jack Angel. Read your Greek history. It's in there. Just know that God communicates through *me*. I hand out *His* retribution. *His* purification. *His* cleansing."

Hellfire eternal.
Infernal obedience.
Neverending.

"A trial by fire?" Jack asked referring to the pastors who killed themselves with fire.

"Not a trial. Consider it a judgment."

"And Julian Watts?"

"His judgment is coming forthwith. No need to worry about him."

Jack actually felt a sense of relief. For him, the Julian Watts case was finally closed.

"And what about Ray and Marcus."

"Let me worry about them. You have other matters to tend to."

Jack had a question he needed answered. It was the same question he had when he met Ray Stevens, but felt still unanswered in his mind. "Ray Stevens said if I investigated the suicides, I would find the answers I needed in finding my daughter's killer. I still don't know who her killer is."

The Gray Man shook his head in disappointment. "That's not at all what he said Mr. Angel. He said that you would find the answers you've been seeking since your wife left you."

"That's the same thing!"

"No. It's not. You've been wondering *why*. *Why* did this happen to you? *Why* did she leave? Now you know why."

Jack was silent. He thought for a moment. "She left because what I'd become after our Ainslie died."

The Gray Man nodded. "You forgot who you were. Now you know. You became something else. Something you're not. You couldn't focus and sunk deep into despair. But now, now you know what type of person, what type of *killer* you are. You are strong once again. Finally, you can go and find your daughter's killer."

Jack knew the Gray Man was right. His words pierced his heart and Jack accepted them as the truth he needed to move forward. But Jack was still unsatisfied.

"You know you can't punish Ray and Julian and Marcus for what happened," Jack said trying to change the subject. "As much as I want to see Julian suffer, he must go through the judicial system along with Ray Stevens and Marcus Rand."

"I'm sorry Jack, but as I've said, they are no longer yours to worry about. The judge they must answer to is not *your* judge."

"What you're planning on doing is not your right. It is not your role."

"My *role*? Is that what you think this is about? *Roles?* You're so infantile in your reasoning. What you have yet to learn is that we all are pawns in a plan that is greater than we all are. You are here for a single purpose."

"And what purpose is that?"

"You're wasting my time Mr. Angel. You already know. You're here as a killer and I'm here for another purpose."

"And that is?"

"That is between me and the supreme Judge. As you figure out more of what you *are* you will realize you can only control what is afforded to you. To catch the person it is you seek, often times people, even innocent ones, will have to be expended along the way. Like *tonight*. It' the natural order of things. Do not mourn them. It is part of His ultimate plan. The sooner you accept that, a more efficient Hunter Killer you will become"

Jack struggled hearing the words spoken to him. As much as he knew the words spoken were true, it was the one part of being a detective he struggled with the most. He wanted to protect all of the innocent and mourned those he couldn't save. It was the fundamental part of him he could not let go. Often times, he refused the reality of collateral damage.

Tonight was one of those times.

"Where are they?" he asked again, grabbing the Gray Man's forearm, stressing his frustration. "*TELL ME!*"

With a flurry and speed Jack wasn't expecting, the Gray Man grabbed Jack by his throat and slammed him into the side of an SUV. Jack bent his feet forward, his toes barley nicking the ground, as he gagged for air. "Don't you *EVER* touch me again! Are we clear on that?"

Jack nodded.

"I'm not your friend. I'm here to guide you, making sure His will is done. And right now, you are *done* when it comes to *His* will regarding this situation. You have other matters to tend to and some you may not even be aware of. For now, I suggest you refine your skills on discovering your daughter's killer. He's out there. Time's a wasting. Better find him."

The Gray Man released Jack's throat, who collapsed to the blacktop pavement, still holding his throat and gagging.

"Oh, before I forget," the Gray Man said kneeling down to Jack's ear. "Forget about Stefan Cooper. He's a deviant, yes, but of no concern to you. Stop wasting your skills on the likes of him. Are we clear?"

Jack nodded, his eyes staring at the ground and hands still clutching his throat.

"Good night Mr. Angel. I'll be in touch."

The Gray Man left Jack who continued gagging and trying to catch a breath. Jack turned his head and watched as the Gray Man walked between two vehicles, a van and a truck. Jack stumbled trying to stand up and chase behind him. He walked between the same two cars the Gray Man past just seconds prior, but when he came out on their front end, the Gray Man was nowhere to be seen. Jack looked to his right, studied the area and then looked left and repeated the same surveillance. It was obvious, but to Jack's disbelief, the Gray Man was gone.

Vanished.

Nowhere to be found.

"Jack!" he heard his wife shout. "Aren't you bringing the car around?"

Jack quickly scanned the parking lot. All he saw were people coming and leaving.

No Gray Man in sight.

"Yeah, I'll be right there."

He turned and walked back to his car knowing what the future held for him.

Find Ainslie's killer.

Jack would forever be grateful to his friend Frank who helped bring him back from the brink of self-destruction. His head was back in the game. He was living again. When life settled down and Jack took some time he knew he would begin the task of finding Ainslie's killer and finally close the chapter on the most horrific time in his family's life.

88

Jack drove his car around to the front of *The Pinecrest* restaurant to pick up Dani. He saw his beautiful wife standing on the curb waving to alert him to where she was standing. As he neared her, bits of conversations from the last twenty-four hours pelted his memory like a hailstorm.

Julian Watts: *"No matter what happens to me, I'm still going to deliver God's message and rid the world of the whores, murderers, judgers, and all that are immoral."*

Barry Spencer: *"Julian felt judged. He encouraged David to see how the eyes of others were the eyes of condemnation."*

Barry Spencer: *"I didn't understand what David was talking about until I took his Bible and saw his notes"*

Julian Watts: *"Because the task isn't finished!"*

Julian Watts: *"Others needed to prepare for what is to come."*

Barry Spencer: *"I'm getting ready for a candle light service tomorrow night to remember this week's fallen Christian brothers."*

The Gray Man: *"...you can only control what is afforded to you."*

The Gray Man: *"...often times people, even innocent ones, will have to be expended along the way."*

The Gray Man: *"Like tonight.* It' the natural order of things."

The Gray Man: *"Do not mourn them. It is part of His ultimate plan."*

The Gray Man: *"You have other matters to tend to and some you may not even be aware of."*

Jack slammed on his brakes, yanked his cell phone and punched in Frank's number. He was waving Dani to get into the car when Frank picked up.

"This is Frank."

"Frank? It's Jack. Listen to me. Don't question me. Just listen."

"Okay."

"I don't know why, but bits of conversations I've had with Barry and Julian just flooded my mind," Jack refrained from mentioning the Gray Man, wanting to keep that to himself. "I need you to meet me at River of Life Community Church."

"Barry Spencer's church?"

"Yes," Jack said already pulling out of the parking lot and driving towards River of Life.

"Why? Can't this wait till tomorrow?"

"No!"

"What's wrong Jack? You sound panicked."

"I am! You know how we found the cyanide at Julian's church? I think Barry was going to do the same to his congregation. They were *both* going to have their congregation drink cyanide."

"Holy shit! Why do you think that?"

"I can't go into how I know. Believe me when I say that I just do."

"What about Pastor Sullivan and Reverend Ray's church?"

"No. Something tells me they're fine. This one has a different feel. Barry was working with Julian. Remember?"

"Okay, I'll call the Lou and send as many cars as we can to the church."

"Have them call EMS too. I'm about forty-five minutes out. We don't have a lot of time and I hope we're not too late."

"Okay, calling now! Anything else I should say?"

"Yeah," Jack inhaled deeply. "If I'm right about this, have them bring a lot of body bags."

89

To Jack's horror, what he feared came to fruition. Turning onto River Parkway, he saw his prediction now a mortal reality. A dozen squad cars were strung along the street, their red and blue lights flashing. EMS vehicles were backed up to the church and crime scene tape was already being wrapped to cordon off the area. As Jack and Dani exited the car, the first of many bodies, covered by a white sheet, was being wheeled out of the church on a gurney. Jack saw Frank standing by one of the officers giving him the few details he'd known.

"How many bodies are in there?" Jack asked finally standing next to Frank.

"Maybe a hundred."

"Had everyone taken the Lord's Supper?"

"Looks that way."

"Any children?"

"No. The kids were found in the sanctuary next to their parents. Some were crying for their mom and dad to wake up. Others had no idea what happened." Frank pulled Jack to the side and out of earshot. "How did you know this was going to happen?"

"It's hard to explain it Frank," but Jack tried anyway. "I was pulling the car around to pick up Dani and pieces of comments from Barry and Julian flashed in my memory."

"And you saw this happening?"

"Not like I'm used to, this time was different. It was more like putting the pieces of a jigsaw puzzle together. One piece after another and then the picture became visible. I saw where each part of the puzzle went. I placed them together and saw this outcome." Jack paused a beat and cursed under his breath. "But I was too late."

"Jack," Frank said trying to comfort his friend. "How could we've known?"

"I don't know. We should've though. Barry became a follower of Julian and believed his twisted theology. He thought the judgers needed to pay. He believed it. Julian had him convinced. Maybe we should've looked deeper into him yesterday. If we did we could've stopped this."

"Jack, we can't stop every crime and unfortunately, innocent people fall victim along the way."

Frank's words pierced Jack. *That's what the Gray Man was saying to him. As if he'd known this was going to happen and Jack would assemble the parts and piece it together. He knew Jack wouldn't be able to stop this mass execution.*

His guided words acted as a sign to Jack.

Just like a reminder.

In his cryptic way of speaking, he'd reminded Jack that bad things happen to good people and Jack wasn't going to be able to stop it all.

Just accept it and remain focused on the task given.

"I know we can't stop everything Frank. I just didn't want this to be a reality. A part of me feels Julian and Barry still got what they wanted."

"And what's that?"

"To punish their judgers."

"Don't worry Jack. We'll find Julian and when we do, he will get the full punishment of the law. That is one judge he will have to answer to and we will both be there watching him receive his sentence."

Jack turned from Frank, grabbed Dani's hand, and walked away. He thought about the Gray Man telling him that Julian was going to answer to a higher authority.

I'm not his judge. Just the executioner that was sent to deliver His judgment. The judge they must answer to is not your judge.

"You're right Frank. He *will* answer for what he's done. I just wish I could be there to see it when it happens."

The Cleansing: A Thriller

Jack finally understood and accepted that the verdict Julian would receive from the Higher Authority, would be far more deserving than any sentence handed down from an Earthly court.

304

SATURDAY

90

A sea of candles filled the ornate chamber along with an altar and a pulpit. There was no electricity to light the area, only the candles, which numbered to a few hundred. In the middle of the chamber, two men were bound to a chair with a black hood over their head. The door leading into the chamber opened as two men entered in full ceremonial regalia. They walked up to the bound men with one of the two men who entered taking a standing position now beside them.

The Gray Man took his place at the podium as Marcus Rand stood by the bound men. The Gray Man did not open a book. Instead, he took an authoritative position at the podium.

"You two were given a task to complete. You were to atone for your sins through a cleansing of fire. One of you, unfortunately, was stopped by his congregation. The other completely ignored the charge. Your evil actions and vile filth are but a putrid taste in His mouth. Therefore, He will spit you out. You must account for what you did. You became blind in your actions and so you will remain blinded by what you cannot see here. I now summon before me, Ray Stevens. Please rise."

Marcus helped Ray stand to his feet.

"Ray Stevens, I know that you tried to remain faithful, but still judgment awaited you. You know what your sentence must be. Do you accept this condemnation on your soul?"

Ray Stevens nodded.

"So it shall be. Remove his hood."

Marcus did as the Gray Man directed.

"Julian Watts. Please rise."

Once again, Marcus helped Julian stand to his feet.

R. G. Huxley

"Julian Watts. Your dark heart and evil mind inflicted pain on the innocent. The idea that *you* were His instrument to leverage judgment on man consumed you. You were wrong. You were blind. You lost the ability to speak truth. And now you stand here, before me, blind and unable to speak. Remove his hood."

Marcus did as the Gray Man directed him.

Julian stood before the three men. His eye sockets were bloody black holes from his eyes being gouged out. Blood covered his front as a result of it pouring from his mouth and down his neck. The red liquid, leaving a stained reminder where his tongue, now a bloody meat-stump, used to be.

"In Leviticus, the third book of the Old Testament, the author, Moses, wrote in the fifteenth and sixteenth verse of the twenty-fourth chapter, 'Then you shall speak to the children of Israel, saying: 'Whoever curses his God shall bear his sin. And whoever blasphemes the name of the Lord shall surely be put to death. All the congregation shall certainly stone him, the stranger as well as him who is born in the land. When he blasphemes the name of the Lord, he shall be put to death.' Julian Watts? You know what your judgment is to be. It is a sentence of death. You refused it in the past, but do you now willingly accept what must become of you for your actions and deeds?"

Julian Watts didn't respond.

"Do not have me ask again. I can assure you, if you do not answer me or the Lord, your punishment will include an intense level of anguish far more than you could imagine."

Finally, Julian nodded slowly.

"So it shall be."

The Gray Man walked past all three men, motioning for Marcus to follow him.

"Take this," he said handing the jug of gasoline to Marcus. "Dowse them and light them on fire. They are to be cleansed."

Marcus took the jug and poured it over both men while the Gray Man returned to the podium. He continued pouring; making certain no drop remained left behind. When he was

The Cleansing: A Thriller

done, he stood next to the two men waiting for the Gray Man's next command.

The Gray Man watched and continued. "Surely there is a day that is coming. This will be a day that will burn like the intensity of a furnace. The smell of brimstone. The heat of fire. The pain of the unrighteous at their final judgment. The haughty and conceited. The sexually immoral. The ignorant. All evildoers alike, they will become hot burning coals in the lake of fire. The Psalmist in the eleventh chapter and sixth verse wrote, 'Upon the wicked he shall rain snares, fire and brimstone, and a horrible tempest: this shall be the portion of their cup.'"

The Gray Man nodded at Marcus.

"It is time."

Marcus turned and lit Ray Stevens and Julian Watts on fire. Their mouths, void of screams since their speech and sound now belonged to the Gray Man, were hollow chasms of silence. Both men fell to the ground, feeling their wicked souls abandon their bodies and replaced by death. The searing pain of the flames burned deep into their flesh. This was the hellfire eternal, the infernal obedience neverending, meant for the wicked. The Gray Man, *Theion*, was pleased to see their charred remains lay on the floor, God's altar, with the smell of their burning flesh permeating the air as an offering made by fire; a sweet aroma to the Lord.

Marcus turned and looked at the Gray Man.

"Marcus Rand, you thought you were doing what was right, but in your actions, you brought a sentence of death that needn't be rendered. Your dark heart and wicked ways require judgment. Each must face accountability for their actions. Consequences shall be meted out. As your intermediary, I have been given authority to give you a choice in your sentence. You will be able to decide your outcome. Do you understand my words?"

Marcus nodded

"Then realize now, as you stand before me, these two wicked men, who lay lifeless before you shall become the ashes beneath their feet - the feet of the righteous and the just. They, the righteous and the just, shall be able to walk over the wicked's burning retched flesh and not feel the lick of the flames that has already consumed them. They, the righteous and the just, shall walk to glory. On that day, the day that sets the evildoers on fire, you, Marcus Rand, will either be the one consumed by flames and try to flee like a frightened animal from a burning stable or you, Marcus Rand, shall become the one walking over the fire and into victory. Do you understand this?"

Again, Marcus nodded.

"And so now I ask, which should happen to you? Shall you be the one consumed by the fire or the one who walks over the fire into victory along with the righteous and the just?"

Tears streamed down his cheeks. "I'm an evildoer. I accept my wrongdoings. I understand I am one that should be consumed by fire. The righteous and the just shall walk over my burning flesh and not feel the fire that consumes my wickedness."

"So it shall be."

The Gray Man walked over to Marcus and handed him another jug of gasoline. Marcus willingly accepted the jug and poured its contents over his head. When the flammable liquid fully doused Marcus, he took the lighter and set himself on fire.

The Gray Man stood and watched and said a prayer for Marcus and then asked God for what His next mission shall be.

"I am yours Lord. I am Theion. I am *Your* Ion. I am here. Send me."

SUNDAY

312

91

Jack sat in his car finishing his call to Frank Madiolie. Frank called him to let him know officers recovered the bodies of Ray Stevens, Julian Watts, and Marcus Rand. All three of them charred.

"Is this what you expected Jack?"

"Yeah. Not surprised."

"I'm a little disappointed myself. Would've loved nothing more than to see Julian fry for his crimes, but sometimes we can't be judge, jury, and executioner."

"I'm starting to learn that," Jack replied thinking about what the Gray Man said to him.

"Do you think he had anything to do with their deaths?"

"Who?" Jack asked, playing ignorant.

"You know who," Frank said referring to the Gray Man.

"No one else entered my mind," Jack said thinking of the Gray Man.

"Yeah, me either. We've launched an investigation here into who he is and where he's from."

"You won't find *him* or anything about *him*. You realize that right? He does what he wants on his own terms."

"I know, but it's part of the process. You know that. He's a suspect and there are questions that need answered."

Frank and Jack both sat in silence, knowing the Gray Man would one day make himself relevant again, but it would be on his terms and in his own time. There's a role he played and it was a role Jack wanted more information on and was determined to find out. And was willing to confront it like all the demons in his past.

"So," Frank finally blurted, breaking the silence and changing the subject. "How are things with Dani?"

"Good. I'm going to meet her in a few minutes."

Frank was silent. He was glad for Jack and simply didn't know what else to say to his longtime partner and friend.

"Frank?"

"Yeah?"

"I don't know if I'm coming back to work."

The words stung Frank's heart. He was afraid that's what Jack would say, but he held out hope that he was wrong.

"Why not? I thought you liked working again."

"I do and I'm finally feeling like myself, but I need to find Ainslie's killer. I'm more focused on that than ever and I feel like my mind is finally clear. The way it needs to be. To do this right, I need to find her killer my own way. Not bound by the rules of engagement."

Frank chuckled a bit. "I understand. Disappointed, but I understand. You always were a maverick when it came to investigations. You're not going to be a stranger around the station are you?"

"Absolutely not. I still enjoy the camaraderie. You're my family."

"Understood. I'm here for ya. You know that right?"

"I do."

"By the way Jack. You still owe me a hundred dollars from last Saturday's fight."

Jack busted out laughing. He'd forgotten all about it with everything that had gone on that week.

"Well Frank how about this. I'd rather owe you than cheat you out of it."

It was Frank's turn to laugh.

"And where did you hear that line from?"

"A longtime friend. I think he goes by the name of Frank Madiolie."

"He sounds like a wise man."

Jack smiled. "I wouldn't go *that* far, but I will say I learned a lot from him."

The Cleansing: A Thriller

"Well here's something more, you need to learn to be on time."

Jack grimaced. "What do you mean?"

"You're late for church Jack."

"Talk to ya later Frank," Jack said in a hurry, turning off his phone and exiting the car, not waiting for a response from Frank."

Frank continued sitting in his office after hanging up with Jack. He reached across his desk and grabbed the picture of his walleye trip with Jack taken a few years ago. It was a picture he'd looked at many times over the last few years and wondered if those were days gone by for good. Feeling certain of a horizon for a new tomorrow, Frank set the picture down and smiled. He looked forward once again being able to spend time with the Jack Angel he knew best.

His longtime partner.

And friend.

92

Jack walked into the sanctuary and saw the congregation standing and finishing their song. He looked around for Dani and found her when he saw her familiar hand waving for him.

Jack scooted past the people in the pew repeating, "Excuse me" several times.

"I'm glad you're here," she whispered and giving him a kiss on the cheek.

"Me too," he whispered back.

"I didn't know if you'd show."

"Well, I needed to be here. I think it'll be good me."

"Really?" Dani asked surprised by his comment.

"Yeah...really."

Dani smiled and turned back around to listen to the pastor. After a few brief announcements the pastor asked the congregation members to stand and for the visitors to remain seated so the church could greet them.

Jack looked a little uncomfortable knowing that if he stayed seated he was going to have to shake hands with people he didn't know.

"Don't worry," Dani said knowing how Jack felt. "It'll be over sooner than you know it."

Jack smiled and remained seated.

The pianist played a hymn song while the members stood and walked across the aisle meeting and greeting one another. A short older lady who was sitting in front of Dani and Jack turned back to welcome them.

"And who's this handsome guy you brought with you Dani?" the woman asked extending her hand to meet Jack.

The Cleansing: A Thriller

Dani stood proud. "This handsome guy is my husband Jack."

Jack's heart warmed as it had been awhile since he heard Dani refer to him as her husband. He stood, returned the woman's handshake and then turned to receive multiple handshakes and welcome hugs by many of the church's congregation.

When the music stopped, the congregation returned to their seats and the pastor came to the pulpit. He opened his Bible and took a sip of water.

"Today, church family, I'm going to preach on the goodness of life. The life God wanted each of us to have, and how to achieve and live such a life. Yes church family, life is good. Do you believe that? Say amen!"

"Amen!" the church shouted.

"Amen!" Jack whispered leaning into Dani's ear.

"I love you Jack."

"I love you too." Jack reached over and grabbed onto Dani's hand and listened to the sermon on how to have the good life God intended for everyone.

A NOTE ON *THE CLEANSING:*

Books are a journey. Plain and simple. They are a journey to write as an author, seeing an idea come to life and watching the characters interact with one another and then finally bringing the story to a close. For the reader, it's a journey as well. You invest time into the characters and hopefully you feel the struggles and victories along the way. My sincerest hope is that when you finish reading, you're completely satisfied and felt the return on your investment was well worth it. If not, please let me know as I would love to hear from you. If you *were* satisfied, again, please let me know as I want to hear what you have to say.

As for *The Cleansing*, my journey into this novel started in 2009. I had written stories prior to 2009 and had even written and directed numerous plays. I had always wanted to write a novel, even had many ideas for a variety of books, but when I sat down to write, the fire would just fizzle and nothing to show for my efforts except 50 or 60 pages of a story going nowhere. I started to think that I was only cut out for play writing. Which was fine, but I wanted more. I love to read and investing my time into characters and I wanted to do the same when I created Jack Angel. I would like as a reader and hopefully other readers would as well.

So, The Cleansing came to me one day out of nowhere. I was sitting at my desk and happened to be watching a fan-made video trailer for a movie. In it, it showed a character in the movie walking around the woods and engulfed in flames. I asked myself, "What if he had set himself on fire? Why would he do that? What if he set himself on fire in front of his church while he was preaching and other pastors did as well. And!!!! What if they were preaching on the same message to their congregation and they set themselves on fire at the same time?"

Well I couldn't stop thinking about it. I wrote the first chapter and shared it with my friend Patrick Toler who said I needed to continue. I was afraid that this novel would end up like all the others…a good start, but nothing more after page 50.

But that didn't happen.

Something was different.

For the first time ever, I actually saw the entire story in my head. I saw the characters. I saw them interacting with one another and I just couldn't get them to go away. Which is a good thing I guess. And on top of all that, I saw the novel broken into 3 acts. Just like a play.

A beginning. A middle. And the end. All 3 acts.

That had never happened before and in a short time I had completed the first draft. When the draft was completed I faced an even bigger mountain.

The story was extremely dark and graphic. I knew that some people could possibly be put off by its subject matter. And by some people, I am referring to those who know me best. I told them I had written a novel and they wanted to read it. Naturally of course since they knew me and wanted to read what I had written. I warned them upfront and kept reminding them that the characters in the story were not me, but they were just characters.

I don't know why I felt so compelled to tell them, but I did. But I also knew that, to me, the story would not have been the same if I went back and changed it. My goal was to take the reader into the darkest regions of man's heart and have them see what Jack saw. The cruel and painful world that exists because absolute evil *does* exist. But then I wanted to take the reader, and Jack, and show them there is true light as well. There *is* absolute goodness, but often times a person cannot see the light and appreciate it until they have been subjected to the darkest of night.

I experienced that once when we had a horrible windstorm one fall and our power was out for days. Every night our house was just black. No light except for whatever flashlights we had, but even the little bit of light those gave off didn't compare to the absolute light we needed and craved. When our power was restored we all breathed a sigh of relief.

The light was back! The darkness retreated.

During that time I realized the truth behind real darkness and what it really was. Pure darkness is the absence of light. Plain and simple. There is relief when a person follows the light and emerges from the dark.

And that's what I wanted to convey in *The Cleansing*. I wanted you, Dear Reader, and Jack to breathe a sigh of relief when the light finally shown through at the end. The darkness retreated...and the light was there to offer warmth and comfort once again. But to appreciate the light, I wanted the darkness to be long and intense.

So after sitting on the draft of *The Cleansing* for so long, I knew it had to be completed. Family and friends loved the story and wanted me to see it through to the end. I delayed in editing it...and quite frankly I hated editing the story. I was told you write the first draft with your heart, but the second, third, and fourth with your mind.

They weren't lying!

Then I was fortunate in the fall of 2011 to meet an author named Jonas Saul who didn't know me from a hole in the ground and asked to read my draft. He came back after a few days of reading it and basically kicked me in the pants to get the novel done. His words were encouraging and exactly what I needed to make this the best novel it could be.

I owe him the deepest of gratitude because if it were not for him, Jack Angel would still be sitting on my computer in a very rough form. Jonas, you are a true friend.

So where do you and I go from here Dear Reader? Oh, there are many investigations awaiting our friend Jack Angel and his quest to bring his daughter's killer to justice. I can assure you, the Gray Man will be watching, and Frank will be there to assist Jack as he ventures into a dark world…where the light will be waiting to assure Jack…and you…that hope is just around the corner.

R. G. Huxley April 2012

ABOUT THE AUTHOR

R.G. Huxley lives in Ohio with his wife Heather and their three daughters: Taylor, Hannah Grace, and Reagan. When he isn't writing, he can be found on the lake competing in the American Bass Anglers Weekend Series bass tournaments or enjoying a quiet ride through the country on his motorcycle. To keep up to date with R. G. Huxley, you can go to his website at www.rghuxley.com or email him at rghuxley@rghuxley.com

Made in the USA
Charleston, SC
24 May 2012